Love at the Fall Fair

by

J.R. Boles

The Wild Rose Press, Inc.
PO Box 708
Adams Basin, NY 14410-0708
Visit us at www.thewildrosepress.com

Publishing History
First Edition, 2025
Trade Paperback ISBN 978-1-5092-6286-1
Digital ISBN 978-1-5092-6287-8

Published in the United States of America

Dedication

For my captain and for friends who feel like family.

Acknowledgements

This book wouldn't exist without my husband and his service in the US Air Force. He's always my first beta reader and my favorite brainstorming partner.

I'm lucky to have local Kansas City authors who encouraged me and kept this story going. Jennifer Fujita, Margaret Rose, and Amber A. Logan were beta readers. My amazing writing group, the Foo Writers and Heather McFeely, provided guidance and feedback. My parents and my aunt are always part of my writing journey, and I'm forever grateful for their support.

Thank you to Stacey Donovan and Leanne Morgena for their insightful edits that helped this story shine. Thank you to my sensitivity reader, Elizabeth Boresow.

Chapter One

For Katy Caterby, autumn in Delaware meant windy days filled with fresh coffee and a colder ocean breeze. Fall always meant harvest time and community dinners back home, with the chaos of people packing into the church multi-purpose room to celebrate with tables full of fry bread, pan-seared pork and beans with *banaha* bread, and grape dumplings. Katy Caterby created her own traditions to pay homage to her Choctaw upbringing in Oklahoma. One of those ways was a random act of kindness every Friday.

She stepped out her green apartment door and took a deep breath of the crisp fall air. A bright redheaded woodpecker swooped past her, so close she could feel the pressure of the wind beating from its wings. She gasped and jumped back, brushing her long hair from her face.

The bird flew into another tree.

She released a big breath with a sigh. *I do not have time to count to ten.* Rushing back into her apartment, she set her bag down and counted to ten. Gran always told her to keep an eye out for redheaded woodpeckers.

They're signal birds, Katy Cat. If one visits your house, then danger is near. If one crosses your path when you're starting something new, start again. We have to listen to the world. It's always telling us something we need to know.

Before leaving the apartment again, she pictured Gran. Until she passed away, Emma Caterby was the family matriarch and lived with Katy's family. A lifetime of gardening had weathered Gran's skin, and she grew and dried herbs as gifts. Hugging her meant walking away smelling a little like thyme and rosemary. She was the best storyteller Katy had ever met, and Gran made sure she and her brother Joe learned all the old Choctaw stories like Grandmother Spider and how Possum lost his tail.

Running late for work, Katy rushed into her friend McKenna's coffee shop, Brewed Awakenings, in downtown Dover. The shop was Katy's third favorite place in town, after the library where she worked and the local bookstore. The coffee shop sat nestled along the historic storefronts. A full pot of coffee right next to the name popped in white print on the bright-green awning.

McKenna ran Brewed Awakenings like a mother hen. Photos of her family graced the wall with half of their faces covered by bold-colored coffee mugs. The place was full of history as a small family business.

Orange twinkle lights and garlands of faux leaves in gold, red, and orange covered every available surface. Chalk pumpkins and vines trailed the edges of the drink menu board. Bright-yellow and red mums in little mason jars decorated every table.

A tall guy blocked a toddler from running out the front door. The mom threw away their cups and rushed over to collect her would-be escape artist.

The guy just shrugged at the mom's thanks. He was in an Air Force uniform, but he was turned away. She pivoted before he caught her staring. *Because wow*.

"Good morning, girl. You're late." McKenna adjusted her purple cat's-eye glasses. Her dark-blue eyes were bright.

"Ran into some trouble, but I'm ready to spread the Friday love." Katy breathed in the espresso, toasted bakery bread, and pumpkin spice scent filling the coffee shop.

"I'll get your usual going. I refilled the ground cinnamon, too." McKenna pointed toward the counter at the back where she kept all the coffee extras.

Katy paid cash with enough to cover a drink for whoever ordered after her. She tried not to be nosy every week and see who ended up getting a coffee, so she scooted over to scroll her phone by the extra napkins and spices. When her order was ready, she took the top off to add a little more cinnamon.

Her family called their shared order the Caterby latte because they all ordered a latte with ground cinnamon on top. Even though she lived so far from Oklahoma, she stayed close with little things like her father's recipes and their family coffee drink.

"Katy?"

That voice. Her breath hitched, and a familiar shiver quivered down her spine. She whirled around— and nearly dropped the cinnamon container right into her latte. The toddler-rescuing officer stopped in front of her. *Luke Taylor? In uniform? Luke Taylor from Durant High School?*

And he stood there with a lopsided grin.

The very same Luke Taylor who broke her heart and humiliated her in high school. His green eyes took her in.

3

She did the same, searching for the kid she remembered.

His broad shoulders filled out his uniform, and his light-brown hair was cropped short. Dover was an Air Force town, so she had no reason to wonder how he'd ended up in Delaware.

"Katy Caterby, I can't believe you're here. Thank you for the coffee." He held his cup with a tiny heart swirled into the steamed milk.

She shook her head to dispel the way his deep gravelly voice still gave her immediate shivers. *The coffee?* "Wait, you're my Friday random act of kindness?" She flinched, wishing she'd kept her cool. Katy tugged at the hem of her favorite sunflower-yellow sweater. She'd never worn bright colors in high school, and she'd kept her hair half covering her face. He shouldn't have recognized her so easily from across the sunny coffee shop.

Her heart sped up. Katy widened her stance and ordered her heart to chill out. She would not notice the snug fit of his uniform on his arms or the way his green eyes had an intently listening vibe.

"Yeah, McKenna said you do buy a coffee for a stranger every Friday. That's so you," he said.

How would he know? They hadn't spoken in years. They weren't even friends on social media—even if she had searched. Realizing she still held the cinnamon shaker, she set the tiny glass jar down to secure the lid back on her latte. She took a deep breath. *Calm down, heart.*

"How in the heck are you? How is your dad? And Joe?" He relaxed against the counter.

Of course, he would ask about Joe. "My dad is

good. The hardware store is going strong. And Joe is Joe. He was elected to the Tribal Council last year." She swallowed.

Delaware was the first place nobody knew Joe, and she didn't have anyone expecting her to be more like her extroverted and athletic big brother. In Dover, she started a new story where she wasn't left behind or disappointing. Luke Taylor would *not* change her path. Never again. "How's your mom? And Jackie?" Katy flushed, squaring her shoulders. Brewed Awakenings was her coffee shop, and she would not run because the boy who broke her heart had grown up with the same rumbling baritone.

"Mom stays busy. And Jackie is happy with her job. Though she'd be happier if I texted her more often. She likes video calls now, too." He softened his eyes when he mentioned his autistic sister. His large hands gripped her coffee cup, pressing the lid down.

She shivered from the contact. "Th-thanks. I'm, um, glad she feels comfortable with video calls." Katy checked her watch. "I need to scoot. I don't want to be late for work."

"Where do you work? I'm at Dover Air Force Base." He pointed south with his thumb.

"I'm an information services librarian at the library just down the road." She studied the orange coffee sleeve on her cinnamon latte. Her heart pounded in her ears. *How had the morning gone so wrong?*

"Information services?" He cocked his head to the side.

"I work the front welcome desk, managing the collection to make sure the books are all where they need to be, and I help with both kids and adult programs." Katy shuffled her feet.

Luke leaned back, running a hand through his cropped hair. "I bet you're the greatest. I'd love to catch up more. Can you meet me here later? I'd like to buy you a coffee to say thanks."

Of course, he would. He was always so polite—another thing she'd liked about him. "Y-you don't need to." She waved a hand.

"I do. Not only to say thanks, but I want to hear all about how you ended up in Dover. What are the chances we'd end up in the same town?" He leaned closer.

His green eyes were every bit as bright and hypnotizing as they'd been in high school. The woodsy scent wafting over her was downright dangerous. Her whole body shivered, and she fought the urge to take a nice long luxurious breath of grown-up Luke Taylor. What if he and Jolie were still together? What if he ghosted her again after she started to care? Getting close again wasn't worth the risk. The humiliation he'd caused was like a live wire under her skin.

McKenna caught her eye from across the shop and waggled her thick eyebrows. Matchmaking gears turned in her eyes behind her purple glasses.

Katy needed to fill her in on the backstory sooner rather than later. Luke had already caused her enough heartache. Katy's phone buzzed a reminder for the first meeting of the day, and she jumped. "Oh, I have to go, Luke. Have a great day."

She let her feet do what they'd been itching to do from the moment his green eyes lit up. She sped out of the coffee shop like a coward. The signal bird started to make complete sense. What person wanted to run into a walking reminder of teenage mortification? Nobody. Definitely not Katy.

****

The red-brick Dover Public Library was modern and welcoming with great pillars and green space calling readers to stop by and read. When she stepped inside, Katy took a deep breath of paper and bindings. Her new life was here. She wasn't the same unseen kid anymore. Under the tall arched ceilings, Katy breezed by the welcome desk. As the heart of the library, the desk hummed with activity. Especially on Fridays when the library hosted story time with a small group of moms and their rambunctious toddlers.

In the back offices, the library director, Mae Adams, stepped out of her office, wearing dark leggings and a gray wool sweater dress with suede camel-colored boots. Mae was a slim Afro-Indigenous woman with shoulder-length hair. Her steps were strong and steady on the blue industrial carpet. "Hey, Katy. Come talk for a minute before you head out front." Mae motioned toward her office. "The banned book week setup you suggested is going to be fantastic."

Katy stepped inside and took a seat. Mae's husband had reupholstered the two chairs across from her desk with soft wool in two red tones and warm gray. "Thank you. I'm excited to set the display." Katy squared her shoulders. She needed to shake off the memories Luke Taylor stirred up. Never mind the way her body reacted like he was her favorite flavor of ice cream. Now was not the time to sort through her feelings.

"You keep those ideas coming," Mae said. "Did you hear Darcy's baby boy came early?"

"What? No, I didn't know." Katy covered her

mouth with a hand.

"She was matched earlier than expected, and she started her maternity leave yesterday." Mae's eyes sparkled.

For Darcy, the lead events librarian, the adoption was a dream come true. Katy would have to research what she could do to help a new mom.

"I can see the wheels spinning. We'll get a meal calendar going and support her as a team. Don't you worry. But her joy also means sharing the load of what Darcy had on her plate with community events." Mae cleared her throat.

Katy lifted her chin. "Anything you need. You know I'm ready and willing to pitch in." She would prove herself—prove to Mae she was the right person to hire. She blinked rapidly, knowing she couldn't disappoint her greatest champion. Mae supported her and mentored her through her master's thesis. She owed every good thing in her life to Mae.

"Well, I'll need more than a team player. I'm putting you in charge of Darcy's new idea to sell used books as a fundraiser at the Fall Fair. She was developing all the processes and plans to use for future community sales." Mae eased back in her creaky office chair.

Katy had never been in charge of something so big. Books would be coming from other branches. The event had hundreds of to-dos. She swallowed down the rising panic. *I can do the book sale. I won't let Mae down.*

"Here are Darcy's project notes. You'll also be the lead at the Fall Fair, running the stall." The notes were haphazardly shoved into a bright-orange folder.

"Where are the donation books stored?" Katy struggled to keep her breathing even as she picked up the folder. They had a Friends of the Library used bookstore on the first floor, but she hoped the books set aside for the fair were somewhere else. She didn't want to disrupt the bookstore volunteers with fair prep. Katy cringed at the idea of being in the way.

"Come with me."

The office was a disaster of used books stacked high along three of the walls. She must've had a hard time getting around in here. A chair in the corner had two boxes with fall decorations spilling out. Orange twinkle lights tangled with tiny pumpkin garlands.

"Darcy was falling a little behind before she left. The timeline in her notes is only about five days behind, though." Mae sounded as though she were checking the box on her Katy to-do list and moving on to the next item. "Use Darcy's office for the project. We can't use the space for anything else right now anyway. Books, books, and more books," Mae sang as she left.

At Darcy's desk, Katy opened the folder to read through the detailed timeline and notes. She had five weeks until the first day of the Fall Fair. Her nerves fluttered. If she hustled, she could start inventorying the books, figure out pricing, and start the marketing campaign. Right now, though, she needed to start her shift at the welcome desk.

Dom was already at his usual spot with all the computers up and running.

She joined him at the welcome desk. He was the resident sports aficionado, and the nonfiction shelves were his territory. He was quiet about his college football team's success, but Darcy had told her he'd led the Delaware State Hornets to quite a few wins. He was much taller than Katy with dark mahogany skin.

He had his screen open to his ever-growing list of books for a sports-themed book display. He clicked on another page.

In the quiet before the library opened, the clack of the keyboard nearly echoed.

"Mornin'. Did you hear about Darcy?" Dom fixed the collar on his red polo. His dark-brown eyes opened wide.

"Mae said she has a baby boy." Katy's cheeks hurt from smiling so wide.

Dom flipped his name badge back and forth. "She waited a long time, and the adoption falling through last year was so hard on her."

"I can't wait to meet the baby. Do we know his name?"

"Nope. Did Mae tell you she's going to set up a meal calendar?" Dom rubbed the back of his neck.

Katy nodded.

"The concept was new, but I'll cook her dinner one night." He shrugged his wide shoulders.

"We all will." Her computer dinged, signaling the library was ready to open. She pressed a hand against her stomach and took a deep breath. She couldn't let Darcy down while her dream of being a mom finally came true. What kind of person would she be if she did?

****

After covering a shift on the second floor, Katy stopped midway down the wide stairs. The light coming through the two-story windows warmed her soul. The children's librarian, Ava Reyna, waved her over to help set up the next story time. Ava was local, like Mae, having grown up in a town north of Dover called Smyrna. Her shoulder-length black hair was curled back from her round face.

"You okay today?" Ava wore a book-themed T-shirt with a bright-blue cardigan, and nobody would mistake her for anything but a children's librarian. She was energetic and supportive of her tiny patrons' efforts, even when the rhymes were new and they struggled.

Katy wasn't sure how long she'd been staring out the window in the small story-time room. A hawk swooped down from one of the small trees dotting their campus, and she sighed. "I might have run into someone at the coffee shop, and he wasn't a welcome sight." Katy raised a shoulder and then helped sort the bins for the shaky eggs and silk scarves. The smooth slips of polyester smelled like hand wipes and fruit snacks.

Ava knelt beside her and raised a dark-brown eyebrow. "Isaac?"

"No Isaac sighting, thankfully." Katy hugged her arms across her chest. She didn't need to add her ex-boyfriend into the mix of today's weirdness.

Ava waved a hand for more.

"I bought a coffee for someone behind me, who ended up being a guy from back home. He's stationed here in Dover." Katy tried not to frown. "Small world."

"So, we're hoping not to see him again?"

"Exactly." Katy blew out a deep breath.

Ava handed Katy a shaky egg. "Shake the bad feels off, lovely. We have library work to do, but I'll expect to hear all about him tonight."

After a little shake, Katy tossed the wooden egg filled with rice back into the bin. If only she could shake away the memory of her humiliation running like a current under her skin. Grounding herself in the present, Katy narrowed her gaze.

Ava's posture was straight, and tight lines tugged around her eyes.

"How did the appointment go with your grandma yesterday?" Katy crossed the room to stand shoulder to shoulder. Ava's grandma had fallen a few days ago and sprained her wrist. As the only granddaughter, Ava was the first call and the main caregiver.

"You know how my *abuela* is. Dr. Ross suggested she move into assisted living again. The ride home was long and filled with her tirade about never giving up her independence." Ava threw her hands up in the air.

"I'm sorry. I keep hoping she'll see how her friends like living together and change her mind." Katy sighed.

"That's my hope, too," Ava said.

Katy slid an arm around Ava. They would get through the next few weeks together.

****

After lunch, Katy scanned the monochrome storage room. A wall of boxes were all labeled with *Festival Donations* in Darcy's boxy handwriting. The sheer number of white document boxes made Katy's stomach tighten. She slid the lid back on one and found tidy stacks of books. They weren't price tagged, but they were in the spreadsheet printout in Darcy's folder with the price already researched. Most of the books were priced by hardback or paperback, but one box had signed and vintage books with special pricing.

The box in front of her held food mystery novels. She slid the lid back on another box and found children's picture books. Each box had already been sorted by genre. Darcy was more organized than Katy had imagined. Katy sat on a hard metal chair in the storage room, jotting down notes with her favorite blue pen. The *scritch-scratch* of the felt tip was soothing in the face of ten shelves of book boxes. The cold metal warmed under her arm where she leaned sideways.

Ava popped her head through the door, scanning the rows of gray metal shelves. "Katy?"

"What's wrong?" Worst-case scenarios spun through her mind like an out-of-control carousel. The metal chair legs screeched across the linoleum floor as Katy stood.

"Isaac is out in the stacks right now." Her sultry voice was high.

"He's writing his thesis, so I should have expected him to show back up this fall." Katy kept her face neutral, but she tightened a hand around her lanyard. He'd been gone all summer.

Ava thinned her plump lips. "Do you want me to deal with him? You're scheduled out here, but I can cover. I'm finished with story time for now."

"If he's fine with seeing me, then I can do the same." Katy lifted her chin. She slipped her trembling hand into her pocket. One day they were making plans for summer trips, and the next they were done. He'd asked her out to coffee and told her he didn't see the relationship going anywhere. The abruptness left her wondering why she was discarded without a second glance. What had she done wrong? She swallowed.

"So, I shouldn't warn you then?" Ava's eyes narrowed.

The entire day rattled Katy. Between the signal bird and running into two guys who bruised her heart, she should have stayed home. *I can and will handle Isaac.* "Forewarned is better. Thank you." She stuck her notes into an orange folder. She would not change her shift upstairs because of him.

Isaac piled records in their bound books on the table like a little fort. He wore a blazer and a graphic T-shirt with an ancient computer. He didn't even glance her way, but he sat there, reading and tapping his high-top sneakers under the table to his own unidentified rhythm.

Katy settled into her favorite spot at the second-floor information desk. When Isaac's cologne wafted over her, she forced a wobbly smile. She'd given him the crisp scent for his birthday. Tall and lanky, Isaac was born to be a college professor. Did hoodies come with elbow patches? His perpetual five-o'clock shadow was dark, and she hated remembering how soft his dark-brown hair was.

"Hey, Katy." He raised his voice to cover the distance between them.

Were they suddenly a Regency couple? Did they really need six feet? Isaac was far from a Regency hero. He was more Mr. Collins than Mr. Darcy.

Katy sighed. "Do you need help finding something?" She fidgeted with the blue pen she kept on her library ID lanyard.

"I mostly wanted to say hey. I don't want everything to be weird." He slumped his shoulders.

"Our new normal takes time." Why was she

making the breakup easier? People broke up all the time, and the world kept spinning. She glanced toward the stairway.

"I bet you're right. You know, I actually could use some more help. I found what I need from the county commissioners. Any ideas on other places to research?" He stepped closer.

They brainstormed nonprofits in the area, and Isaac kept inching closer.

She scrolled through the search results. He smelled like his citrus cologne. The little buzz under her skin from when they were first dating was gone. When had she stopped feeling *something* toward him?

Isaac pressed a hand over hers to control the curser like he'd done hundreds of times when they were together.

She slipped her hand away. The escape from the slick clamminess of his skin made the air colder, sharper. Maybe the signal bird was a fluke? She'd get to McKenna's earlier next time. Isaac wouldn't always research during her shift. She was convinced until she left the library to the wing beats of another signal bird.

Chapter Two

On base, Luke Taylor searched for Katy on his phone during the slow process of logging onto his computer. He found the library hiring announcement with a great photo of her in front of a wall of books. Her long golden-brown hair was half up, and her heart-shaped face was bright.

She'd been there a little over a year, and he couldn't help but wonder how many times they'd been in Brewed Awakenings or on Dupont Highway at the same time. Dover wasn't a big place. He didn't see any guys on her bookish social media pages filled with reading recommendations and book-inspired food. He cracked his neck. Katy Caterby, in Dover of all places.

His phone pinged with a text from Major McClain to come to her office. He racked his brain for something he might have done wrong to warrant the terse text. *Today was apparently a what-did-you-do kind of morning.* He left his computer to do its slow morning routine and made his way to Major McClain's office. Her long, dark-brown hair was in a tight bun. She punched the keys like she was angry typing. Her jaw wasn't clenched, so maybe he wasn't in trouble.

She motioned toward the black plastic chair across from her desk.

Luke sat on the edge. He clutched his notepad ready on his lap.

"Morning, Captain. I received the most interesting email about you. Turns out there might be a spot at Squadron Officer Training." She raised a manicured eyebrow. Her espresso-brown eyes gave nothing away.

Luke sat up straight. Actually going in person was a big deal. The PCS—Permanent Change of Station— was the chance of a lifetime and his way out of Dover. He'd never lived anywhere for more than three years, and the itch to leave was like ants running across his skin. *Four years.* Too long to stay in one place.

"I'm not even going to ask if you're interested. You'd be a fool not to want the opportunity, and I've known you long enough to know better." She waved her palms in front of her.

"Yes, ma'am. I'm very interested. Even being considered is an honor." Luke pressed his lips firmly together. He was stir-crazy in Delaware. As Mom would say, *The grass was growing under his feet.*

"You apparently impressed the wing commander on your last deployment, but I need to see a big change if you want my endorsement. You've been 'the job' for too long. There's no story. You have to be the full person. In the meantime, you're tasked as the rover today." She turned back to her computer, clacking out a loud email.

He nodded. Her written endorsement would be a game-changer for his chance of being chosen. He kept his expression flat. How many times had a ranking officer thrown the "full person" line around? Like active-duty military officers had all the free time in the world to somehow make a relationship work with their hours and deployments. Oh, and find time to regularly volunteer in the community. Being "the job" was all

Luke was good at. He'd have to find somewhere to volunteer, fast. Surely, community engagement would be enough for Major McClain.

"So, get out there and keep things moving on time." She waved him off.

"Thanks, Major." Getting to attend Squadron Officer School in person would open doors he couldn't open any other way. He would meet officers who could help him get better assignments and kick-start his career. Anyone paying attention would know he was a top performer. He could sign up for a few volunteer shifts. His ticket out of Dover was within reach.

His phone buzzed on the way back to his desk.

"Captain, Aircrew is out to prep the aircraft, and the cargo isn't ready to go."

Those were not words he ever wanted to hear from the control tower. Was someone asleep at the wheel? Luke tensed his shoulders. "I'll check in with outbound and circle back."

When he spotted the problem at the outbound desk, he thinned his lips.

The new sergeant responsible for outbound had schoolwork on his lap. His screen had gone to sleep.

Luke's scowl reflected back on the black screen. "What's the status on the next outbound?" The sergeant had no idea, but Luke needed to give him a chance.

The bald-headed sergeant dropped his textbook and highlighter. His textbook landed with a thud, and the highlighter rolled to a stop against Luke's boot.

"Are we in study hall, Sgt Groves? The aircrew is standing at an aircraft without its load. What is the status?" He punctuated each word in a staccato rhythm.

The guy shifted to his screen and called his

counterpart. "Where's my k-loader, Dan?"

Luke called the aircrew and the control tower to identify the timeline he was now working with. If they didn't get the cargo all sorted before the aircrew's hours reset, the load would be delayed. The cargo was on an aircraft and not a ship for a reason.

He hustled out to join the crew and bark at the k-loader driver to hurry up. Luke huffed after the fourth call to get the load back on track. Why, in the midst of everything, was his mind squarely on a librarian? Figuring out the mystery of Katy Caterby would have to wait.

****

The following Friday, Luke sat at a table in Brewed Awakenings, hoping to catch sight of Katy. Since high school graduation, bookstores and hardware shops always reminded him of her. Her golden-brown hair and heart-shaped face brought back so many memories from Oklahoma. Over the last few days, he'd prepped loads, tracked parts, and tried to make time to volunteer while Katy popped into his mind on repeat. He had to fix whatever he'd broken in their friendship back in high school, or he'd never get a moment's peace again.

McKenna had tall cabinets behind the counter with vintage coffee tins lined across the top, including an ancient red tin of chicory coffee. Her espresso machine was newer and her pride and joy. Grinding and blending filled the air as the baristas filled order after order.

He slid the mason jar of sunflowers around the table for the fifth time.

The door chimed open again.

Katy breezed in, beaming like the best part of her day was about to happen. She'd changed so much since high school, but in some moments, she was still the same girl who'd been his closest friend. She wore gray leggings with a dark-blue sweater. Her long brown hair flowed down her back, and he couldn't take his gaze off her. His heart jumped into his throat.

He tried to pay for her coffee, but McKenna wouldn't interrupt Katy's plans. He stood and waited by the order counter, hoping to catch her before she ran off again.

She spotted him and tripped over her own feet, stumbling to catch herself.

He steadied her arm.

But she tensed.

He leaned back, missing the softness of her sweater against his fingertips. "Hey, Katy, will you join me for coffee?" He wiped a slick palm on his jeans.

"She'd love to," McKenna yelled from behind the counter.

Katy sucked in a breath, snapping her head toward the owner.

Luke imagined the expression wasn't the nicest.

McKenna pursed her lips.

"I start work late today, so I was planning to stay for a while." She bit her lip.

He sputtered, searching for something to say, but she wasn't helping the situation with the frown taking up half of her face.

"McKenna told me to wait a minute before ordering my coffee, and now I see why. Should we go order? I could leave my book here to save the table?" She slipped a book from her purse. Her slim fingers danced over the cover.

"Sure. Good thinking. What's your standard coffee order?" He pointed to the chalkboard menu with orange and green pumpkin vines.

Her dark-blue sweater hugged her hips.

"Cinnamon latte. The Caterby latte back home." Her dark hazel eyes grew warmer.

"I'll have to order one of those. I'm a chai latte with an extra shot kind of guy. Though McKenna will tell you I drink cold coffee in the summer. I'm convinced she thinks iced coffee is a character flaw or something." He rubbed the back of his neck. He was rambling. How did he turn the words off?

"Could be," Katy said.

Luke relaxed his shoulders. He liked the way her lips quirked in the corner.

McKenna leaned toward them. "I'll get your usuals going. I have a few cider donuts left. You want me to plate those?" She pointed over to the case with the donuts.

Her pastry case had pumpkin spice muffins, apple turnovers, and cinnamon swirl scones. Luke would have said *yes* to anything McKenna baked.

"I think we better take those. I have a firm 'always say yes to donuts' policy." Katy shifted toward her friend.

The two women had a whole conversation with their facial expressions. McKenna smirked, raising her eyebrows. Katy pursed her lips. Luke needed a translator. He paid for their treats.

She tightened her lips but let him pay. She handed McKenna enough to cover the next person's drink order.

McKenna took the cash and winked.

Katy's book guarded the table. She took a seat and slipped the book back into her sunflower-yellow bag.

"What book are you reading?" He couldn't think of a safer topic. If only he could get her to remember how good they were together as friends. Neither of them had ever held back. She was the one person he'd never had to police his words with. Books and Katy matched together in his mind like peanut butter and jelly. She'd always been reading back in high school, and with her being a librarian, he hoped the topic would ease her into talking.

"Which one? My current list includes a car book, a bedside book, a work break book, and a purse book." She bounced in her chair, and she was no longer sitting with her back rigid.

"I'm not surprised in the least. I want the whole list. I'll have you know I became quite the reader on my first deployment. After my first thriller, I was hooked."

She nodded. "I love a good gateway book."

"What exactly is a 'gateway book'?" He scrunched his brow.

"The book responsible for your reading habit."

When she smiled, her hazel eyes had flecks of gold.

She listed her current reads.

"So, what brought you to Dover? My story isn't much of a mystery since I go where the Air Force sends me." The application form for the training program sitting on his desk popped into his head, but he didn't say anything. Even the smallest thing might jinx his chance of going in person—of moving on.

"I met my current boss while working on a project

in grad school with the Mini Community Library's Indigenous Library Project. Do you know what a Mini Community Library is?" The corner of her mouth curved upward.

"Those little book stands you see in front of houses or at parks? We have them back home in Durant now."

Her chin lifted higher. "I helped set those up in Durant, actually. My boss is a resource for their initiative, and she was my mentor. She called after I graduated and said she had an opening here at the Dover Public Library."

Her passion for the tiny libraries sparked in her eyes. He leaned toward her like a moth to a flame. "Sounds like the job was meant to be." He was even more determined to earn her friendship back.

"I couldn't believe she hired me. I still can't quite believe I got the job. I was so excited to leave Oklahoma and live close to the ocean." She drew her brows together. "Nobody knows Joe here. Not once has anyone stopped to tell me how different I am from my brother like I'm a disappointment."

Katy and her brother were complete opposites. Joe was the high school quarterback and stickball champion. He'd even been class president every year. If they hadn't shared the same golden-brown hair, heart-shaped faces, and dark hazel eyes, Luke would've had a hard time believing they were siblings. Where Joe would talk to anyone, Katy was quiet and only talked to a few people. He'd been one of her select few—at least for a while. He'd never been anyone's first choice before.

Why had he let her friendship go? "I understand. One of the things I like about being in the Air Force is moving around. I've been a lot of places, and they're all so different from back home." He bounced his foot. He more than liked to move around. He'd spent his childhood moving between posts while Mom served. After almost four years in Dover, he was close to begging for a new assignment—a new adventure.

"I'm surprised you ended up in the Air Force. You used to wear all those Army shirts."

He winced. "My mom retired from the Army, so I was given a lot of Army shirts back then. She still gives me a hard time for choosing the Air Force. But I'll tell you, I figured out real fast the Air Force was better for me. And maybe I wanted to go my own way." Luke understood wanting to escape someone else's shadow. His mother was a decorated Army veteran, and Luke hoped he'd serve as well as his mother had.

"I bet she's proud of you." Katy squeezed his forearm in her slender hand.

The contact sent an electric shock wave up his arm. He cleared his throat. "She sent me boxes of full-sized candy bars during my last deployment. When the mail delivery arrived, I was fairly popular."

"Where did you deploy?" she asked.

"Iraq."

Katy covered her mouth.

He wanted to rest a hand on hers to reassure her, but he wouldn't push his luck. "I'm a logistics guy, a loggie, so I did similar stuff as here. Making sure everyone has the equipment they need and running flight line schedules. Though I don't miss the thirty-hour days or sleeping in a tin box with jets taking off over me." He rubbed the back of his neck. He didn't miss the sand either. He shifted in his seat.

She leaned forward, resting her elbows on the table. "I can't imagine. How did you even sleep at all?"

A barista called his name, or rather a different Luke's order, and he was jarred out of the bubble they'd created merely by being together. The grinding and steaming roared back into his awareness. For a moment, only Katy had existed. He shook his head. He'd been so tired on deployment. Thirty-six-hour days would cure even the worst insomnia. "Like anything else, you get used to new situations." He lifted his chin.

"I'm glad you came back." She scrunched her brows together.

"Thanks, Katy. I can't quite believe we ended up in the same town." He forced a laugh. People thanking him for his service or talking about how dangerous deployments could be just made him want to disappear into a bush. He'd made the commitment, and he wouldn't waste time worrying.

"Seeing you was quite the shock." She glanced at the door, tucking a strand of her long brown hair back behind her ear.

He wanted to ask why.

McKenna slid their drinks and donuts onto the table.

Were they calling his name earlier? He needed to get his head on straight.

"I'm going to need the backstory here." McKenna rested against the back of Katy's chair. Her dark-blonde hair was pulled up into a fancy knot, and her purple apron had coffee smeared across her store logo on the front.

"We were lab partners in high school. You were only in Durant for a year, right?" Katy fidgeted with her napkin.

"Yeah, just a little over a year in Oklahoma. Dover actually just crossed the finish line for the longest I've ever lived somewhere." And he was ready to live somewhere else. He could practically smell the moving boxes and freedom.

"So, why did you two lose track of each other?" McKenna adjusted her apron. Her T-shirt had tiny pumpkins dotted all over in green and cream.

"He moved away." Katy grimaced.

He blew out a breath. "I was an idiot? I'm hoping we can be friends now, though. When I enlisted, I should have kept in touch. Jolie, my ex, wasn't your biggest fan, so I guess I cruised down the easy route and let our friendship go. You two never really got along."

Katy stiffened. "My childhood nightmare? *Not getting along* might be underselling the situation." She dropped her cider donut onto the plate. Loose sugar flew around like confetti.

Her nightmare? Was she exaggerating? Or was he part of the nightmare by association?

"Nightmare? Was she a bully?" McKenna squeezed Katy's shoulder.

Luke opened his mouth to defend Jolie, but the tightness around Katy's eyes stopped him. "Was she?" he asked softly.

Katy squared her shoulders. "You have no idea how mean girls can be to each other."

"Jolie isn't a bad person." He couldn't sort out the picture Katy was painting with his own memories.

"I'm not saying she didn't grow up and become a better person." Katy hugged her arms around her stomach. "Jolie was different with you."

"You never said anything." Why hadn't she confided in him back then? He tried to remember what Jolie told him. Katy had gotten a spot on the yearbook over Jolie, and his ex was convinced Joe sweet-talked them into giving her the position. Jolie's issues were typical high school stuff.

"Teenagers aren't always equipped to name their hurts." Katy clutched the coffee cup.

Luke sat back. He didn't know the whole story. What had happened between them? He'd missed all the drama. Some friend he'd been.

"Amen." McKenna glanced at the growing line of customers. "Now, you two enjoy these donuts."

"I should have stood up for you back then. I should have kept in touch after I enlisted. I can't go back and fix my mistakes, but I can tell you I'm sorry." Luke hung his head. How hadn't he known Jolie bullied Katy?

"You two aren't together anymore?" Her cheeks were flushed.

"No, she ended things to move back home for her dream job after she finished college. She wants a life in Oklahoma teaching in the school where she grew up. I'd be miserable if I wasn't out in the world experiencing new things. We grew up and wanted different things."

He stared at Jolie's pink suitcases by their apartment door. Was she going somewhere?

"Hey." Jolie dropped another bag by the door.

"What's going on?" Luke swallowed.

She stared at her bags. "I got my dream job, and there's no point in asking you to come with me. You're not a hometown kind of guy. You're an on the move, no permanent address, only good for leaving—"

"That's not fair. Where is this job?" His eyes stung, but he would stay calm. She went on the offensive any time he got upset. He couldn't handle being attacked. She was leaving him. They were breaking up. Had she even mentioned applying for jobs somewhere else?

"Back home in Durant. And I accepted it. I'm going home where I belong. I can't live like this anymore. I hate it here. I hate not knowing where we'll be next year. I deserve to have neighbors who know me and to visit my mama any time I want. This is the life you want, not me." She pursed her lips.

"Jolie—"

"Goodbye, Luke. You take care of yourself." She opened the door.

Her dad stepped up to grab her bags.

Luke hadn't even known her dad was in town. He watched them leave without another word. What could he have said? She hated his life.

He wanted to find a safer topic, but he floundered, scanning around the shop. "You and McKenna are friends?"

Katy wavered in her chair.

He waited to see if she'd let him off—if she wanted to change the subject as much as he did.

"She and my coworker, Ava, met in high school, and now, the three of us are friends. I can't imagine life without them." Katy's smile lit up her hazel eyes. She relaxed her shoulders.

"Friends make everything better. And coffee. Coffee definitely helps." He lifted his cup in salute.

Luke tapped his foot, desperate to fill the silence stretching out like the dunes in Iraq.

Katy lifted her cup in cheers. A sly grin spread across her face. "Remember how Mr. Wegman would do those morning dances with his coffee? I'll never forget the first time we caught him in his room, shimmying around to ABBA with coffee splashing everywhere." She shimmied her shoulders.

Luke couldn't contain his grin. "Oh, man, I'd forgotten about Wegman's dancing hijinks. Most days, little coffee splatters speckled the floor. I've never met anyone else obsessed with disco music like he was."

"Want to know a secret?" She leaned in.

"Always." He held perfectly still. He didn't want her shifting mood to change.

"On hard-to-get-moving mornings, I channel my inner Mr. Wegman and dance with my morning coffee. The moment is messy and ridiculous, but I'm ready to conquer the whole world afterward." She blushed.

He sat back with a smile, picturing quiet Katy jumping and dancing around her kitchen first thing in the morning. "What's the soundtrack, though? The vibe is a very important part of releasing your inner Wegman." He wanted to know everything about grown-up Katy. He'd missed too much. In high school, he'd known her favorite bands. Her music might have changed, but her eyes still were warm and open.

"The songs aren't disco. Am I dishonoring his memory by choosing my own songs? Or is the key to find music you can't help but dance to?" She tilted her head to the side like the soundtrack was a deep and essential question for a life well-lived.

"I have a morning playlist for my run. I'll share my

jams if you share your coffee dance tunes."

"Maybe someday." She took the last bite of her donut. Katy's phone buzzed. "I need to head to work. My coworker is out for the next few months, so the rest of us are stepping in to cover."

"I hope everything is okay." He gathered their plates and empty cups.

She stopped in the process of getting her bag and studied him with her big hazel eyes. "She's a new mom, so she's tired but okay. I bet I'll see you around."

"We could meet for coffee again." He gulped. The chances she would say *no* were too high.

Katy bit her lower lip.

His shoulders started to droop.

She smoothed out her silky hair. "A-are you still a hug person?" She opened her arms.

"Definitely." He leaned in for a quick hug. She smelled like cinnamon, coffee, and home. He reluctantly let her go. Luke took a step back. What was his problem? He kept standing there. How in the world had he ended up in a coffee shop with the woman he never could forget?

****

"Captain Taylor, come with me. Bring a pen and your notebook." Major McClain snapped her fingers.

Luke locked his computer screen and followed her. Their boots echoed in the narrow hallway lined with portraits of Dover AFB's wing commanders. Fall brought a reprieve along the corridor lined with wide windows. Warm but not sweltering was a win.

Major McClain exhaled a long, slow breath, bracing a hand on the chipped oak doorjamb. She entered a conference room filled with other officers and took an open seat.

"Glad you could join us, Major McClain. Who did you bring today?" a full-bird colonel asked from the other side of the conference table.

"Captain Luke Taylor is one of my flight line loggies. We're happy to participate. Our community on base is always a top priority." She smoothed her shiny hair back.

Luke took a seat like he had a clue. The wheels squeaked, so he stopped before scooting all the way in. As the lowest-ranked officer in the room, he had no intention of receiving more attention.

"Welcome to the table, Captain." The colonel adjusted his thin wire glasses. "Now, you all know we're here to deal with a new literacy program being rolled out. Reading levels for the kids on base are sliding, so our goal is to improve literacy over the next three years. Let me hear your ideas."

Everyone froze. The room smelled like boot polish and discomfort.

Hazel eyes and a heart-shaped face popped into Luke's mind.

"Sir, shouldn't we be asking the school librarian for guidance?" Major McClain sat up straight. "Literacy isn't my expertise. But I'm a mom of kids on base."

"Great idea, and of course, your perspective will be invaluable to the project. Reach out to the school library on base and let me know what action items you come up with." The colonel slid a printout across the table. "Make sure the plan works within the original initiative parameters."

To her credit, she didn't bat an eye when she was placed in charge of all the brainstorming.

He stood, meaning everyone followed and left.

Except Major McClain, who plopped back into a chair and reviewed the initiative paperwork. She tapped her pen on the page. Major McClain glanced up. "I'll need you to call the school and talk to the librarian tomorrow. Let me know what they say, and we'll come up with a list of options."

Luke nodded. Would Katy be willing to help? "I know a librarian at Dover Public Library. You okay if I reach out to my friend first? She did her whole masters on youth engagement." Was he jumping the gun by calling her his friend? Maybe. But he was a big believer in visualizing goals. He'd win her back.

Major McClain cocked an eyebrow. Smiling, she revealed a big gap between her front two teeth. "Great idea, Captain. I've known you long enough to know you'll take the initiative seriously. Let me know when you talk to an expert."

"Yes, ma'am." Luke returned to the duty officer desk with a spring in his step. Recruiting Katy had nothing to do with the way he kept wanting to see her. Absolutely nothing…

Chapter Three

Katy sat outside the library with a coffee and her current book—a cozy mystery set in a coastal town all decorated for the "ber" months. Her work phone buzzed. She let the call go to voicemail. She'd handle the call when her break was over.

Her phone rang again after the first call had gone to voicemail. She gazed up at the puffy white clouds in the sky, shaking her head. Answering with her memorized library spiel, she smiled as the words rolled off her tongue without pause.

"Hey, Katy. This is Luke."

She gulped. Why was Luke Taylor calling her—repeatedly—at work? "You're persistent."

"You used to like my inability to give up."

His voice was deep and warm. She ignored the shiver running down her back.

"How many hours did we spend on those lab assignments we failed? You stuck with me no matter how many times we had to try again." He chuckled.

She'd mistakenly assumed the time they'd spent together made them actual friends. She couldn't make the same mistake again. "Countless hours. All right, Mr. Persistent. What's going on?" She stowed her book in her yellow bag and wandered under the canopy of newly turning trees.

"I ended up in a meeting today. We're launching a

literacy initiative on base. I need an expert to help me with some ideas to present to my boss and others."

His tone shifted from playful to what she imagined was his captain voice. *Oh.* She pressed a hand to the rough bark of a tree with leaves slowly turning scarlet. "Adult literacy?"

"For the kids. You know I was an Army brat, and I want to do right by the kids on base."

He'd moved to Durant the summer before their senior year, and he'd had no problem making friends. The track team claimed him on day one. After a summer where she was his only friend, she'd expected him to ditch her like everyone else. He had eventually. She could still feel the sting in her heart. "I'm done here at seven. You want to meet somewhere? I need to see the initiative." She couldn't say *no* to helping kids increase their reading skills, especially kids with parents serving in the Air Force.

In their own way, the kids were a big part of the support network. A life of service needed support from the whole family.

"How about the Lobby House? I can meet you there around seven thirty?"

Luke sounded more excited than she was. "You mean Fraizer's?" She chuckled. When she'd first moved to Dover, the name was already Fraizer's. Anyone who grew up there or had lived there longer than a year had a hard time switching to the new name.

"As far as I'm concerned, the Lobby House is the restaurant at the edge of downtown."

"For you and everyone else."

"Should we swap phone numbers? Just in case something comes up?" Luke cleared his throat.

She rattled off her phone number. "Okay, I'll see you then." She added a reminder on her phone, so she wouldn't drive home on autopilot.

Her heartbeat drummed in her ears. He'd asked for her number. He'd tracked her down at work. *Did the persistence mean anything?*

The sliding glass library doors closed behind her with a whoosh of air. She breathed in the paper and bindings scent of her favorite place.

"What's with the moony eyes?" Ava's tone was soft.

"Funny story, I ran into the guy from high school again at Brewed Awakenings." Katy studied the industrial blue carpet. She blinked, willing her eyes to hold zero moons. Her heart was not hammering in her ears over having drinks with Luke.

"What a small world. You like him?" Ava waved her on.

Ava needed to get her own life. She hadn't dated in months. Her ex married her former best friend over the summer. Dating someone new would help Ava move on, but she adamantly refused.

Katy joined her at the welcome desk and sighed. She didn't want to like Luke, but just his voice had made her heart race and her whole body shiver. "I asked him out in high school, but he sort of blew me off. And then he ghosted me after we graduated." An image of his smirking high school girlfriend popped up uninvited, and Katy slumped her shoulders.

Jolie was bright and shiny with her dark-red hair and gymnast's physique. She was a ruby tiara while Katy was a vintage pair of sneakers.

"Quiet, bookish kid takes a risk only to be shut

down. I think most of us have lived a similar story at one time or another. So, why the smile?" Ava tilted her head and waited.

Katy shrugged. "Because he's been assigned to a literacy initiative for kids on base, and he wants my help. We don't get to serve their community as much as I'd like, so I'm excited." Her joy was bookish—completely bookish. Luke remembering her and acting like they were old friends had nothing to do with her excitement.

"Well, be careful." Ava popped a hand on her hip. *Easier said than done.*

****

Back in Darcy's office, Katy spread out thick poster paper ready for selfie station sketches. Her office smelled like graphite and permanent markers. Her broad pencil strokes made her think of the way Luke had always paid so much attention to her classroom doodles. Nobody else had ever noticed.

"The photo booth is coming together." Mae stepped into the doorway. Reading glasses hung around her neck, and the red shiny beaded chain blended in with her red blazer.

"The Adventure Girls leader volunteered to make signs for the different areas in the stall. They also offered to make bookmarks for freebee gifts." Katy twirled a permanent marker around her fingers.

"Sounds great." Mae added notes to her ever-present red notebook.

They chatted about the details, and Katy started to feel like she could manage the Fall Fair stall. Maybe she wouldn't let everyone down after all.

"I talked to Darcy. She and baby Charlie are

finding a rhythm." Mae's wistful expression softened into a contented sigh.

"What a great name! Did she say if we could do anything to help?" Maybe she should leave diapers on Darcy's doorstep?

"Her dog has moved in with me for a little while. Fitzwilliam has already settled right in."

Fitzwilliam was a terrier mix with white-and-brown patches on his fur. Katy set down her permanent marker. "Fitz is such a good dog. I'm so glad he has a place to stay while Darcy spends her days with baby Charlie."

The dark skin around Mae's eyes was wrinkled from years of easy joy. "We look out for our own here."

Katy and Mae shut down the library for the night, running through their end-of-the-day checklists. Isaac's slow shuffling steps caught her off guard.

He stopped and adjusted his battered leather satchel. He shifted from foot to foot.

Her stomach filled with bees. "Hey, Isaac, have a good night." She didn't raise her gaze from shutting down the last computer.

"I need to set an alarm on my phone, so I'm not the last one out anymore. I'm headed to get a drink. Do you want to join me?" He adjusted his black plastic glasses.

Did he mean…like a date? No, obviously not. And she didn't want a date. He wanted to hang out as friends. Like she was doing with Luke. She sighed with a twinge of wistfulness. "I have plans, but you have fun." She kept her voice even.

The doors closed behind him with a rush of chilly fall air. What was he doing? He'd broken things off in such a casual way. Was he trying to pick things back up? She wasn't sure how to handle his renewed interest. Did she want him back? She rubbed her temples.

Mae turned the lock with an echoing click. She was wearing long black-and-white beaded earrings.

"Did you make your earrings with your mom?" Katy asked.

"These were the last pair we made before she passed. Thank you for remembering. Wearing them makes me feel like she's with me." Mae clasped one of her dangling earrings.

Katy had never had the patience for beading, but she'd spent hours sorting tiny glass beads as her contribution. Gran had made some incredible jewelry and even added beads to her puckered moccasins sometimes—just because she could. She'd been gone for three years, but Katy didn't miss her any less. She'd been Katy's mother figure—the gentle hand to her father's hard-line rules. What would Gran make of Isaac?

Mae cleared her throat. "I appreciate the way you've stepped up to run the book sale. I'm impressed."

"Thank you, Mae. I've come a long way from the Mini Community Library project in Oklahoma."

Mae softened her expression. "I know the MCL projects will always be your favorite, though. You and those mini libraries. I've never seen anyone champion those like you do."

Katy pressed a hand over her heart. "Books out in the community? Available to anyone? Reaching new readers? Are you kidding? They're the greatest." When a teen found a graphic novel and lost complete track of the world around her, Katy's life had changed, inspiring her to become a librarian.

****

At Frazier's, Luke stood and waved from a bar-top table. He was wearing jeans and a button-up. His shirt was army-green and made his green eyes bolder even in the darker bar lighting. She tried not to notice the way the shirt clung to his muscular arms and failed. Why did her body react like a magnet any time he was in the same room?

"Hey, thanks again for meeting me." He ran a hand through his short, sandy-brown hair. He had dark circles under his eyes.

How stressful was his job on base?

"What can I order for you?" He pulled out a wooden high-top chair. "You hungry? I'm putting in an order for nachos."

"Fried avocados and a lager beer—your pick. I'm game for whatever." She shrugged.

He returned from ordering at the bar and slipped a little memo notebook out of his back pocket. "I'm ready to be schooled on youth literacy."

She swallowed against the picture he made with his pen and earnest expression. Why did he have to be so...*Luke*? His full attention was addicting. "How did you end up on a literacy project?" She tugged the cuff of her dark-blue sweater. The creamy fabric was soft enough to be a reading blanket. Part of her wished she was curled up at home with her favorite book, but part of her was thrilled to be out with Luke.

"I was 'voluntold' by my boss to figure the initiative out. She spoke up in a meeting and ended up point person. But you know I'm game for volunteering. Sharing books could help kids connect when they end up stationed here."

"You'd be the expert. You moved around a lot before Durant. You always made those Army brat references."

"Military families have a different way of approaching life. If I can help ease those transitions, then I'm in." He stared at his blank page and tapped his pen.

She'd spent her whole life in the same house in a small town until college, so he was the expert. "I did a little research after we talked, and I think you should get them to add Mini Community Libraries by the school or playground on base." She shared every statistic she could think of.

He jotted down notes and chewed on the top of his pen. "A park in Durant had one. Do they all have to be small boxes, or can they be bigger? You'll need books for a wide range of ages, right?"

"Is the initiative targeting elementary school age kids? Did you bring the initiative?" She swallowed. She'd jumped ahead without reading the instructions again.

"Oh, right. Here." He unfolded a sheet from the back of his notepad.

They expected the project to span early readers to high school, but the goal was to increase literacy. Straight forward enough, and the MCL would definitely achieve a boost. She bit her bottom lip. "Maybe we could use three boxes together. One door opens to picture books, one to early chapters, and one to middle grade and young adult." She sorted through her bag for a mechanical pencil. No way was she borrowing his chewed-on pen. She slid his notepad over and sketched out what she had in mind.

"Can you paint characters? Like you did in Durant?" He tapped her doodle page.

She dropped her mouth open. "You really stopped at the one back home?"

"Well, yeah, I checked the library out last time I visited my mom and Jackie. I'd never seen one in person before." He shrugged.

"Thanks." Heat crept into her cheeks. He noticed one of her Durant MCLs? Her dad was the only one from back home who ever sent her photos of the small book-lending library. Hundreds of questions leaped to the tip of her tongue. Had he seen them at the big park back home and taken a closer look? Did his sister Jackie swap books there?

"Do you think the park or the school would be better?" He took a few more notes.

"I would place the library as close to the park as possible. When school is out, do kids play on the school's playground? Like back home?" The closer they built the mini library to where kids played, the better. She pictured the sheer joy of a bookish kid discovering new reads at the park.

He eased his broad shoulders back. "I'm not sure. I don't live on base, so I'm not an expert there. My boss has kids in the elementary school, so I'll ask her."

"Checking with an expert is always a good start," Katy said.

A server stopped by with their drinks and food.

Luke's nachos towered over the table, threatening to topple at any moment under the weight of cheese, beans, and chicken. Katy wished she'd ordered her own. "Those nachos are slightly epic."

Luke leaned back. "You've been in Dover for how

long, and you've never had Lobby House nachos? You are hanging around with the wrong crowd." He waved at a platter the size of two plates with a mound of cheesy goodness.

"Good thing I have you to correct my Dover food education." She snagged a chip loaded with toppings. The sour cream was packed full of taco seasoning. She was officially impressed.

He tapped his notebook. "I'll take these notes to my boss and let you know what she says."

"She'll be the one to approve?"

"Partly. She'll take the plan back to the colonel who assigned her the project for his thumbs-up or down. But I bet they'll defer to her. If we get the go-ahead, any chance you'll help me?" He smoothed his shirt and straightened his back.

"You know I can't say *no* to an MCL." She lifted her hands in defeat. Did she have time to take on another project? No. She'd help anyway to help kids on base. Gran always said the Choctaw did good things but didn't talk about them, so she'd bring the light of literacy everywhere she went.

"MCL?" He raised an eyebrow.

"Mini Community Library."

"Even librarians have acronym soup." He chuckled.

"I'm sorry, but you absolutely have to explain acronym soup." She sipped her sweet amber beer.

His face lit up. "The Air Force has acronyms for everything. I could easily have an entire conversation in acronyms without the other officer even getting lost or annoyed."

Katy would pay good money to see him try. "Okay,

so MCLs. We added one outside the library and one to a park last year. I didn't know we could add one on base, but I found plenty of them around the country." She should have called and asked the principal at the elementary school on base. Disappointed, she vowed never to leave the base out of her outreach plans again.

"Makes sense. We kept a table in our offices on deployment where people would share extra food or books they finished reading." He finished off his nachos.

"Oh, wow. I bet people who didn't have anyone to send them treats appreciated everyone sharing." She squeezed his forearm. His army-green shirt was soft cotton. How many people served without support systems at home?

"Definitely. Adventure Girls cookie season was the best. My mom sent me a few boxes she ordered from a neighbor's kid. I shared them, even though I kind of wanted to eat them all." He brushed her hand, reaching for one of her avocado fries.

Her skin buzzed like Fourth of July fireworks. "Well, who wouldn't want to eat those?"

"Right? But yeah, we shared what we had." He shrugged.

She imagined the sharing table had probably meant a lot to others serving with him. "Did you find any good books?" She had to know what they were reading overseas. His patron population remained a mystery.

"You'll laugh, but I packed the *Dune* books. The books were my mom's idea of a joke, but I'll tell you what. I liked them. I'm usually a mystery thriller kind of guy, but reading about a desert people in the desert was cool."

She dropped her jaw. "Oh, my gosh. You took a fantasy book about a hot desert to a hot desert?"

"Yep, a fantasy book about the military." He held his chin higher.

His reading journey was undeniably cool. "You let me know if you need book recommendations for more mystery thrillers. My coworker, Dom, is all nonfiction sports books and thrillers. I bet he has a list ready to go for anyone willing to listen. No, I know he does. We're librarians." She was more of a cozy mystery reader, but she listed off at least four titles she could bring him the next time they met up.

Luke leaned forward. "Thanks. Send his list my way, too. I'm always ready for a new book. I don't go to the library." He ducked his head. "The Last Chapter bookshop down the street from Brewed Awakenings has been my go-to shop. The owner has been good with book recs, too."

Katy clasped her hands to her chest. "Shopping local isn't something to feel sheepish about. You didn't know how great the library was yet."

The corner of his full lip pinched upward. "I sure do now. What genres do you read? I rambled too much and didn't find out the other day. I was too nervous."

Katy bit her lower lip. "You were nervous?"

"You didn't want to see me, and I didn't get why." He threw up his hands. "I disappeared on you, so the mystery is solved."

"I have no choice in the matter. Readers need me." She sighed, staring at her glass. Why did he have to be so sweet? Part of her wanted to explain, but she wasn't sure what to say. *Everyone else in my life left, so when you did, too, the silence wrecked me.* She'd been a dramatic teenager at the time. She would keep their time together all about the kids on base. *Focus on the work. Keep your heart safe.*

"I knew you couldn't say *no* to helping kids find more books." He slid a hand along her forearm.

His rough palm was warm against her exposed skin. She bit her lip. "What monster could?" She gasped in an overdramatic display of horror.

He laughed.

She'd missed his deep baritone more than she wanted to admit. He'd been one of the few people she'd let herself be goofy around in high school. Was letting her guard down again a good idea?

"Truth. Now, don't think I'm dropping my question." His full attention landed on her.

"I read a lot of different things." She smirked.

"You mentioned you have books for different places. I remember way back, you had a bus book and an under-the-desk-during-class book. What else was there? I used to know the whole list."

His smile was lopsided and distracting. He remembered? She leaned toward him, relishing how Luke Taylor really listened when she talked. "My reading habits haven't changed much. I do read more learning theory books, though. But I read a lot of mystery and romance."

"Back then, you were already planning to be a librarian, and nothing would stop you."

"Books are my safe space." She swallowed. The awkward years of high school weren't ones she liked to revisit.

He took a sip of his dark beer. "See? You were always going to be an expert. So, what do you think about the MCL? Do you have time to help me?"

"Look at you picking up the librarian lingo. I'll help you with the *MCL* project from start to finish." She beamed.

He relaxed his whole body.

What had she just done? "Work is a little wild right now. I ended up in charge of the library's used book sale at the Fall Fair." The box of tangled orange twinkle lights was waiting back at the library.

"Wait, so how does the sale work? Will you have a stand at the fair?" When he swallowed, his Adam's apple bobbled.

"A stall, yeah. I have the books, and I'm working on getting price tags on them all. We have a Friends of the Library bookstore, so the sales system is ready to go. I just have to make sure we have staffing." She patted her bag where she kept her new orange notebook dedicated to the Fall Fair stall.

He raised his eyebrows. "Oh, *just*, huh? Sounds like a lot. Any chance you'll let me volunteer since you're helping me? I do work in logistics, you know." He leaned closer.

His aftershave was subtle and made her picture him hiking in the woods. Sandalwood, maybe? *Get your head on straight, Caterby!* Maybe she could accept help, though—for the library. Definitely not because she wanted to spend more time with him. "Any chance you have a truck and don't mind carrying heavy boxes of books? I have pushcart dollies." When she pictured the daily set up and break down, her head swam.

He chuckled. "Count me in. When do you get to set up?"

"We set up and break down every day since the

city can't ensure overnight security." She struggled with asking for help. The Fall Fair was her responsibility, but she couldn't cart everything back and forth alone. *Many hands.*

"Oh, right. I guess I never realized how much goes into those fair stalls. I'll be there to help set up and break down. I'm your guy." His green eyes lit up.

"I appreciate any and all help." When the fair started, she would have to hustle, and the more help she set up now, the smoother the sale would go. She added his offer to her list of things to accomplish in her official fair planning spiral notebook.

He gazed at her notes.

"I'll make a volunteer sign-up form. I'll email you so you can see what the options are. Okay?" She set her green pen down.

"You want me to send the form around the office and see if others want to help, too? We're highly trained with moving supplies." He tilted his head and lifted an eyebrow.

"Oh yeah?" She cocked her head to the side with a smirk. Joking around was as natural as breathing. If his wide grin told her anything, he'd pull out all the stops.

"We're loggies. My day-to-day is all about transporting equipment and people from place to place." He scooted his chair closer.

"Do you like your job?" She brushed her long hair over her shoulder.

"Well, sure. You know how I like a good challenge." He rubbed his chin.

He'd been the first to raise a hand to volunteer for the extra credit challenge experiments in high school. She hadn't known the last experiment would be the final time they cozied up at their black lab table. After the disastrous date—her first—where he brought his girlfriend and two buddies, she never offered to help him again. "I'm having a hard time picturing you as organized. Remember, I've seen your high school locker." She mock-shuddered at the memory.

Luke rested his calloused hand on her arm. "We should keep my past disaster status between us. I don't think anyone needs to know about the level of slob I was back then. You'd be surprised. I live for color-coded spreadsheets these days. Sure, my desk is covered in sticky notes, but I don't lose track of things like I did back then. The Air Force was good for me. I grew up a lot."

She couldn't picture him hyper-focused on a spreadsheet.

"Katy?"

She jerked her head to the side.

Isaac shuffled to a stop by their table.

Why was Isaac here? Was today ghosts of heartbreak past day?

Chapter Four

Luke was a fairly good judge of character, and his gut said, *don't trust him*. The noise in the bar around them ebbed and flowed, but Luke's heart thrummed in his ears. Who was this guy to Katy?

He was tall and skinny with thick-framed glasses and a jacket over a snarky T-shirt. His friends shuffled like they'd rather be anywhere else.

Protectiveness surged within Luke, and he swallowed down the urge to fix whatever was causing Katy discomfort. She didn't need him to rescue her, even if he wanted to.

"Hi, Isaac."

Katy's tone had more pep than her body language could support. Luke had never seen her fake pleasant. Well, except for their first run-in at Brewed Awakenings. He rubbed his neck.

"Isaac, meet my friend from Durant, Luke." Katy waved a hand toward Luke.

"Hey, man. Good to meet you." Luke flexed his arms, resisting the urge to rest an arm along the back of Katy's chair to provide some kind of shelter from the tense situation. Isaac must be an ex of some kind, which did not bother him. He wasn't interested in Katy as more than friends. If things worked out, he'd be leaving Dover soon. Now wasn't the time to start something. Even if Katy was, well, Katy.

"From Durant? Oh, cool. Good to meet you. If you want to join us later, you're more than welcome." Isaac adjusted his thick black glasses.

Luke frowned. He didn't appreciate being invited to the awkward party.

Katy had a death grip on her pencil. "We're about to head out." She pushed up her sleeves again.

"Oh, okay. I'll see you at the library then." Isaac softened his gaze.

His friends ushered him away without looking back.

She scowled. "So weird."

"What's the story there?" Luke rested a hand over hers.

She squeezed his hand, gazing too long at their entwined fingers.

Her hand fit perfectly into his, but where his hands were rough from years on the flight line, hers were smooth and silky.

"I'm not ready to share. Okay?" She glanced beyond the bar to where Isaac and his friends were laughing.

"I'm here if you need to talk." He wished they'd been friends again long enough for her to confide in him like she'd done when they were younger. He'd missed out on a big part of her life. He was such an idiot for letting her friendship go—for letting *her* go.

"Exes are always awkward, right?" She curved her shoulders forward.

"I only have the one." He winced. He'd been bullied a time or two, but Jolie had made Katy miserable for years. He couldn't imagine Jolie being mean, but he believed Katy. He didn't want her to shut him out. "And I can say without a doubt dealing with an ex is a special kind of awkward. You two broke up recently?" He was fishing. Luke fought the urge to glare at Isaac, who was leaning toward the server. Was he flirting? What could the ladies possibly see in skinny Isaac? Luke doubted he could even carry boxes of books.

"Just before summer. And then he wasn't around the library much because he had an internship up in Philly, but now he's back at my library, researching for his thesis." She raised her hands palms up and shook her head.

He had a few ideas about what she should say to her ex. Most of them included kicking Isaac to the curb. "Sounds awful. You can get another librarian to help him, right?"

"I should." Her tone was flat.

"Nobody would think any less of you if you didn't want to be the librarian helping your ex research." He shouldn't be getting so invested in her life, but the idea of Isaac hanging around and making her uncomfortable didn't sit well. He leaned toward her again like she was a magnet. "I should get going. I have to work an earlier shift tomorrow."

"Right, no problem. Just let me know what your boss says."

He reached for the last chip and brushed Katy's soft hand. Electricity zipped up his arm. He gulped. "You'll be my first call." Why did the idea of seeing her or talking to her again make his heart hammer like a one-man construction crew?

****

Major McClain reviewed the notes on the MCL

and the statistics Katy sent.

He'd also printed some photos of actual MCLs from across the country, including the one Jackie had taken of Katy's MCLs in Durant. His little sister was always game to help with photos.

As was her usual, Major McClain's face gave nothing away. Her tidy office had a wall of metal file cabinets behind her. Everything was beige except the bright-red, apple-scented lotion she had on her desk. He'd worked with her long enough to know not to ask questions or rush her when she read the details. He had to sit on his hands to keep himself from tapping on the table.

"A full plan isn't what I had in mind when I asked you to brainstorm." Major McClain's mouth stretched into a frown.

"My friend Katy installed a few back home in Oklahoma, and she's added one to a park here in Dover. The statistics she gave me were convincing." He sat straight. He might not know up from down about getting kids to read, but Katy did.

"Were these her words? 'The MCL is the joy of the library at its most reachable, most available incarnation.' " The major ran her thin finger over the line.

"Yes, ma'am. We'll do a community book drive to build an inventory of books for the MCL, and I called the school to talk to the librarian. He said, and I quote, 'The MCL is brilliant.' "

The school librarian, Josh, had gushed over the idea for a solid twenty minutes. He had even offered to manage the book supply at the park.

"So, two experts." She pursed her lips.

"Leaving the third expert. You, ma'am."

She raised her eyebrows, and she chuckled. "The mom approval?"

"Absolutely." He pressed his lips together to keep from smiling.

"I've never heard of an MCL, but these photos are inviting. My kids will want to open the little door to find out what's inside. Let me take the suggestion to the colonel, and we'll see what's next." When she mentioned her kids, she softened her gaze.

Luke followed her out of her office. The morning sun filtered through the wall-sized windows overlooking the flight line. Luke knew better than to make direct eye contact with the window early in the day. He'd be blinded.

"You did a good job. Talking to two librarians and preparing the proposal was well done." She nodded and left.

He was one step closer to her letter of support for the in-person training opportunity, and he should have been relieved. His mouth was dry, and his throat was tight. Why wasn't he excited to leave Dover?

****

When Luke finished his shift on the flight line, he stopped by the major's office to ask about a shift detail for the following day. She was massaging her temples—never a good sign.

She narrowed her espresso-brown eyes. "Taylor. Good. You have approval for the MCL. Here's the list of forms you need to fill out. I'm counting on you. I might even be inspired to write a letter in support of Squadron Officer Training, depending on how well the initiative goes." She popped an antacid tab into her mouth, filling the small office with peppermint.

"Thank you, ma'am." He shut his mouth so he wouldn't say something stupid. A letter from his commanding officer while the powers that be made their decision would be a game-changer. "I won't let you down." Moving boxes danced in his head.

She handed him a stack of forms and the checklist for building something on base. She dismissed him.

He hadn't even had a chance to ask about the scheduled flights for the next morning, but he would email his question and give her some space. He stashed the lists on his desk in the MCL folder where he had all of his notes from Katy and the school librarian. What dimensions would work? He'd built birdhouses as a kid, and these were giant versions of those…with front doors and hinges. Completely doable. *Maybe.*

"What's with the photos?" Ryan Hart pointed to the page and clenched his square jaw. His dark hair was buzzed on the sides.

"I'm working on a community project on base. We're going to build one of these once I fill out a million forms. We'll stock books in them for the kids on base. Take one, leave one, and pass one on kind of a thing for kids to pick out books at the park." Luke knocked his knuckles against the inch-thick stack of forms. He couldn't afford to mess the MCL up. He'd never lived anywhere as long as he'd been in Dover, and he itched to be somewhere new. He wasn't the staying kind—just ask his ex.

Ryan picked up the sheet. "If the box needs to look presentable, Major's going to be sorely disappointed. I've seen you try to sketch. Stick figures are too much." He slapped the papers back with a chuckle.

"Hey! My stick figures were fine. Everyone understood where they needed to be." They'd had a complicated situation a while back, and he'd needed a new game plan and a diagram. His stick figures were too confusing, and he'd resorted to Xs and Os. Everyone reached their locations. The rest were details. "I've called in an expert," he said. "Lucky for us, she's advanced way past stick figures."

Ryan adjusted his hat while they made their way out to the parking lot. "Since when do you know experts?"

"I know people." Luke squinted. "I ran into a friend from back home. She's a librarian, and I can vouch for her artistic abilities. We'll be fine. Any chance you want to help me fill out forms?"

The late afternoon light was hazy over the parking lot. Base didn't have many trees, but the maple across the lot had changed to a brilliant yellow for fall.

"No, but when you need to build the thing, let me know. I have all my tools at my dad's house."

Mr. Hart had relocated to Delaware while Ryan was in college.

"Will do. She has a plan for a three-door MCL beyond my limited tool supplies. Thanks, man." Luke sighed, relieved he wouldn't need to requisition a long list of tools.

Ryan mock-saluted, revved his motorcycle, and took off.

The days with weather warm enough to ride were numbered. Luke preferred hiking in the fall, so he welcomed the milder days. He called her number and waited.

"Hey, Mr. Persistent. Any word on the MCL?"

Katy cleared her throat.

Luke leaned against his truck. "We have approval. Any chance you can meet to work on the details?"

She cheered. "Yes, if you can help me pick up a bookstand for the book sale. I told you I would need your truck."

"Every truck owner has to bear this burden. But the drive is for a good cause, so you know I'm in." He fought the urge to move closer. His heart rate picked up. He didn't think a trip to pick up furniture worked for his keep-his-distance plan. What was he doing?

****

Luke showed up at Brewed Awakenings early to get a table. The spicy scent of pumpkin and cloves filled the sleepy coffee shop. Two regulars had claimed their corners with their silver laptops. Luke stopped in his tracks.

Katy was already there, talking to McKenna.

What was he doing? Her smile was no reason for his mind to go blank. "Good morning, ladies." Luke stood beside Katy, close enough to breathe in her cinnamon scent.

"What did I miss?" He raised his eyebrows.

Katy's warm hazel eyes lit up. She shifted to stand next to McKenna.

Her casual inclusion was so different from the way she'd reacted at first. He nudged her with a shoulder.

"One of McKenna's favorite authors has an author event at the library next month. She's a little excited." Katy motioned toward her friend.

"I'm going to get all the things signed. And maybe a mug, too. If she signs with a permanent marker, then I can save the moment forever." McKenna hugged her arms around her stomach.

Luke liked McKenna more and more. Book people were his people.

"I ordered you a chai tea latte." Katy smirked.

"Well, hey now. I showed up early to order one of those lattes with the cinnamon on top. You stole my gameplay." He nudged her playfully.

"Gameplay? You sound like Dom at work. He's always making sports references I have to research. He called me the 'Hank Aaron of goal-getting' the other day, and I fell down a baseball rabbit hole." Katy chuckled.

Heat spread through him. Her little laugh was pure sunshine. "Sounds like a good guy. And don't you have to know a little bit about everything to be a librarian?" He gazed into her hazel eyes.

"You joke. We spend so much time skimming resources to answer questions and find reference materials. I'm constantly researching the most random topics. When we had a big boom in yarn crafts last February, I had to speed-read about the difference between crochet and knitting. My days are constant crash courses."

"I'm going to pretend like I don't know the difference, even though I grew up holding the yarn ball for my mom while she crocheted." He stretched his arms like he was fine with his craft knowledge. Nothing to see here.

"That's adorable." Katy nudged him. Her shoulder lingered against him.

"I am. It's true." He laughed, but he liked the way she never wavered her gaze.

McKenna called out their drinks. The espresso

machine purred, and she quickly sold out of pumpkin scones.

By the time they returned to their table, the line was almost to the door of the sunny coffee shop.

"I'm glad I showed up early, or we'd be standing to drink our lattes." Katy motioned toward the line as the door chimed.

"Her coffee is worth the line." Luke took a sip of his dirty chai. The espresso hit just right.

McKenna managed her shop with a sort of organized chaos. She was tall and curvy and, per usual, completely focused on the customer in front of her. Her dangling pumpkin earrings glistened as she laughed at something her customer said.

"Agreed. So, the project was approved?" Katy sipped her latte.

Luke didn't know how McKenna created those foam shapes. He'd tried to follow the tiny movements she made, but no luck. "I talked to the school librarian and combined the notes from both conversations into a proposal for my boss. She took the idea to her boss, and what happened after is above my pay grade. You both made strong cases for increasing youth access to books and the mighty power of the MCLs. The proposal was already written before I logged in. I have to fill out a bunch of forms so we can plant the box into the ground." The moving parts lined up in Luke's thoughts like a spreadsheet.

" '*Plant*?' I'm never describing new MCLs any other way." She sketched a small doodle of an MCL with leaves and a flower-shaped box.

"I mean, I guess I could say 'install.' " He cleared his throat.

"Nonsense. I'm committed to library plantings. 'Installing' sounds like a construction project. 'Planting' sounds like readers will be blooming." She tapped her pen against her lips.

He was distracted by the way her lips pursed. "If you say so. Did you have a chance to reach out to your MCL contact?"

She closed her notebook and gazed across the table.

He leaned in so he wouldn't miss anything.

"I did. She was so excited we were even talking about adding an MCL on base. I found some successful MCLs on military bases around the country." Katy scooted to the edge of her chair.

"Okay, so we build the box. What else do we need to do?" He focused on her, shifting closer. Luke was happy to defer to her expertise, and his interest had nothing to do with the way she bounced in her chair whenever they talked about the mini libraries.

"Well, in Durant, we did a book drive to fill the MCLs, and then we hope the community will keep them going." She tapped the pen again.

Luke didn't need more of a reason to stare at her full lips. *Get a grip, Taylor.* "'A book drive,' " he repeated to get his head back on track as he jotted down notes. "I have the sketch you made with the three doors, and my buddy Ryan said he'd help me build them." He fully planned to do his share of the work on the project.

The idea for the book drive was a good one. His major already approved of the community engagement off base. He also recognized he was a little *too* pleased with the prospect of spending more time with Katy.

She flipped open her blue notebook and started

adding to the list she'd started earlier. "Okay, so we'll need to go visit some businesses."

He hopped up and stood at the back of the line.

"Hey, you want another latte to go?" McKenna waved an empty cup with tiny pumpkin-shaped polka dots.

He nodded and also ordered Katy's cinnamon latte.

McKenna called out their drinks. "Anything else?"

"Yeah, actually. I was wondering if we could place a box out by the front door for book donations for kids on base. Katy and I plan to install one of those Mini Community Libraries like the ones she installed at the park and in front of the library."

McKenna beamed. "Count me in."

He paid for their lattes and gave Katy a thumbs-up. "One business owner already agreed."

She beamed at McKenna.

Katy had always sort of been on her own in high school, so he was glad she had such good friends in Dover. He was the only one she'd talked to in their class. He'd liked being her person, though. Being in on her doodles had always been important. Why had he ever given her up?

"McKenna is the best. Do you have boxes at work? We tend to use ours for projects at the library." She started a new list of businesses to visit.

Luke chuckled. "Oh, we have boxes. I'll bring one with a flier."

"Better wrap the boxes in bright paper to catch people's attention." She scanned her notebook while she talked.

"See, you're the expert." He jotted down more notes. "So, where are we getting the shelf?"

"From a local carpenter. We need to stop by her workshop before noon."

"We have time to stop at a couple of businesses first."

Lattes in hand, they wandered to the sidewalk under the thick canopy of trees. Red and orange leaves transformed the street. Shadows danced across the sidewalk.

When he moved on, he'd miss Dover. The small coastal town had gotten under his skin—into his heart. But he was born with an unquenchable wanderlust. He wasn't the staying kind, or at least, Jolie thought so. Her final words jangled around his head like loose change.

"I like when the leaves change color. The whole downtown transforms." Katy's red fingerless gloves were bright against the pumpkin polka-dotted cup.

She slowly drifted her gaze down the street. "The trees make a fall-colored canopy over the street here. Hey, you want to stop by the bookstore?"

He gasped. "*You* want to go to a bookstore?"

She squeezed his arm, leaning into him. "Well, the shop next door is an obvious place to start."

Side by side, they headed down the cozy street with their shoulders bumping together, causing him to feel completely aware of her—like she was more real than anyone else in the world.

"Do we need to limit how many books we walk out of here with?" he asked. "You know thrillers are my genre of choice, and I feel like going to a bookstore with you is dangerous for my budget."

"I promise to use my powers for good," she said solemnly.

The Last Chapter was a small bookshop with narrow aisles and limited selections. A chalkboard sign on the sidewalk listed story times and a book club meeting.

Spencer Price was Luke's mom's age. He'd learned everything he could about Luke's book preferences during his first visit to the store.

"Well, now, what brings you back in so soon? You can't have finished your latest treasures quite so fast." He stepped out from behind the counter. He had thinning gray hair and a well-groomed mustache. The guy always seemed like he'd fit more into an early 1900s black-and-white film.

"Good morning, Mr. Price. We're actually here to ask for a favor." She motioned toward Luke.

"I didn't realize you two knew each other. Luke here has been working his way through my thriller section book-by-book for years." Price tugged on the sleeves of his corduroy jacket.

"Can you believe we went to high school together in Oklahoma?" Luke shook Price's hand.

"Happens all the time. Life is always ready to surprise you with how small the world can be. So, what's this about a favor?" Price raised his bushy eyebrows.

Luke explained the MCL project. "We're hoping you'd be willing to have a box by your front door for donations."

"I'll do you one better and have a box by the register with options for books. I've helped with other book drives, and I'd be more than happy to help the two of you. What ages?" Price's computer hummed to life. "Excuse me a moment. I have to get my notes all typed up. My handwriting would be indecipherable later."

His handwriting sometimes threw people for a loop. Luke was kind of relieved to know he wasn't the only one.

"Luke is the same way." Katy nudged him with her elbow. "His handwriting is awful. Do you still write all boxy caps?"

Luke leaned back. They hadn't seen each other in years, but she remembered more about him than most of the people in his life. Being an Army brat, he didn't have many childhood friends. Katy was his first friend in Durant. He'd never even told her she was his oldest friend. They had history he didn't share with anyone else but Jolie, and with their breakup, he didn't find much comfort in their shared past now. With Katy, he had a chance to maintain a friendship stretching back to his teens. "I scribble to the best of my ability and use all caps when anything needs to be readable." Luke kept his face as serious as possible.

"We all have our strengths." Price leaned against the wide oak counter, scanning the wall behind them stacked floor to ceiling with colorful children's titles. A bright-yellow sign warned kids not to climb the ladder.

"We're planning to have three different boxes attached together with picture books, early chapters, and middle grade or young adult—all separated." Katy tucked her fingerless gloves into her pocket.

"Well, I can certainly get behind reaching all those ages. I had a mother in last week letting her daughter pick out a new book for the MCL at the library. Her excitement over sharing books was such a joy to see." Price slowly typed his notes.

"MCLs are magic. I never tire of the way they

connect readers." She sighed dreamily.

Could anyone love those book boxes as much as Katy?

They talked about timelines and when they'd be by to pick up the books.

Luke couldn't believe how lucky they were to have Price's support. Dover might seem big, but at its heart was a small town full of people ready to help.

"Do you need a book before we leave?" Katy batted her eyes.

Luke was momentarily distracted by the gold flecks in her hazel gaze. "I might." He squinted. He stopped in front of his favorite shelves and picked up a new thriller by one of his favorite authors. The back of the book had secret societies and something to do with Atlantis in the description. He stuck the book in the crook of his arm.

"I didn't even have to talk you into anything." Katy popped her hands on her hips.

"I don't need much encouragement to buy a book. Just ask Mr. Price. You want to shop for something, or are you good from your last visit?" He raised an eyebrow, remembering Price's initial reaction.

"Maybe a peek at the mysteries." She scooted around the corner.

He followed her around another corner to the mystery section. She inspected cover after cover, and he was content to stand there all day.

Her fingerless gloves matched her red knit sweater where they stuck out of her back pocket. She ended up with not one, but two books hugged to her chest on the way to the front of the shop.

Luke handed Mr. Price his credit card.

"You don't need to buy my books, Luke." She offered Price her card.

"Ms. Caterby, when books are offered as gifts, you say 'thank you' and then go read them." Price's brown eyes sparkled.

"You're right, Mr. Price. Thank you." She held out her hands expectantly. She tucked the books into her magical purse.

The sunflower-yellow crossbody somehow held more than his standard-issue backpack.

"You two let me know if I can help more with your book drive. I'm very proud of our military, and I'd be happy to support their families, especially with books." Price tucked the receipt into Luke's book.

The few blocks to the hardware store passed too quickly. Usually, he rushed through tasks to get back to work, but with Katy, he needed to slow down. "I didn't expect book donations to go so well."

"Mr. Price is good people." She peered over her shoulder.

Her long golden-brown hair swung easily. The sun reflected off her shining hair, almost creating an ethereal glow to the sunshiny librarian beside him. "My first week here, he was the first local to make me feel welcome, and he sent me to McKenna. I owe him for all the good things I have right now." He softened his gaze.

"You should be buying him books then, not me." She nudged him with her shoulder.

"Listen, I haven't seen anyone as giddy to buy books in my life. You can't judge me for sponsoring your reading habit. And…when you let me tag along on your breaks, I always wanted to buy you a book. I didn't have any money then because I kept mowing over roots and having to replace parts, but you were my first friend, and I guess…"

"I had no idea. You had plenty of other people—other friends—once school started, though. The summer we hung out was my best summer during high school." She snapped her lips shut and swallowed.

"Mine, too." Luke cleared his throat.

Gourds, pumpkins, and scarecrows lined the hardware store walkway. Haybales were covered in red, yellow, and purple mums.

Luke tugged at his collar. "I haven't been in here yet. No real need for a hardware store living in an apartment." Would the aisles of nuts and bolts remind Katy of her dad's store back home?

"I bought some new pots for my patio plants here last summer." Katy shook her head with a rueful smile. "When he was here, my dad had to stop by."

"Professional curiosity?" Luke pressed his palm to the small of her back. The doors swung open. Her red sweater was warm and soft under his hand.

Katy nodded. "My dad is always curious about how other hardware stores are run."

"You worked a lot of weekends." He'd made excuses to shop there more often than strictly necessary, especially when she was his only friend in town.

Between lawn bags and replacement cables for his lawn-mowing business, he was in at least once a week during the summer. Her dad was a big guy with a great memory and an easygoing disposition. His story was the epitome of small-town life.

But Katy was the real reason Luke liked going to

the hardware store on Main Street. He could picture her in her green polo with the shop logo on the sleeve. She always kept a flat pencil tucked behind her ear.

She laughed. "I know way more than I want to about lawn mower parts. All those years in my dad's shop have come in handy with the Do-It-Yourselfers searching for books at the library."

The wind rushed from the closing doors, carrying the scent of paint, sawdust, and birdseed.

"Lucky them, they have a hardware store clerk at the ready." He reluctantly removed his hand from her lower back.

"Hey, is Mr. Zhang around?" Katy asked a young clerk.

"He was restocking on aisle six last time I saw him. Do you want me to check?" he asked.

"We'll find him. Thanks." Katy waved before heading toward the back of the shop.

They found him back by the bird feed section, hanging up a new bright-copper squirrel-proof feeder.

His face lit up. "Hi, Katy. What brings you in today?" A middle-aged man with a thick head of dark-gray hair and golden-toned skin stepped toward them.

"Hi, Mr. Zhang. Do you have a minute? We have a favor to ask." She introduced Luke. "He's an Air Force officer, working on a literacy initiative for kids living on base. We're asking local businesses if they'd be willing to host donation boxes for books."

Zhang leaned back but only for a moment. "I thought for sure you were going to need something for the Fall Fair. Darcy was in here for measuring tape and wooden crates about a month ago."

"I'm planning to paint those crates, so I'll be back

for something to go over my acrylics." She wrung her hands.

"Have I ever told you my daughter is a teacher? She teaches middle school down in Milford. I can't wait to tell her the hardware store is helping with a book drive." Zhang stood taller.

"I didn't know. Well, if she ever needs book recommendations for students, then I hope you'll send her my way." Katy relaxed her hands to her sides.

"Thank you for hosting a book drive box." Luke shook the man's hand. "We appreciate the help."

"You might be Air Force, but not everyone can be a Marine like me." He pointed to his chest. "We all have to stick together regardless."

"That we do, sir," Luke said. "I'll drop off a box."

"And fliers if you're willing to have them at checkout?" Katy magically had her blue notebook out.

"Yes, sure. Did you stop in and ask Mr. Price over at the Last Chapter?" He pointed toward Price's shop.

"We did. Thank you. We're going to build a Mini Community Library by our park on base like the one Katy added at the park down the street." Luke smoothed the front of his shirt.

"Oh, the one with all the characters? Come see me when you're ready to build." Zhang's smile split his face in two.

"Thank you." Katy's eyes doubled in size. When they left the hardware store, she had a bounce in her step from their success.

"The shop owners didn't take much convincing." Luke climbed back into his truck.

"Feels like back home, right? I didn't think Dover would have the small-town feel when I first moved here, but I'm so happy I was wrong."

"Today reminded me of Oklahoma." He meant more than the shop owners who all adored Katy. Being around her was like no time had passed at all. Their friendship was as easy and important now as when he was a teenager. Only this time, he would protect their friendship. He wasn't a stupid kid who couldn't see what was right in front of him anymore.

She navigated them toward the furniture shop. "I bet you spend a lot of time helping people move since you have a truck."

"I've helped my fair share of people move into new apartments." He chuckled. "But I don't mind. Hey, by the way, I texted my mom when I first ran into you. She hopes you're doing okay."

"I liked when your mom and Jackie stopped into the hardware store to buy flowers every spring. Your mom knows way more than I do about plants, so I always ended up learning so much." She leaned her head back against the seat.

"Her garden is her happy place. A magazine interviewed her last year, and she framed the article for the mantle. I think the frame will live there forever." The article was in a gold frame with flowers Jackie found online.

"A magazine article is a big deal for a gardener." Katy threw her hands up.

"Believe me, I know." He sighed. Gardening was new in Oklahoma. What was the point in roots when they were always going to leave? The gardening hadn't come naturally to Jackie, but she wanted to please their mom. When they found gardening gloves she said *felt right*, he ordered cases of them.

"I know you dug all the garden beds in high school, so you helped, too." She nudged him with her shoulder.

"You think I should remind her I get credit, too?" He smirked.

"Somehow, I don't think she wants to hear about sharing credit." Katy rolled her eyes.

"No, no, she definitely doesn't. But thanks. I dug a lot of dirt in her yard over the years. I kind of forget I worked on her garden, too, sometimes. The whole yard was a family effort."

They pulled into a strip mall with a small furniture shop. He lingered a minute, not in any hurry to finish their errands. He searched his mind for excuses to spend more time with her.

No. He shook his head. A new assignment would drop in a couple months, and he didn't want to give her the wrong impression. They needed to keep some kind of distance. *No roots.*

Chapter Five

Katy reheated her bright-red mug of cinnamon coffee for the third time and settled into her favorite spot in her kitchen. After staying up later than she wanted to think about, Katy had a spreadsheet for all the books they'd collected for the MCL so far. She emailed Luke and shut her laptop. Her day was just getting started. Five boxes of books needed price tags. She had a few more graphics to make for their social media accounts. Her advertising plan was delayed, but she would turn everything around today.

She opened her apartment door with an eye out for the redheaded woodpecker. Was she being a little ridiculous? She didn't have time to run back in and count to ten. The signal bird had nested in the trees outside her apartment's front door.

The bright-yellow and orange leaves fluttered in the chilly breeze. With no flash of red in sight, she headed to work. She was earlier than the others but not the first one there. Mae always beat everyone to the office.

"You're early." Mae filled her coffee cup in the break room.

Katy tucked a lock of hair behind her ear. She had a big project, and she wasn't about to let them down. Part of not being in her brother's shadow was making her own way and proving she was worth the risk Mae

71

took on her.

Mae narrowed her eyes. "How's the fair prep going?"

"Good. I need to make a couple more graphics today for social media. The Adventure Girls are working on their posters today."

"You've really brought the community on board. The Last Chapter had a donation box for the MCL drive on base. Just how much time are you devoting to the Air Force project?" Mae cocked an eyebrow.

"My friend is collecting and adding all the books to a spreadsheet. I'm organizing them." Katy shuffled.

Mae leaned her hip against the counter and pursed her lips over her coffee cup before she took a sip. "Just let me know if you need more help with the fair. I know MCLs are your passion, but I don't want the sale to fall any farther behind."

Katy winced. "I'm almost caught up to Darcy's timelines. Oh, she sent me a text with photos of little Charlie yesterday. He's so cute."

"I see you working hard, but please remember to ask for help. The Fall Fair was always meant to be a team rollout. Now, show me these photos."

Katy nodded and showed her the photos of the newborn baby boy with sunlight cast across his sleepy face. Little Charlie was sound asleep in a puppy onesie and a soft green blanket in Darcy's arms.

Back in Darcy's office, she hedged around a book stack, but she checked a corner with her hip and froze. The whole stack wobbled. Gingerly setting her coffee on the edge of the desk, she used her back to press the books against the wall. Breathing heavily, she dropped into her desk chair before any other calamities unfolded. Her phone buzzed. "Good morning," she said. Why did she sound out of breath? Her heartbeat thumped into her throat.

"Hey, the spreadsheet is amazing. Thank you so much."

From the background whoosh of wind, Luke was out on the flight line. He raised his voice over the gust.

He cleared his throat.

"You already have so many books. You might not need to keep those donation boxes out for much longer," she said. The MCL wouldn't need as many books as they had.

"Should we wrap some for welcome gifts when new families move on base? Or when families have new kids?" Luke shouted over the roar of a jet taking off.

A door slammed, muffling the wind's roar.

"Did you just get in a car? I can hear you so much better." She swiped away an incoming text from her brother.

"Sorry, yeah. I should have waited to call you from my truck." His deep rumbly voice vibrated through the phone.

Katy shivered. "Wrapping the books will make them extra special. How will they get the books, though?"

"A volunteer committee will handle the actual handing out of books. We could get different wrapping paper for each age group."

"You want to color coordinate the books by reading level? I want to go back and tell high school Luke. He'd be aghast." Katy pressed a hand to her chest.

"You can thank the Air Force for my addiction to color coding. And I don't know if I would have believed you. I was committed to being disorganized. Chaos was a lifestyle." He chuckled.

"I remember all too well." The corner of her lip turned up. He hadn't even used folders for homework. He shoved his papers loose into his backpack. She bet their teachers had known which assignments were his by their crumpled state alone. "Listen, I have to catch back up on some things for the fair, so I better let you go. Count me in for wrapping books, though."

"Thank you. I remember how nicely you wrapped stuff at the hardware store when you had the wrapping table during the holidays. I need an expert again."

The smell of scotch tape and brown craft paper flooded her memory. "Yeah, yeah. You want free labor." Katy jotted a note on her to-do list about wrapping books.

"I mean, I need volunteers, too." He swallowed. "Seriously though, I'll let you get back to work. I know you're taking time from your big project, and I appreciate all your help."

"I'm always game to help with a new MCL project. Just text me the details when you have them."

"Will do. Oh, hey— Any chance you can go with me to an Air Force formal event tonight? I'm staring at a text saying I'm supposed to make an announcement about the literacy initiative. You'd get to see me in what my mom calls my 'server uniform' and talk about MCLs all night after the announcement. I know I'm throwing the formal at you last minute."

His tone was apologetic and adorably hopeful.

"H-how fancy are we talking?" She had a little

black dress.

"Our formals are like black tie for the civilian world."

The dress could be elevated with borrowed heels. She'd get to see him in another uniform. She bit her lower lip. "I think I have something. What time?"

He promised to send a text with all the details.

Going to a fancy Air Force ball with Luke had nothing to do with the butterflies in her stomach. She was happy about the MCL. *I'm going for the books, not Luke.* She thanked him and stashed her phone away with her mind racing.

"Durant Guy called?" Ava stepped around a stack of books. She had a *booked and spooked* T-shirt with tiny white ghosts surrounded by a stack of gold, orange, and red books. Her shoulder-length black hair was in a smooth ponytail with a bright-orange headband with little white pumpkins dotting the fabric.

Ava might be a summer person, but she fully committed to every season. Katy rolled her eyes. "Durant Guy's name is Luke." Saying his name made her want to shake her head. How was he back in her life? Katy should have taken the signal bird to heart. She needed to keep her distance to protect her heart. Life was making physical distance impossible, but she couldn't go through a second ghosting from Luke Taylor.

"Uh-huh. If I'm supposed to learn his name, I need to meet him, especially if a phone call has you practically drooling." Ava tightened her high ponytail and squared her shoulders.

"I'm happy about a new MCL." Katy flipped her name badge the right way.

Ava sighed. "You love those mini libraries to an obsessive degree, but your glow has more than a little to do with High School Heartbreak."

"I like Durant Guy better." Her personal favorite was Mr. Persistent.

Ava cocked her head to the side. "Both are accurate."

"We were friends in high school, and we get along. He's a good human." Katy flipped her badge again. The whole situation was too complicated. "Um, speaking of Luke, can I borrow some heels for an Air Force dinner tonight?"

"Like a military formal? What dress are you pairing? Those are pretty fancy. Cocktail probably isn't nice enough."

"I have a black cocktail dress from the county banquet." Katy slumped.

Ava pursed her lips. "With fancy hair and my heels, your dress should be okay. You won't be the least dressed-up, and you won't be the most—nice and in the middle."

"Um, fancy hair is not in my wheelhouse." Katy brushed her long silky hair over her shoulder.

"I'll head to your place after I grab the heels after work. I've got you. A fancy formal with High School Heartbreak, huh?" She waggled her thick eyebrows.

"Can we talk about anything else?" Katy groaned.

"You're no fun. Now, show me the new graphics, and let's get this show on the road." Ava maneuvered around to see the computer screen. "Katy, Katy, Katy. We can slide the logo up here, and the whole thing comes together in a defined color palette." Ava clicked a few things, and the whole graphic transformed into the three colors of their logo.

"Oh, for goodness' sake." Katy leaned back and crossed her arms. She'd struggled for hours with the designs.

"You should have asked me for help in the first place. We're all here to help you." Ava's large eyes were warm.

"The graphics were okay…" Katy saved the changes, sighing. "Can I send you the other ones?"

"I'll get them all fixed up. Do you want me to send them straight to Kylie so she can post them?"

"Are you sure you have time? I don't want to make you fall behind on your own projects." Katy wanted to give her an out. The fair stall was her project, and Ava didn't need to carry the weight. Why was asking for help so darn hard?

"What's that? You love me, and I'm the bestest at graphics? Truth. And I love you, too. Now, if you'll excuse me, I have to journey through your book jungle and go find my puppets." Ava did some fancy ballet poses on her way out of the office.

Katy planned to channel Ava's energy to make it through the evening. She shouldn't be going to a formal with Luke, but community events supporting books were mandatory as far as she was concerned.

She emailed the rest of her social media plan and what she'd created to Ava's work account and then shut everything down. She was overwhelmed and operating strictly in the extra perky zone—her personal version of "fake it 'til you make it."

"Hey there."

His rich, rumbly baritone carried across the small office. Katy jumped. Luke took up half of her doorway in his uniform. His short, cropped hair had the telltale lines of his hat. The green-and-khaki camo brightened his eyes, and she tried not to stare.

Luke lowered his head. "Sorry, Katy. I didn't mean to startle you. I knocked on the doorframe, too."

She couldn't figure out what Luke Taylor was doing in the employee-only area of the library until she spotted a to-go cup from Brewed Awakenings. "I hope the coffee is for me." She shifted toward him like a magnet.

"I figured you could use a pick-me-up. The spreadsheet must have kept you up half the night. And I wanted to say thanks for being my plus-one for the dinner tonight." He held up her latte.

"Thanks, Luke. I'd offer you a seat, but I've piled them all with books." She took the offered coffee and took a sip of the cinnamon-y goodness.

Luke nodded toward a stack of books. "Will moving them ruin your organization?"

"No, but I'm overdue for a break. Let's go outside." She stood and stretched, ready to take a break from the cramped office.

"You found her." Mae offered a hand. "I'm Mae Adams."

"The library director." Luke shook her hand. "Katy has told me so much about you."

"Has she?" Mae rested a hand on her chest. "All good things, I hope."

"Definitely, ma'am." Luke stood straight.

"You have a truck, don't you?" Mae pursed her lips and tapped her mechanical pencil on her notebook.

"I do." He gulped.

"How would you feel about meeting a group of

librarians at a pumpkin patch tomorrow? You could drive our pumpkins back to the library afterward." She squinted her coffee-brown eyes.

Oh, my goodness. Mae had just met Luke, and she was already asking him a huge favor on very short notice. Luke didn't seem to mind. Whenever Dad asked him for a quick hand at the hardware store, he jumped right in without pause. "We're setting up our October First Fridays activities for the kids." Katy stuck a bright-blue knit hat on her head and picked up her latte. "And one of those activities involves a lot of little pumpkins. But we all have trunks, and between all of us, I'm sure we can manage."

Luke eyed her hat. "Or I could meet you. I'm off tomorrow. I'd be happy to help, ma'am. I've been meaning to pick up a pumpkin for my balcony, anyway. I usually buy one at the grocery store."

"A grocery store pumpkin?" Mae gasped. "Well, you'd better go to the patch then."

Wait. Was Mae trying to...*set her up*? Katy's cheeks warmed. "If you don't mind," Katy said, giving up.

"Well, good. Katy can share the details. Thank you for volunteering your time." Mae patted his arm absently. She glided away.

"You didn't prepare me." Luke shook his head. "Can I be her when I grow up?"

Katy shook her finger. "No, I already called dibs."

"Well, how is that fair?" He released an appreciative sigh.

"Hmm." She chuckled. "Come on, we can go out the back way." She tugged on the sleeve of his starched uniform and led him out a side exit. She ignored the way his body radiated heat, making her want nothing more than to lean closer. She stumbled and forced herself to think about the Dewey decimal system.

She sat on a bench in the sun and inhaled the sweet scent of her cinnamon latte and the cool salty air. The trees around them had tips of yellows and reds like the world was starting anew.

"How's the prep going for your fair? And you have the First Friday thing coming up, too?" He leaned back with a leg crossed over his knee. He had one arm extended across the back of the bench.

If she leaned back a little, she could feel the heat from his skin. A tingle she wasn't ready to deal with swept over her. "I have a plan, and I'm being better about accepting help." She brushed her hair behind her ear. Why couldn't she be strong and direct like Mae?

"Why would asking for help be hard?" Luke leaned away to scan her face.

"I think a lot of women struggle with needing help. We have an odd sort of pressure like we have to do everything all on our own to sort of 'make it.' " Katy wasn't sure how else to explain.

"I'm not going to pretend like I understand, but I hope you know I *want* to help." Luke stretched out his long legs.

Katy took a sip of her creamy latte and leaned back against Luke's arm. A little comfort wouldn't hurt. Being with him was like the eye of a storm. Her mile-long to-do list was waiting, but in her small coffee with Luke bubble, the weight of potentially letting Mae down and failing the after-school kids wasn't as crushing.

"You'll let me know if I can help. I shared the

sign-up you sent. My buddy will show up early to help set up, too. We don't always get to be a part of things off base." He slowly edged a hand down toward her shoulder.

"Hey, Katy." Isaac stopped by the bench, furrowing his brow.

To stay calm, she took a deep breath. She'd been staring intently at Luke and missed Isaac's approach. Isaac had his hair styled with too much gel, and he was wearing a nice green button-up again. Who was he dressing up for? "Hi, Isaac. You remember my friend Luke?"

"Good to see you." Isaac barely nodded in Luke's direction. "When you're done, can you help me find a local history section?"

"Sure, but you know a-any of the librarians can help you." She released a deep breath.

"You know my thesis, though." Isaac gripped the strap on his satchel.

She forced her smile to be even perkier. "I'm on break for a bit."

"You know where to find me." He winked.

He held his eye shut too long like a slow-motion awkward train. Katy shivered. Whatever he was up to, she was not interested.

"Now I need the story." Luke had scooted closer at some point.

His arm was warm against her neck. The tingles intensified, and she shivered. "We dated for a while, but in May, he asked me to coffee and told me he wasn't *feeling* it and we shouldn't see each other anymore." She sighed. Maybe he'd done them both a favor...but she didn't understand what she'd done wrong.

Luke gulped. "Like the big, forever *it*?"

"I guess so? He didn't get into a lengthy explanation, and for obvious reasons, I didn't ask for more details." She closed her eyes, willing her memories of the humiliating moment to stay locked away.

"Guy clearly regrets his terrible life choices." Luke glared in Isaac's general direction. He cleared his throat.

Katy leaned forward a little.

He eased back to the other end of the bench.

The fall breeze whipped through the space between them. He smelled like spicy chai and cedar. "I seriously doubt he has any regrets, but I could live without him making my work life much more awkward than the situation needs to be." Her phone alarm buzzed. She only had a few more hours of work. She could handle a little more time with her ex.

Luke took another sip of his drink.

"I better head back in there. Thanks again for the coffee. A girl could get used to Brewed Awakenings coffee breaks." She gazed into his green eyes, hesitant to leave.

"Any time, Katy. You want me to come hang around? Is your ex making you uncomfortable?" He adjusted the bill of his hat with one hand. "I'm here if you need me."

"He's confusing me, but I'll be fine." She shrugged. "I'll see you tonight."

Inside the library, Mae waved her over. "Can you cover for Ava at the welcome desk? I need her to finish the First Friday graphics."

"I'll head out there right now." She hustled out to

take Ava's place. With the slower time of the day, she was the only one at the welcome desk.

"Was that Durant Guy outside? Because you were holding out on me. He's *cuuuute*." Ava happy danced, shimmying her shoulders.

"Yep. And he's okay for…" Katy blushed. She had no idea how to describe him. The air rushed from her lungs. She was failing to protect her heart from cut-and-run Luke Taylor.

"For a handsome guy who makes you smile?" Ava smirked.

"I'm sure I don't know what you're talking about. Besides, Mae wants you to finish the graphics for First Friday." Katy fluttered her eyelashes.

"We are in no way done talking about him. I need the details. I have no life, so you have to have one for me to live vicariously through." Ava logged out.

Katy kept hoping Ava's grandmother would agree to move into the assisted living where most of her friends lived, but she was still firmly against moving. Ava's last boyfriend dumped her because she spent too much time caregiving. She hadn't tried dating since.

A flash of green plaid caught her attention. Katy slumped and waited for Isaac to close the distance between them.

Isaac beelined straight toward her. "You on welcome desk duty?" He adjusted his glasses.

She'd forgotten about him, and she winced. "What did you need help with?" Her voice pitched too high.

"No problem. I'm hoping to find more statistics on volunteer rates. I've exhausted all the local ideas for the case study portion." He absently played with his hoody's drawstrings.

"Have you checked the Office of Management and Budget for statistics? Didn't you mention them once?" She scrunched her eyebrows.

"I have. I didn't know if you had any other ideas." He shuffled his sneakers.

Was he making excuses to spend more time with her?

"We can check the sociology shelf," she said.

His face lit up.

She was half tempted to ask another librarian to show him where the shelf was.

"I knew you'd think of something." He bumped her with his shoulder.

She stepped farther away. "I'm happy to be helpful." She straightened her juniper-green cardigan.

"I might have to write you into my acknowledgments. Thanks for always helping me work through my thesis. Do you think you'd have time to edit the file before I send the whole paper to the committee?" He tilted his head to the side.

Katy formed an *O* with her mouth. She would need hours and hours to review his thesis. Not to mention, she was more than a little sick of the subject after months of discussion centered around civic engagement. Katy tightened the low bun in her hair. "You can find great editing services out there. I can share the contact info for the editor I hired to clean up my thesis."

The rows of low shelves transitioned into tall metal shelves packed with knowledge. Instead of comfort, her safe space was claustrophobic with Isaac leaning against her. Light touches used to be their norm, but now, she needed at least a football stadium between them.

"So, who's the guy you're always with now?" Isaac asked.

She stopped in front of the sociology books and studied Isaac's face.

He clenched his square jaw.

"He's a friend from back home. We're helping each other with work projects." She wished she was anywhere else right now.

"Oh, well. I just wondered. When we were, you know, hanging out, you never mentioned him." He adjusted his glasses.

Hanging out? They'd dated for seven months. And then, for some reason, he'd decided she wasn't worth any more of his time. She schooled her face and hoped he couldn't see the tears threatening to spill. She took several deep breaths and made herself think about the scratchy blue carpet beneath her feet.

Isaac pursed his lips.

"He's great." She shifted into full librarian mode and told him way more than he needed to know about sociology and handed him a stack of books. She helped him carry the books to the table he'd claimed.

The books were lined around his silver laptop. He lingered his gaze on her curves, and he bit his lower lip.

She waited to feel something, anything, but her body didn't respond.

"Can I buy you a slice of pie at the diner to say thanks for helping me?" He studied a blue cover with one sociologist's take on the reduction in civic engagement.

Seriously? Connection between them was off the table. He'd asked her out the first time the same way.

Was he acting like they'd never dated? Or was he starting things again?

Either way, Katy wasn't interested. "I don't think pie is a good idea, Isaac. We need to keep clear boundaries, and spending time together outside of research for your thesis is blurry. I can't handle *blurry*." Her stomach dropped. Was she being professional or harsh? Even if he'd casually crushed her, she wouldn't hurt him.

"Hey, Katy, can you help me with the First Friday signs?" Ava glared at Isaac.

When had she joined them? "Sure." Katy's extra perky was showing again. "Good luck with the statistics hunt." She followed Ava to the offices in the back. Katy sagged her shoulders. She had emotional whiplash.

"What's his deal?" Ava pursed her lips. "Other librarians could help him find books." Her black ballet flats tapped on the floor in a brisk staccato rhythm.

"Maybe seeing me with Luke is making him jealous?" He'd shown his cards, and his motivations were all shaking out in her mind.

"Ugh. Boys." Ava brushed her bangs aside and opened the screen with all her graphics leading to their next First Friday. Downtown Dover would have events like pie flights at the local diner and activities all afternoon and into the evening at the library.

Katy loved the bright designs Ava had created. The dancing pumpkins were her favorite.

Ava cocked her head to the side. "Can you let someone else deal with Isaac next time he's here? Can you tell him *nope* for the thesis review?"

She sighed. "I don't want to be *that* girl."

"The girl who doesn't want her weird ex hanging

onto her at work? If our roles were reversed, you'd have pushed me out of the way and helped my ex instead. Don't tell me otherwise. I know you and Isaac weren't together very long, but you two spent all your minutes together. He shouldn't be super needy while you're at work." Ava clenched her fists.

"I hear you, and I'll talk to him. He should be finished with the research phase. I'm surprised he's not busy writing right now." Katy stepped into Ava's line of sight.

"See, look at you caring and being concerned. He ended things, and you don't have to help him anymore." Ava brushed her bangs.

Katy searched around for some way to change the topic and distract Ava. Her friend was right, but she'd never been in a situation where setting boundaries with an ex could be unprofessional. "Did I tell you Mae invited Luke to pick pumpkins with us tomorrow?" She tugged on her cardigan sleeve.

"What? Mae is a woman of action. I can't wait to meet Durant Guy. Was he happy?" Ava picked up a stack of abandoned fall gardening guides.

"She asked him to volunteer his truck, and he didn't hesitate. I wonder when his last trip to a real pumpkin patch was. I can't imagine buying a grocery store pumpkin." Store pumpkins were great for cooking, but the joy of decorating for autumn required a trek through tightly packed rows of green pumpkin vines.

"Yes, but you love the fall in the way most people love summer or Christmas. You've been waiting for all the fall things for months while I was busy holding onto every last drop of summer sun." Ava sighed.

"Fall is my favorite." Katy waited all year long for the leaves to change colors and the chilly mornings to make everything fresh and new. Harvest time was around the Choctaw New Year, and this year was vibrant in a way she wasn't ready to admit. For her, fall always felt like hope.

"And now, you have an Air Force formal and a pumpkin patch with High School Heartbreak." Ava had a Cheshire cat grin. She wandered toward the stacks of wayward books.

Right. The formal with Luke where she would have to hold tight to her weakening boundaries. Surely, she could manage one dance without falling in love.

****

By the time her makeup was finished, Katy barely recognized herself in her bathroom mirror. Her hair was curled and half up, cascading down her shoulders in soft waves. A small voice in the back of her mind whispered of almost-proms, but she shut those thoughts down as fast as she could. The fancy dinner was for the literacy initiative.

She paced her cozy living room, afraid to sit down and wrinkle her silk dress. Ava's heels were strappy and comfortable, which was a relief. Her friend had a penchant for ridiculously high heels, but these were a happy medium. Katy might even survive the night without tripping over her own feet. She opened the door at the first knock. She pressed a hand to her chest.

His dark-blue uniform for the night made him taller and more muscular. He wasn't wearing a hat, and every sun streak shone in his carefully combed hair. His lapel was full of little ribbons with round medals, and the librarian in Katy wanted to know what each one meant to catalog them.

Luke exhaled a sigh. "You look incredible. And with hours for notice, too."

"Thanks. You clean up pretty nice, Mr. Persistent." Katy brushed her curled hair over her shoulder.

"Come on. I can't be late, or I'll be the first one sent to the grog." Luke fidgeted with his keys.

"Do I even want to know what the grog is?" She grabbed her little black clutch and followed him.

He chuckled. "Imagine a mix of the most random and terrible liquors, and you have the grog bowl. We have to follow a list of rules, and if we're caught breaking them, we get sent to the bowl in front of the room."

"Rules? I don't want to drink disgusting punch." Katy stumbled a little. Being singled out and called to the carpet in front of a room full of strangers and drinking some awful concoction sounded vaguely like her worst nightmare.

"No, not you, Katy. Guests are exempt. We'll try to trip my buddy Ryan up tonight." Mischief sparked in his eyes.

She let out a deep breath. "You want to make your friend drink something so terrible?"

"He'll be doing the same thing." He narrowed his eyes with a playful grin. "Just promise me you won't help him. You have to be on my side."

"No promises." She chuckled.

He opened the passenger door, offering her a hand to climb into the cab.

His calloused palm was rough and warm. Katy flexed her tingling hand and settled into the seat.

"You ready for this?" He revved the engine and

headed toward the highway.

The sun was already low in the sky, lighting the horizon in cotton-candy pink and purple. "But they won't send me to the grog if I make a mistake, right?" She ran a hand over the smooth fabric of her silk dress.

"No, you're safe. And even if you weren't, I'd take the grog for you." He checked the rearview mirror.

"Ever the gentleman." She bit her lower lip, trying not to smile.

He parked at a nondescript building on base.

A rush of uniforms filled the parking lot. The civilian men were all decked out in black tie, and a few women wore full-length blue and black ball gowns. Several women close to her age were wearing similar little black dresses, and Katy relaxed her shoulders. She was right in the middle, just like Ava said.

Luke rested a hand on the small of her back to lead her into the open reception area with clusters of high-top tables without chairs. The bar was lit with twinkle lights on the far wall, and two open doorways led into the red-white-and-blue decorated banquet hall.

Luke stopped at a table with two men and a woman standing around with drinks.

An officer close to their age nodded to Luke. His black hair was gelled up with the sides buzzed short.

"Hey, Hart," Luke said. "Meet my friend from back home, Katy Caterby. She's a librarian here in Dover. Katy, meet a fellow member of the flight line, Captain Ryan Hart."

Ryan quickly welcomed her to the table.

Luke left to get her a drink.

"So, what was Tyler like?" Ryan barely waited for Luke to be out of earshot.

"About the same as now, but less organized." She shifted. Luke wouldn't want her to share stories.

Ryan snickered.

"Why is there evil laughter?" Luke handed Katy a glass of chardonnay.

"That's between me and Katy." Ryan motioned between them, leaning toward her like they had an agreement.

Luke narrowed his eyes, but he stood shoulder to shoulder with Katy.

His warmth mingled with hers, and she leaned against him. "So, what is the dinner for tonight?" She'd searched online, but she couldn't find an obvious answer like the Air Force birthday. They were weeks too late for a birthday party.

"Commander called for a celebration. We reached the ten-year mark for partnering with the rec center in town. I should have told you. A few people from the rec center will celebrate with us." Luke nudged her shoulder.

"So, a bunch of you volunteer there?" Katy warmed to the idea. A number of their after-school regulars were in a bunch of programs there.

"Hart, here, is one of their regular coaches for soccer and basketball." Luke raised his beer toward Hart before setting the bottle on the table.

"They couldn't find anyone better and got stuck with me." Ryan scowled.

"Take a compliment, man. You're doing a good thing for those kids." Luke shook his head.

The two loggies argued like an old married couple. Katy leaned away, trying not to laugh.

"Anyway, we'll toast to the partnership and make

some promises about the years to come. A bunch of us volunteer regularly. No big deal." Ryan narrowed his eyes. He took a sip of his beer and left without a word.

"Prickly?" Katy raised an eyebrow.

"Paints an accurate description. He doesn't volunteer for praise, so he won't hear any." Luke shrugged. "I'll still tell him he's doing good work."

Katy nudged him with a shoulder. "You're a good friend."

"I do my best." He stepped away and rubbed his hands together. "Okay, your goal is to make sure he carries his beer into the dining room. He'll get called out and sent to the grog."

The absence of his warmth sent a chill down her spine. She gasped. "You weren't kidding? And I just complimented your friendship skills."

"I never kid about the grog."

His deep whisper made her whole body take notice. "I'm not helping." She set her drink down next to his and crossed her arms.

"Somebody's in trouble." Ryan set his fresh beer on the table.

"All good here." Luke smirked.

They were called into the dining room.

Ryan left his drink behind.

"Don't you want your beer, Hart?" Luke raised an eyebrow.

Ryan snorted. "Not my first rodeo. Don't let him rope you into the grog nonsense. That stuff is terrible. Nobody deserves grog."

Luke motioned Katy into the dining room.

She hoped she remembered which fork to use first. She surveyed the fancy table setting. Each table held a vase filled with blue Christmas ball ornaments with the Air Force logo lit by tiny twinkle lights.

He showed her to their table and pulled out her chair.

The commander waved.

Luke took center stage with a microphone.

Several of the higher-ranking officers at the head table turned to face him.

"I get the honor of telling y'all about a literacy initiative here on base. A local Dover librarian, Katy Caterby, has been working with our elementary school librarian to create a welcome gift for new kids on base with an age-appropriate book and a Mini Community Library for kids to enjoy here on base. Katy's here tonight. Katy, wave to the nice people."

Katy stood on shaky legs to offer a hesitant wave. She sat so fast the drinks on the table wobbled. "Sorry." She glanced at Ryan.

He steadied his glass of water. "Rickety tables."

"With Katy's and Joshua's help, kids on base will develop better habits for lifelong reading." He named the members of the literacy initiative committee, thanked the commander for his support, and beelined for their table.

"You could have warned me," she whispered.

His forehead glistened with sweat. "If I'd known, I would have. I should have taken my notes. I blanked." He scanned the table.

The seat next to Katy was empty, but the other three officers at their table were chuckling.

"Your secret is safe." She squeezed his arm. His starched uniform was scratchy under her fingertips. "Now, what's the plan to get Ryan to the grog bowl?"

Being with Luke under the lowered lights of the banquet hall made her forget her plan. Operation Keep Her Distance was a failure.

A slow grin transformed his face. "I knew you'd get on board. Just get him to talk about our job."

What was she doing? Katy shook her head. She had no interest in turning the grump into even more of a curmudgeon. She bit her lip.

A server brought stuffed chicken for the main course, baskets of bread, and gold-wrapped butter squares. Room-temperature peas and mashed potatoes filled the rest of the plate.

Luke scowled.

"Food touching?" Katy covered her mouth.

Luke sighed. "You remember I hate when my food gets mixed up?"

"Maybe." She shrugged. The large banquet hall had filled with the scent of roasted chicken, potatoes, and bacon. Silverware scratched white plates, creating a soft soundtrack for the evening.

Ryan chatted with the couple to his right about fishing.

"Chickening out?" Luke whispered.

"He's just kind of…" She waved a hand back and forth.

"Surly?"

"Yeah, and I don't want him to turn on me." She leaned closer, seeking shelter from a potential storm.

They were between courses, waiting on dessert and coffee. Luke stretched an arm across the back of her chair. "Don't worry." His thumb rested against her shoulder blade. "Oh, I think you're about to see the grog bowl in action." He pointed across the room to where a young man stood and fixed his clip-on bow tie. "Crooked bow tie." Luke tsked.

The young man stood in front of the main table, saluted the officer in the middle, and filled a small plastic cup from the bowl. "To the mess." He chugged the neon-green liquid.

Luke and Ryan puckered their lips and swallowed in unison.

The officer at the grog bowl turned the cup upside down over his head, returned the cup to the grog table, and saluted the officer with the silver shoulder bars at the main table again.

"Those clip-on bow ties will get you every time." Ryan shivered.

"What tripped you up?" Katy leaned back against Luke's arm.

"I didn't know which way the cummerbund went. What did they ping you for in February?" Ryan patted his dark-blue cummerbund.

Luke groaned. "I forgot I had a glass in my hand on my way into dinner."

"Why do you even have a grog bowl?" Katy eyed the glass punch bowl like the crystal bowl was full of live ammunition.

"Tradition." Luke lifted a shoulder.

Katy chuckled.

After dinner, they were surrounded by officers and family members asking questions about the MCL. Katy understood why Luke wanted her to join him. He could answer some things, but more often than not, he deferred to her.

"Let's give this fine librarian a break from the twenty questions." A middle-aged gentleman from the main table offered his hand. He introduced himself as General Rodkey. "Mind if we get the dancing started?"

She followed him to the square parquet dance floor. Her heels clacked loudly against the polished wood tiles. "We're the only ones dancing."

"Give them a minute to get over themselves. Air Force formals can feel like a middle school dance at first. I didn't mean to put you on the spot. Seems I've failed at my rescue attempt." He kept pace with the instrumental song, keeping the box shape and measured steps Katy knew from dancing with Dad.

Was he dancing the foxtrot? She skimmed her fingers over the silver bar on his shoulder, counting three stars. She gulped.

Servers entered the room to clear the tables.

"I'll take any chance to dance." Katy's heart raced. Would anyone else join them on the large parquet dance floor? *Was the whole room watching them?*

A slower song started, and several couples joined them on the small dance floor.

"Your help means a lot to all of us. My sincere thanks." He bowed a little, stepping to the side to make room. The bald crown of his head gleamed under the banquet hall lighting.

Luke walked across the dance floor and offered his hand.

She shifted her body toward him like a magnet. *Traitor.* "Dream a Little Dream" crooned from the speakers. He swept her across the dance floor. She relaxed into his lead, gliding around. Luke Tayler could dance. His palm was warm on her lower back. "I can't remember the last time I danced. You're suspiciously good."

"When we lived in North Carolina at Fort Bragg, my mom made me take these etiquette classes with Ms. Kitty. Ballroom dancing was a big part of the six months of classes. I can't tell you how relieved I was when those things were over." He smirked.

His deep baritone laugh made her shiver. "But I bet you know which fork to use." She waved at the silver table setting.

"I sure do. And you can count on me for a slow dance." He spun them around another couple.

Her heart thundered. The world around them disappeared. How did he always create a bubble around them? His hand was warm against her back. She relaxed into the steady rhythm of the dance and brushed fingers over his captain's shoulder board. The two silver stripes at the end were smooth.

He tensed until another slow song eased from the speakers.

"Uh-oh. What happens to your moves when they play a faster song?"

"Don't worry. I'm proficient at the lawn mower, the grocery shopper, and the sprinkler." He almost kept a straight face, but he cracked and laughed.

She gasped in mock horror. Her dad used to threaten to dance those disjointed moves when she was younger as a joke. "You wouldn't."

"No. I'd be too afraid someone would video my moves and post online."

"I'm someone. Or Ryan. You have such good friends." She leaned closer. She didn't want the song to end.

He squinted with a smirk. "You'd make me go viral?"

"Maybe." She shrugged a little.

A fast song blared from the speakers, and he led her from the dance floor.

She laughed and let him take her hand. "No sprinkler, huh?"

"If I make a name for myself here, I hope I'm known for more than my smooth dance moves." He stopped at their table to take a drink of water.

"Ms. Caterby?" a younger woman in a floor-length midnight-blue dress asked.

The metallic color accentuated her eyes and her dark-bronze skin.

A group of higher-ranking officers called for Luke.

"Katy, please. Are you from the rec center?" Katy stuck out a hand.

"I'm Carmen Delgato, director of programs." Carmen limply shook Katy's hand.

"Nice to meet you. I bet we serve a lot of the same kids." Katy raised her chin.

"I know quite a few of the tabletop games group." Carmen smoothed her shiny dress.

"They're such a good bunch." Katy nodded.

Luke crossed the room to talk to another group.

Carmen bit her lower lip.

Was Carmen checking out Luke? Katy swallowed hard. She stopped herself from stepping into Carmen's line of sight. Luke was not hers. *Get a grip.*

"So, how long have you known Captain Taylor? He helps out with Captain Hart sometimes, and he seemed like a really good guy." Carmen took a sip of her drink.

"We went to high school together." Katy pitched her voice higher. Something about Carmen had her extra perky showing. Their overlap was only for a year, but Carmen didn't need to know just how little time they'd actually had. Luke had taken off, and if they hadn't run into each other in McKenna's shop...

"Oh, wow. And you both ended up in Dover? Small world. Are you two, um, dating?" Carmen pressed her lips into a thin line.

She certainly didn't pull any punches. "We're working together on the MCL, and he's helping me with the library's stall at the Fall Fair." Katy's heart pounded in her ears. She knew how she wanted to answer in the moment, but Luke was a known flight risk. Even more so now because his job might send him packing any day. And long-distance friendship was much more realistic than anything else. If he even wanted something more with her. Why was she letting Carmen rile her up? The dance had rattled her.

"So—" Carmen raised a thin eyebrow.

"Hey, Carmen." Ryan angled himself between them.

"Everyone's favorite MVP coach. How are you?" Carmen's eyes flashed, and her mouth barely twitched.

Katy would have missed the expression if she'd blinked.

"You gonna add MVP to my name badge?" Ryan flashed a condescending smile.

What was the deal between these two? Katy expected to see frost form around them.

"I'll see what I can do." Carmen gestured toward the room. "Isn't tonight lovely? I should go share my appreciation with the commander. I'm sure I'll see you around." She wiggled her fingers.

"She's a character." Ryan tracked Carmen with

narrowed eyes.

Luke's broad shoulder brushed against her, sending warmth zinging down her arm. Katy leaned against him. "You escaped." His warmth thawed the frosty moment.

"Yeah, sounds like you might have someone from the rec center calling to ask about building an MCL outside their gym." Luke rested his strong hand on her lower back.

"You let me know if you need another box. I'll build whatever." Ryan's phone buzzed in his pocket, but he couldn't check his screen without earning a trip to the grog.

Katy snapped her head toward Ryan. "Thank you."

"No big deal." He whistled, and his eyes lit up. "The first few folks are heading out."

"Now you can sneak out without anyone saying you weren't social." Luke smirked.

"You should probably get Katy out of here. A few people are eyeing her for more questions." Ryan took one last sip of his water and nodded toward Katy on his way out.

"Not one for chitchat?" Luke's laugh warmed Katy all over. The dark-blue mess dress made his soft green eyes brighter. Her fingers itched to run along the silky lapels.

"No, he's definitely not. If he could skip out, he would. But we can't just be 'the job.' " He rolled his eyes.

"What do you mean?" She leaned closer to hear him over the din of the dining hall.

"We have to be 'the full person'—a term they throw around meaning you have to have a balanced life and not just work. Ryan started volunteering with the rec center so nobody could say he doesn't have 'a story'—another term we hear ad nauseam." Luke shook his head. "And then he was hooked all on his own. I like volunteering with the rec center, but Ryan lives for coaching the way he lives for the Air Force."

Katy glanced at the door where Ryan had disappeared. Her life since high school centered around school and work. She'd dated Isaac, but she hadn't made room in her life—not really. The thought jolted her upright.

He tilted his head.

"The full person, huh? I'm not there yet. Are you?" She bit her lower lip.

"I'm a work in progress." Luke clenched his jaw.

The small ribbons on his mess dress probably all told stories. She cataloged them in her mind for further research. He had more than Ryan, but they were the same rank. "You and Ryan have different ribbons." She brushed a hand over them, feeling firm muscles underneath.

"I'm prior enlisted, so I've been in a lot longer than Ryan. He was in Reserve Officers' Training Corps at his undergrad. Same destination, different paths." He followed the path of her fingers with his gaze.

The purple medal in the tidy row kept distracting her. "And the Purple Heart?"

He lifted a shoulder. "When I was enlisted, one of my jobs on deployment was to collect air frame pallets."

She scrunched her eyebrows, and she bit back a billion questions.

"I know, I know. But we need them, and they don't

always return on their own. My convoy took an Improvised Explosive Device and rolled. I walked away with a broken arm. A lot of people sacrificed a whole lot more for their medals." He scanned the room with his generous lips in a tight line.

A whole stretch of his life was a mystery, but she'd done a fair amount in the time after he'd ditched her, too. And now they had a chance to share those stories.

He shuffled his feet.

"Thank goodness you only broke an arm. Bones can heal." Her voice cracked. The image of his convoy truck rolling wedged itself into her mind.

"You ready to head home?" He motioned to the nearly empty room.

When did everyone leave? "Sure. We have a big morning at the pumpkin patch tomorrow." Her smile was hesitant.

"I can't wait." He slid a hand to the small of her back.

She leaned closer, thankful he was here to discover all over again.

If she was brave enough…

Chapter Six

Luke wasn't sure what he was doing, sitting in his truck outside Katy's apartment complex to drive them to the pumpkin patch. The bright-blue sky overhead promised a crisp fall day. He'd given himself a good pep talk about keeping his distance, only to take her to an Air Force banquet dinner and accept the pumpkin patch invite from her boss. Her ex lurking around the library didn't help him want to stay away, either. He promised himself to keep it "friends only" with Katy to relieve some of his guilt. Was he giving her the wrong impression?

Katy stepped out of her front door and tilted her head toward the trees.

Her expression was tight. Should he get out and help? *Not the right direction.* They were friends, and he was being friendly. Nothing more.

She wore a cream-colored sweater and jeans.

He almost missed her librarian cardigan. Did librarians have a uniform? He jumped out to open the door.

"Thanks for the ride."

Her cinnamon-and-vanilla scent filled his senses. Did she know she smelled amazing? She had to know. Friends could appreciate how the other smelled, right?

Climbing into the cab took longer because she was petite.

He smirked. She'd been touchy about her height even back in high school.

"What's with the smirk, Mr. Persistent?" She tucked a strand of her silky golden-brown hair behind her ear.

"Just wondering if I should offer a leg up next time you need to climb into the truck." He dodged her swat as much as he could. He shut her door and hustled to get the truck started.

"Excuse you. I might be vertically challenged, but I have no problem getting into your truck. And here I was being polite." She ran her tanned hands down her sweater.

"You were. Although, I could live without the nicknames." At least, they were in a place where she was picking out nicknames.

"No? How about Cowboy?"

He'd lived in small towns for most of his life moving from post to post, but he'd never worn a cowboy hat. "What's wrong with my name?"

"Fair enough. But you did spend a good chunk of your life in Oklahoma. You don't have the accent, but you have roots." She mimed putting on her cowgirl hat.

"I've never even ridden a horse. I have no claim to cowboy status." Sweat broke out across his forehead. Why did it have to be horses?

Katy patted his arm. "You're young, yet. We can find you a horse."

Sweat beaded his face. "I'll stick to running, hiking, and kayaking. Thanks."

"Afraid of horses?" Her tone was gentle, but her eyes danced playfully.

The truck rumbled to life.

His pulse pounded. "Not afraid. I have a healthy respect. From the ground." He followed the directions to the pumpkin patch, soothed by the methodical program's voice.

"Oh, wow," she said. "My uncle had a couple of ponies when I was little. I've only done trail rides as an adult, though. A horse ride can't be scarier than rapids when you kayak, right?"

"I can swim. I can't glue my skull back together. Same reason I don't go rock climbing." His stomach churned. He gripped the steering wheel tighter.

Katy eased back into her seat.

She belonged in his truck with her bag tucked under her feet and her cinnamon scent filling his cab.

"I'm not sure climbing the side of a mountain equates to sitting on a horse." She shook her head.

"Agree to disagree." He rubbed the back of his neck with a free hand.

She smirked. "Oh, come on. If I booked us a trail ride, then you wouldn't go with me?"

Was she serious? His palms were sweaty. His heart raced like he was a hundred feet up in the air without a parachute...about to fall. Luke tapped his fingers on the wheel. "Maybe. Listen, can we talk about anything else?"

"Okay. You have horse issues. I have woodpecker issues." She chuckled.

He glanced out the windshield at the cluster of oak trees. "Woodpecker issues? I need to know the story now. I'm picturing dive-bombing woodpeckers."

She straightened again and toyed with her sweater's cuff. "My gran called them 'signal birds.' If one flies by me when I leave the house, then I go back inside, count to ten, and leave again. They mean danger is near. And go figure, one has taken up residence in the trees outside my front door. My new neighbor brought bird feeders, and I think the woodpecker must be eating from them or something."

Luke needed to say the right thing. "What do you think the danger is?" He'd waited too long to respond, but he didn't like the idea of her expecting danger to come out of the woodwork. In high school, she'd rarely shared anything about her Choctaw heritage.

She bit her lower lip. "Honestly? The morning we ran into each other, the woodpecker was why I was late getting to Brewed Awakenings."

Luke chuckled. "So, I'm the danger?"

Katy's cheeks were pink, and she didn't answer.

Considering how she'd responded to running into him, he could put two and two together. He swallowed, his shoulders slumping. "I'm out of the danger zone now, right?"

"My ex also showed back up in the library after a nice long summer without him…so, who's to say my little signal bird wasn't warning me about Isaac?" Her expression softened.

"Definitely the ex then." He nodded. "I like how you carry those stories. I try to do little things to stay connected to family—not the same in any way. I guess I'm saying I know stories and traditions are important." He blew out a breath. "I'm not saying anything right."

She gently rested a hand on his arm. "Tell me one family thing you do."

"I buy cherries every year, even though I don't eat them. My aunt always kept a big bowl of them. She always had fruit in the house for some reason having to do with lace curtains." He turned off the coastal highway and down a two-lane road wedged between two pastures filled with waving golden tall grass.

"Why not buy fruit you want to eat?"

"Listen, I'm not judging you for counting to ten if you see a woodpecker. You leave my cherry buying alone." He chuckled. Some pair they were.

She snorted.

The bowl of cherries made him think of the old pool where he learned to swim. At Aunt Carol's house, they expected him to be a kid. He wasn't a substitute parent or house manager. He paid homage to those moments with a small cherry bowl.

"Next time, you let me know, and I'll help out. What are friends for, after all?" Katy eased back against the seat again.

"Sure, *friend*." He sighed. Not the word he wanted, but the one they both needed. He swallowed. Even if he wanted more—and he'd be an idiot not to—they couldn't start anything because he would hopefully move soon.

They passed bright-yellow and red trees, driving farther into the countryside. Delaware was flat, but he liked driving past open fields and small farms winding down with autumn. "We're almost to the patch. I get to meet your coworkers." Luke tugged at his blue Henley's collar.

Katy snickered. "I should warn you Ava will be overprotective and ask you a billion questions today."

He drew his eyebrows together. "Ava is the one who knows McKenna?"

Katy nodded. "And my best friend. She also possibly calls you Durant Guy."

"I've been called worse." He smirked. "Protective best friend, huh? I'm good with best friends. Just how many pumpkins is your boss planning to load into my truck anyway?"

"Seventy little ones." She raised her finger and thumb to mime *tiny*.

Luke whistled. They'd fit, but he wished he'd known he'd needed boxes.

Katy tapped her finger against her thigh. "Plus a dozen or so bigger ones. And you need one, and I need one. I carve one every year."

"I bet you carve a magazine cover-worthy pumpkin." He couldn't wait to see what she created.

"I make books or characters. Last year, I carved a tiny library scene on my pumpkin with a lion for one of my favorite children's books. I'm not sure what to carve this year." A sad song crooned from the radio, and she changed the station.

How many of her pumpkin carvings had he missed over the years? With her doodling abilities, he bet they were top-notch. "What about the wild teacher with the field trips and school bus? Remember when you drew her on our experiment sheets? When we added heartburn relief tabs to every liquid Mr. Wegman could think of? I'd never seen a drawing so good."

"You remember my little doodle? And she's perfect. Problem solved." She beamed.

The gravel parking lot for the pumpkin patch crunched under his truck tires.

Katy waved to two people standing near the entrance sign.

The guy was built like a linebacker, and the woman was Latinx with black hair tied back in a high ponytail.

Ava jumped up and down, waving.

He was happy to be along for the ride. Sure, he hiked and explored with his buddies, but today wasn't exercise or "mandatory fun" as Ryan called their excursions. A trip to the pumpkin patch was like Saturday mornings with donuts as a kid or trick-or-treating—pure nostalgia.

Katy hugged Ava. "You guys, meet Luke, my friend from back home."

"Durant Guy. We meet at last." Ava popped a hand on her hip.

"Hey, man, good to meet you." Dom shook his hand. He turned to his fellow librarians. "Why do we need so many pumpkins again?"

"Why do you act surprised about the pumpkin display *every year*?" Ava waved toward the pumpkin patch.

Luke and Dom stood shoulder to shoulder.

"I don't remember the last time I was in a pumpkin patch." Luke ran a hand through his hair, turning in a half circle. An expansive view of green rows dotted with orange pumpkins spread out in front of him. The sun peeked through the far tree line, painting the rows of pumpkins gold.

A few parents followed small kids on the hunt.

Luke took a deep breath of air filled with pumpkin and dry dirt.

"You've been missing out. The line for the donuts is already growing." Katy pointed over to a little red barn off to the side.

A small line had formed in front of the ordering window.

"Come on," Dom said. "Last year, they sold out,

and I didn't get seconds."

Katy gave Luke two thumbs-up. She bounced on her toes through the rows of orange pumpkins.

"Man, I'm glad to have help carrying all the food. I mean, I'm glad you're here for your truck, too. But carrying hot cider for a group is a trick." Dom wore an oversized football jersey for a nearby team. His black sneakers kicked up dust from the gravel path.

A family left with at least a dozen bags of donuts.

The fresh dough permeated the air, and Luke took a long slow breath of yeast and cinnamon sugar. He hoped his next post had a pumpkin patch with cider donuts. Grocery store pumpkins would never happen again.

Dom whistled.

Luke leaned back to read the menu board and decided to buy an extra bag. "So, how many pumpkins does the library use every year? I thought you picked one pumpkin and went home."

"Right? I expected one pumpkin, too. Last year, I think we had close to ten at the entrance to the library. Lined both sides of the steps. And then they had to have hay bales. And then corn. Want to guess how much wildlife we invited to the front doors? I couldn't step out without some squirrel or something zooming under me and making me spill my coffee. No man needs squirrel zooms heading into work for the day." Dom shivered, running a hand over his shape-up hairstyle.

"I don't think anyone needs squirrel zooms ever," Luke said. "Did the squirrels eat the library's pumpkins?"

"Oh yeah. I have pictures of the jack-o-lantern massacre. And they'll be back. I bet more than last year. And I'll have to clean the mess and listen to Ava complain about the squirrels eating the pumpkins like I should be stopping them." Dom stepped forward in the line.

The two of them towered over the families in front. Luke wasn't used to being around anyone taller than him. He stood a little straighter to combat his discomfort. "How does one stop a pumpkin-eating squirrel?" Luke asked.

"By not putting a small pumpkin patch on the front step. But the fall stuff was inviting the public in, and I should be on board." Dom raised an eyebrow.

They ordered enough kettle corn, cider donuts, and hot cider to feed at least ten people.

The cider had lids so Luke could at least stack them. He followed Dom into the pumpkin patch.

"So, you and Katy are spending a lot of time together." Dom cleared his throat. "Goes without saying if you hurt her, a gaggle of angry librarians will show up."

"A gaggle?" Luke stumbled over a rough break in the gravel path.

"Like geese, man. We seem real innocuous, but we take care of our own." Dom adjusted his stack of cider cups and shot Luke a sidelong glance.

"I've been Katy's friend since high school. We're good." Luke swallowed. He hoped they were good.

"We'll see." Dom cleared his throat.

"But while we're on the subject of protecting Katy. How often is her ex at the library?" Luke raised his eyebrows. Isaac was ridiculous, expecting her to help him with his research after he dumped her.

"Isaac? I didn't realize he was bothering her." Dom

narrowed his dark-brown eyes.

"Made a big deal about how she was the only one who understood his thesis or whatever. And he wanted her to go sit with him when we were at the Lobby House the other night." Even the crisp scent of fresh apples and spice wafting from the paper cups couldn't shake his Isaac-induced mood.

"I'll keep an eye on the situation. Nonfiction is my jam. I'll bring down a storm of reference materials the likes of which he's never seen." Dom nodded and stared into the distance.

What would a storm of nonfiction look like anyway? "Sounds like a good plan." Luke smirked. He pictured her ex under a giant stack of heavy books. The way Katy let Isaac linger bothered him. If she was done, she'd have sent him packing, right? Her ex wasn't good enough.

They found Katy and Ava circling a boulder-sized pumpkin.

"Nope. The monster pumpkin does not belong at the library." Dom breathed in and out slowly. "What do I even do when a fifty-plus pound pumpkin goes bad? When squirrels eat through its side? I don't have time to be rolling a giant pumpkin."

"I'll help." Luke gazed at the mammoth pumpkin.

"Don't you dare speak any louder." Dom shot him a warning glance. "Gaggles, man. Don't forget the gaggles."

"Beware of geese." Luke chuckled. "Remind me to tell you about guard geese in Europe."

Dom stopped and eased back to give Luke his full attention. "I won't forget."

"Thanks, guys." Katy bounded to them.

She and Ava relieved them of their cider cups and several bags of warm donuts.

"Thanks." Ava stuffed a donut in her mouth. She made appreciative noises and shimmied her shoulders.

"I think these donuts are the best I've ever had. Oh, my gosh, Luke. Do not tell McKenna." Katy flashed her eyes as wide as saucers.

"And get you banned from the best coffee shop in town? Never." He handed her another donut. Loose sugar fell in its path like glitter. He wiped crumbs from her cheek. Her smooth skin was velvety. He flexed his hand, resisting the urge to cup her cheek.

Katy raised a hand to where he'd touched her cheek.

"So, and I need to know before I eat three bags of donuts, are we picking all seventy small pumpkins from the patch?" Luke hoped he was wrong.

"No, man. We'll pick those up at the barn at the end. Katy called in our order. Those little pumpkins go fast." Dom frowned at the giant pumpkin Ava was using as a chair. "Ava, please. I'll trade you my whole bag of donuts if you leave the giant pumpkin here."

"Can you go get one of those big wheelbarrows from the front? No, maybe two of those." Ava pointed toward the big red barn. "Dom Davis, buckle up. Pumpkins are happening."

Dom handed over his cider and donuts. He shook his head with his shoulders slumped and trudged to the front to get a wheelbarrow.

"I'll get the second one." Luke handed Katy his cup. He'd hang onto his donuts, though.

"Durant Guy is helpful," Ava said.

"His name is Luke, and he's not far away enough

yet. He can totally hear you," Katy whispered loudly.

They returned with the wheelbarrows, and he snuck a donut from Katy's bag. The melt-in-his-mouth spiced donut was gone too soon. He stood by her side and surveyed the straight rows of big green leaves. A line of trees at the patch's edge was red at the very top with green clinging around the bottom.

Katy tucked her brown paper bag of donuts into her purse.

"My sister Jackie said to get a particular color of orange pumpkin and send her a picture, so I need help. Orange is orange." Luke drew his brows together.

"How old is your sister?" Ava cocked her head to the side.

Her sweater had three puffed-out pumpkins. The middle pumpkin was maroon and matched her pants. Everything about her said she liked to match, and she had her life in order.

Dom finished his last donut.

"She's nineteen. She takes colors very seriously, so we need to find Pumpkin Orange one fifty-eight." He rubbed the back of his neck. She sent him the official color-tone catalog for the orange he needed. She'd said his pumpkin had to match. Talking about colors and holidays usually kept her interest and filled her cup.

On his last deployment, he'd spent his entire call limit for the week listening to Jackie talk about the Sacagawea quarter error. His mom hadn't even been mad after he'd emailed her the reason he had to wait another week to call her back.

"His sister is basically one of the greatest humans ever. I accept her orange challenge." Katy smiled with her face upturned. Her boots were dusty from the field, and her loose hair was tousled from the wind.

Why had he ever let her go? Visiting with Katy while they shopped for their gardening supplies was always one of Jackie's favorite moments of the year. Katy's dad video called her the first year Katy was in college, and Katy had her dad parade the phone through their garden section. She hadn't even paused to wonder what Jackie wanted before launching into the gardening talk she always gave them.

He followed Katy down a dirt path between patches. He wasn't sure what to search for. What made a good pumpkin? He usually picked the first pumpkin he saw.

Katy smiled, holding a little orange one.

His head went fuzzy like she'd blasted him with sunshine again. He swallowed. "I think she's expecting something big enough for me to carve." He took the tiny gourd and returned it to the patch.

She held his hand, leading them deeper into the patch.

Her slender hand sent a shock of electricity up his arm. Would her touch ever stop making him feel more alive?

Toward the middle, she pointed to a cluster of orange gourds.

Luke knelt closer to a good-sized pumpkin. His sister's color square almost matched. His alarm buzzed with Jackie's favorite song. "I scheduled a video call with Jackie. You okay if I call her now?"

"Can we?" Katy straightened her spine.

He texted Jackie to see if the call would work. She initiated the video call right after the text. Jackie's amber hair was loose, and she was sitting in the living room at home next to Mom. Sometimes, having their mom there helped Jackie feel calm for the calls.

"Hi, Luke." Jackie held the phone back so he could see her full face. She preferred text messages most days, and her green eyes shifted all over the screen.

"Look who I have with me." He shifted the screen over to include Katy.

"Katy Caterby. How are you?" Jackie's frown was a brief shadow when Katy joined on screen.

Why hadn't he remembered to text her a warning? Jackie didn't end the call, so Katy was familiar enough. He'd had more luck with video calls lately. Jackie said seeing his face was easier. He knew better than to throw her a curve ball, though. Surprises had never been Jackie's favorite.

"I'm doing fine, Jackie. How are you doing today?" Katy leaned toward the screen.

Conversations involving Jackie usually had a comfortingly familiar pattern. She greeted people with a list of questions, starting with how they were doing.

"I left work thirty-two minutes ago. My day was busy because Caleb called in sick. I had the only register, but everyone was real nice. Roger Stevens paid me with a two-dollar bill with red ink on the seal. I need to research. I've never seen a red seal on a two-dollar bill." Jackie cleared her throat.

Jackie was passionate about color-tone catalog numbers and rare coins. He guessed she'd add rare bills, as well. Luke smiled, remembering her on her tiptoes, checking out books with her first library card. Nobody could out research his little sister.

"Oh gosh. A busy day for sure, and you'll have to let us know about the two-dollar bill. Can you see where we are?" Katy waved toward the field.

Luke panned the screen to show the acre or so of big green vines dotted with yellow and orange pumpkins.

"A pumpkin patch. Did you find an orange pumpkin?" Jackie scrunched her eyebrows.

Katy showed her the one she'd found.

"Is the pumpkin big enough? My brother found Pumpkin Orange one fifty-eight." Jackie had most of the color-tone catalog and numbers memorized.

Katy lifted the pumpkin higher. "He sure did."

"He needs to carve a face on the pumpkin." Jackie's voice never changed pitch or cadence. "He hasn't been carving them."

Luke angled the screen so Jackie could see him. "I'll carve a scary face and even light a candle in my pumpkin. Scout's honor." He held up three fingers.

Her amber hair swung above her shoulders.

Mom waved at the end, trying not to be more present than necessary on the call while being there if Jackie wanted her to be.

He'd call Mom later.

"Bye." Jackie hung up.

"I miss seeing her. Your sister is wonderful. She loves researching almost as much as I do." Katy shifted his pumpkin closer to her stomach.

"Oh, here, let me." He opened his hands for the pumpkin she was holding. Leaning in, he inhaled her delicious cinnamon-and-vanilla scent.

"You did good." She motioned toward the pumpkin after she tucked a loose strand of hair behind her ear and took the smallest step back.

"I'll never skip another year." He silently promised

Jackie he would do better. She deserved every joy. He spotted the other librarians not too far off in the field. "Well, let's find yours. The vine mate could be a keeper."

"Vine mate?" She chuckled but stepped closer to the pumpkin in question. The sun highlighted her golden skin.

"What else would you call them? Seriously though, my pumpkin is okay, right?" He cleared his throat and motioned toward the pumpkin.

"Your gourd is about as orange as possible," Katy said. "I think the *vine mate* needs to come home with me."

"Did you find your pumpkins?" Dom pushed the heavy wheelbarrow with the fifty-plus pound pumpkin now surrounded by at least half a dozen smaller ones. "You got enough? We have some to spare."

Ava shook her finger. "Those pumpkins will be so welcoming." She squealed and ran toward a large photo station with wooden farmers with face-sized cutouts.

"I get to be the farmer. Katy, you can be the wife," Ava said.

Dom snapped photos.

Katy and Ava made faces.

"Come on, High School Heartbreak, you need to be in the photo, too." Ava raised a hand to cover her mouth.

High School Heartbreak?

Katy's eyes opened wide, and her cheeks flushed bright pink.

What? He'd broken her heart in high school, and he hadn't even known. He stepped behind the wooden farmers, placing his face in the wife's spot while Katy stood on her tippy toes to fill the farmer. He posed "extra perky" as Katy would call his fake enthusiasm.

She breathed unsteadily in the cramped space behind the wooden photo frame.

The side of the barn was less than a foot behind them, casting a shadow over their backs. Her nearness made him too aware of her.

"I can't do this." Katy disappeared behind the red barn.

Luke followed her, hoping she'd explain. "What did Ava mean?" He stood back so she wouldn't feel crowded. The big red barn loomed behind her.

Katy breathed heavily.

He cocked his head to the side and waited. He'd wait as long as she needed, but they weren't leaving until he understood. How could he have broken her heart? His blood froze.

She stared at her boots. "I asked you out right before prom, and you showed up with Jolie and some of the football players to our date. When you were with Jolie, you basically stopped talking to me, and after graduation, you fell off the face of the earth."

His throat felt thick as heat tingled up his neck and cheeks. What an idiot he'd been to hurt her and never realize he'd let his friend down so spectacularly. With her eyes on the ground, he couldn't see her expression. He needed to know if he was saying the right thing, so he took a step to the side and filled her vision.

Her hazel eyes grew stormy.

"I don't remember you asking me out, so I didn't have a clue. I was stupid. You meant the world to me back then. I didn't have to be anything but me. And you shared your doodles and plans for world library domination." What was the right protocol here? His *Air Force Manual*, the *AF Man*, wouldn't line out clean-cut directions.

"I asked you to hang out, so in all fairness, I wasn't very clear." She huffed.

"I need more details. You wanted to date me back then?" His heart rate sped up. What would he have said? How had he missed being asked out by the amazing girl in front of him? If he'd known he had a chance with Katy, would he have started dating Jolie?

She caught a bright-red leaf from the air. She spun the stem back and forth like a tiny dancer. "During our last after-school lab, Mr. Wegman disappeared to find more isomalt sugar… You were being sweet about how you liked our science time, and I asked you if you wanted to hang out at the diner." She bit her lip.

He didn't want to know what happened next—and yet had to know. Just how much had he let her down? "And then what?"

"You said 'sure.' I waited in a corner booth, excited for my first official date. Jolie sauntered in, and you followed. She sat across from me. I hadn't even known you two were dating. And then your friends blocked me in the booth, and I had to sit there. And I felt like…" The corner of her lip quivered.

"Like I'd been hiding my relationship?" He rocked back on his heels. His memory was a complete blank. He couldn't remember the last time they'd worked together after school with Wegman. She'd asked him out in high school. And he'd blown his chance by missing the whole thing and throwing her childhood bully into the situation. Luke hung his head.

"I am glad we found each other." She shuffled her

feet.

"I'm sorry I let you down back then. Seeing you again is like no time has passed—like we're still those kids." He wished he had better words to explain. Being with her reminded him to live more outside of work. She was his favorite song on the radio. She could fix any mood and turn around the worst of days.

"Those hurts are ancient history." She bit her lower lip.

Shadows played over her face. He stared at her full lips for a beat too long. She'd wanted to date *him*. Her hazel eyes glimmered with the sun cascading through tall maple trees.

She hugged both arms across her stomach.

"*Ancient*?" He smoothed his cropped hair. How different would his life be if he'd had the chance to be with her in high school?

"I don't know. I see some gray hair." She raised a hand like she would actually point to some.

"What? I don't have gray hair." He patted his crew cut. "I'd be okay with gray hair. What do they call that?"

"Silver fox. And yeah, you'd be fine with a head full of silver."

She thought he was *fine*? He followed her to the front of the barn. "So Durant Guy and High School Heartbreak, huh?" He folded and unfolded his arms. "I think I liked Mr. Persistent better."

Ava joined them and blanched. "I messed up. You okay?" She angled her body between Katy and Luke.

"We're good. We were way overdue to clear the air." Katy looped an arm through Ava's.

Her voice sounded a little too upbeat like when she

121

was talking to Isaac. He didn't want to be grouped in with her ex. He had to fix their friendship.

"Dom is getting antsy to go pay for the pumpkins. You guys ready?" Ava barely glanced his way.

Luke could spot an out when he needed one. He waited, ready to follow her lead. Some roots he had—Jolie, who said he was too much of a wanderer to make a good husband and Katy, who he'd let down in more ways than he'd ever known. He hadn't kept in touch with any of the guys he'd run track with in Oklahoma. His head swam like he'd been at sea for too long. Maybe Jolie was right.

"Yeah, we should get our little pumpkin order, too." Katy motioned for Ava to follow her to a barn large enough to hold a small market inside.

He bet the barn doubled as an event space during the winter months. The floor was cement, and a few local merchants had signs on the walls—most of them vintage. Luke lagged behind the librarians with the wheelbarrow. He'd missed so much in his teens. He hoped he was doing better with paying attention as an adult. Katy Caterby had asked him out...and he'd missed his chance. He couldn't wrap his head around her liking him—even back in high school.

"Do you remember those award-winning porches back in Durant? When the city council handed out awards for best decorations at harvest time?" Katy waited in a long line weaving through the aisles of the barn.

"What kind of awards are we talking?" Ava motioned toward a trophy case filled to the brim with prizes for largest pumpkin and a pumpkin bread recipe.

"You won a yard sign and your name in the local

paper. The awards are a big deal back home." He chuckled. Growing up, he'd taken the fall decorations for granted. How many of these fall signs and gnomes with acorn hats would take over front porches in Dover?

"Does your mom still go all out?" Katy fiddled with a handmade scarf.

"Like you wouldn't believe. Every year, she adds more and more. She won't quit until she gets the first-place yard sign." Luke ran a hand through his hair. His mom had no fewer than sixteen pumpkins the year before. She hadn't sent him pictures of her new decorations yet. "I should ask for photos of her current setup." He rubbed the back of his neck.

"When you get them, you better share." Katy half-grinned.

She wasn't as pale as she'd been earlier. He had the sudden sensation of being in a fishbowl. He'd forgotten Ava and Dom were there.

Two employees wheeled out with the first two loads of little orange and white pumpkins for the First Friday activity.

Luke climbed into his truck to load the little pumpkins first. The larger pumpkins would go in last so they could be unloaded first. Loggie guys always planned the cargo.

By the end, his white truck bed was packed with a portable pumpkin patch. Who knew librarians needed so many pumpkins? He opened the passenger door for Katy.

She grazed his hand with hers.

Luke swallowed. Her touch zinged up his arm. He shook his head and hopped into the driver's seat.

"Jackie never stays on calls that long. I think she approved." Luke started his truck.

Katy shifted her feet and clenched her jaw. "You did good on the color and the size. Bonus brother points." She crossed her ankles and leaned back in her seat.

"I might have to get a Christmas tree now and keep rolling with the holidays. If a pumpkin makes her happy, I'll deck my apartment all out for every holiday. Even the minor ones." What was the protocol for decorating for Labor Day and Arbor Day anyway? Living halfway across the country, he'd take any chance to be there for Jackie. Even if he had to take the color-tone catalog printouts to the hardware store to get the right green for the tree.

"Well, invite me over for Pi Day then. I'm a big fan." Her eyes twinkled a bit.

"Pie Day? Like apple, pumpkin, or pecan?" He glanced sideways.

"Technically, the day is for Pi the number. Last year, Ava used pie crust to make the Pi symbol on top of her berry pie. I think I have a photo somewhere. How are your pie-baking skills?" She crossed her arms.

"Nonexistent. But I know where to get them at the grocery store." He maneuvered back onto the small state highway. Farms lined the road for miles in every direction.

"Are you at least buying bakery department pie and not freezer pie?" She pouted her full lips.

Luke had to jerk his gaze back to the road. What was he doing? She'd liked him a lifetime ago, and now, he couldn't shake the idea of them together. What could he possibly offer her, though? He would move in a few months or a year tops. He could deploy for as long as a year at a time. Jolie was right. He didn't bring much to the table.

"You back off my freezer pie, or you're not getting any." He kept his tone light. She didn't need to know he couldn't stop imagining what might have been.

"Harsh, Taylor. Harsh." She changed the radio station to something more upbeat.

"I might change my mind by March." He smirked. He couldn't shake the unsettled buzz under his skin. He'd ruined everything. His shoulders slumped. If the mini library worked out, he'd be long gone by spring.

"*Friends* share pie."

He was being friend zoned before anything could even start, but he might score the in-person training opportunity or end up stationed somewhere else. He had no business dating anyone—especially not Katy. He squared his shoulders and promised himself he'd do right by her. She deserved someone she could build a life with here near Ava and McKenna.

Katy drummed her fingers on the console.

"Hey, we finished at the pumpkin patch early. Any chance you want to run to Rehoboth after we drop off the pumpkins? The bookshop on the main strip has a box of books for us." Had he planned to invite her? Nope. His heart and brain were not on the same page.

"You want to take me to the beach bookshop?" She bounced in her seat. "Gee, let me think…"

"Fair enough. Let's drop these pumpkins and go get some books and taffy."

****

Luke found a parking spot a block away from the bookshop. Rehoboth was a 1950s boardwalk town with a taffy pull company right on the beach. The air was sweet and salty. The chilly fall day hadn't slowed beachgoers down.

"Have you played the giant plastic chess set?" Katy pointed toward an alcove where the bright-white-and-black chess pieces glistened in the sun. She flitted her gaze around the small coastal town as they walked to the bookstore.

"Not yet." He wagged his eyebrows.

"How are your chess skills?"

"As a card-carrying Adventure Scout, I have the chops. Chess is pretty much all we did in the evenings or on rainy days at camp." He could practically smell the damp earth and musty camp tents.

She drummed her slender fingers on her knee. "I did not know Adventure Scouts have a chess tradition."

"Everywhere we moved, downtime stayed the same." Luke shrugged.

His mom had signed him up for scouts in every town they lived in. If they lived off base, scouting was the fastest way to make friends. Her dad was an Adventure Scout, and she was set on him achieving the same. He barely attended the bare minimum of meetings and campouts when Mom was sent to a new base every two to three years…or when they lived with Aunt Carol while Mom was deployed.

"After we get the donation books, I challenge you to a game." Her grin was wide. "I haven't been here since early summer. For an Okie, you'd think I'd spend as much time as possible at the beach."

"Do you go to a different one? Or do you just live vicariously through beachy books?" He shoved his hands into his pockets to resist the urge to make a bigger fool of himself.

She chuckled. "I've been to a state park just south of here more than Rehoboth. Ava and McKenna love the dog beach." She kept pace but left extra space between them.

"I'm sold. I've never seen dogs on the beach." Luke opened the door to Browseabout Books, smirking at the *Smart People Shop Here* sign chalked out front.

Katy took a deep breath and sighed, gazing around the shop.

He waited while she had her moment. He'd made the right call inviting her.

"Can I help you?" The sales clerk at the front of the shop stepped out from an aisle with a stack of fall cozy mysteries.

"We're here to pick up a box of books for Dover Air Force Base." Luke squared his shoulders.

"I'll go grab those from the back." The clerk went to find their box in the back.

Katy beelined for the beach reads display while they waited. She drew her slender finger down a couple spines, biting her lower lip.

Luke forgot the rest of the world existed.

She handed him one book before quickly adding three more to the stack. They had bright covers with beach umbrellas and sand dollars.

"You escaping your favorite season?" He raised his eyebrows.

"Oh, I'm saving these for winter. Books keep. And when coastal winds turn bitterly cold, I'll have these to read." She hugged herself. "Here, I can hold them."

"I have one job, and you are not taking it from me." He held her stack high. Her glare spoke volumes.

In high school, she kicked him in the shin if he used his height against her. He smirked.

The sales clerk breezed by them to the front register. "Our regulars had a blast shopping for kids on base." She patted the top of the box. "Can I get a snap of you and the books?"

"Thank you so much." Katy hushed her voice.

Luke and Katy each picked a book and stood by the donations.

He draped his arm around her shoulder and held her close. His heart jumped into his throat. Her hair smelled like cinnamon and vanilla, and he swallowed back the urge to kiss her.

Katy left with a new book tote and a stack of winter reads.

"Let's get these boxes into the truck, and then I'll let you win at chess." Luke set his box full of rainbow board books onto his truck bed, securing the box with bungee cords. He climbed down first. He wasn't sure why she'd climbed in after him, but holding her waist steady made his heart speed up.

Katy laughed. "In your dreams, Taylor. I bet I can beat you in four moves."

"Four? Big talk."

In the sand-colored stone alcove, the chess set was in use. A mom navigated the ever-changing rules of her toddler overlord.

"We'll be done in a minute." The mom barely kept the pieces from wandering away from the board.

The three-year-old was determined to make a sandcastle.

"You're just fine." Luke wandered over. "How do these need to go?"

The pint-sized tot sized him up. "Move the horse over there." She ordered Luke to position piece after piece.

She barely came to his knee. The toddler even offered him a fist bump she finished with jazz hands. How the shape made a sand castle, Luke wasn't sure.

The kid jumped and ran around her creation.

Katy snapped a photo of the mom and her daughter with the chess pieces.

The young girl's gaze sparkled with mischief. She hid behind the bench and slowly crab-walked toward the beach.

"We've got this. There might a crab on the move." Katy pointed to where the toddler was sneaking off again.

"I feel rotten to leave you with our mess." The mom fretted her hands while keeping her attention on her kid.

"No reason to. We helped position the pieces. We'll get them back on the board." Luke waved at the toddler.

The mom chased the little girl back onto the sidewalk.

The sun hung low above the horizon, and the beach town slowed. Their hands brushed over the last chess piece.

Katy froze. Leaning back on her heel, she created space between them.

Luke frowned. Was she still mad from the pumpkin patch? He cleared his throat. "You have time for a game?"

Her eyes sparkled. "Oh, my win won't take long."

The game was over in four moves. Luke stuck his

hands into his pockets and stared at the large chessboard. "You warned me, but I didn't believe you."

"The middle schoolers had a chess craze last year. The fad didn't last long, but I learned a lot." She rubbed her fingernails on a shoulder and then examined her nails. "No big deal."

Luke took a deep breath and rocked on his heels. "Loser buys dinner?" His words were gentle. Dinner wasn't a good idea, but he couldn't help himself.

"You don't need to treat me to dinner." She studied her boots and clenched her jaw.

He couldn't drop her off until they were okay. He'd be pacing his apartment, brainstorming ways to apologize for his teenage stupidity all night.

"Have you ever been to the Irish pub around the corner?"

She raised her gaze. "I haven't."

"I can't believe you haven't been there yet. Come on." He held out a hand and waited.

Her smile was tight. "Sure, I guess I can check out a new pub with a friend." She breezed past him. "Which way?"

The main strip stretched out ahead, and Luke steered them closer to the boardwalk where a pub with a bright-red telephone box waited. Sunset bloomed over the horizon in a frenzy of reds.

The tables inside were mostly empty.

Katy turned back to raise a shoulder.

"A little faith." He motioned toward the stairs. He hung back to wait for the moment. He didn't want to miss her expression when she realized the second floor had wall-to-wall glass windows with a view of the ocean stretching out ahead.

"Wow," Katy whispered.

They snagged the last table by the windows and ordered fish and chips.

"Have you ever been to Ireland?" Katy gazed out the window.

"No. I've been through Germany a time or two. When my mom deployed overseas, she'd always send us to stay with my aunt in Georgia. And she was mostly in Desert Storm, so she didn't go anywhere Jackie and I could go." He shrugged.

Katy nodded, briefly making eye contact. She kept looking out the window at the expansive ocean. The sunset cast a red and pink haze over the water.

He hadn't minded living with Aunt Carol and her family for six months here and there. His older cousin had helped with Jackie, so those months were easier on him in some ways.

"Is your aunt your mom's sister?" Katy leaned her head to the side, turning away from the window.

"She's my dad's big sister. She wanted us in her life, always has. Mom doesn't have any extended family. I won't say the situation wasn't awkward for my mom, but she tried to hide the complications. My grandma lived with my aunt, and I have an older cousin, Cheri. I liked living there, and they were all great with Jackie."

He'd played junior baseball one summer with his uncle coaching. Summers still weren't complete without orange slices and yellow sports drink. Did Aunt Carol know those were the only times he really had a chance to be a kid? Even when she wasn't deployed, Mom worked long hours. He'd been proficient with cooking a few meals and running the washing machine by the time he was nine.

Katy was the only one who knew about his family situation in high school. He hadn't even told Jolie until her first year in college.

"Sounds complicated for your mom, but I'm glad you had a family net when your mom deployed. With your mom working in the lunch room and around all the time, life in Oklahoma was so different." Katy tucked a strand of hair behind her ear.

The server delivered their plates piled high with steaming fried fish and chips.

"Her retirement wasn't the smoothest adjustment. For years, I called most of the shots in the house, and then when she was present, she was in my business." He shook his head. "My issues with her were part of the reason I enlisted right after graduation. Our fighting wasn't good for Jackie. Mom wanted things to go a certain way, but Jackie and I had our own rhythm. She and Jackie found a new one after I left, and I know my decision was the right call. I just wanted Jackie to be okay."

Routines were deal-breakers for her and always had been. She'd been miserable when he and Mom couldn't compromise on the way they both thought things should go. Jackie had started to shut down, and he couldn't live with being the reason.

Katy nodded. "When my dad would date someone new, he would live in this hope bubble. I was happy for him… But I also resented the changes. I don't know how to explain."

"The single parent life is tough. I didn't understand, not really, until I was an adult. Back then, she'd expected me to handle things for years and then took back all the control. Treating me like a kid when I was a senior in high school didn't go over so well." He took another bite of the thickly battered fries with sweet malt vinegar.

He and Mom found a path forward after a few years. Mom never quit fighting for their relationship. Jackie was thriving again with a routine and a quiet life to suit her personality.

"I can't imagine anyone would enjoy having their role reversed so late in the game. I'm glad you found your way even if you ghosted me after graduation." Katy squeezed his hand.

"Ghosting is a harsh way to describe what happened." He leaned forward. "I didn't talk to anyone except..." He swallowed, realizing his mistake.

"Jolie?" She gazed out at the expanse of ocean and the bright-pink horizon.

"Now that I know how it all felt for you, I really am sorry." He rubbed a hand over his face. He'd lost his appetite.

"I know you are, but the disappearing act sucked." Her face was pinched. Her plate was still mostly full.

"I regret not keeping in touch. You know why I stopped into the Last Chapter?"

She jerked her gaze toward him.

"I go into the local bookshops in every town I'm stationed because I remember shopping in a little hole in the wall store with you. I don't have many uncomplicated or good memories left of Oklahoma." He pushed his plate away.

"You remembered?" she whispered.

He'd gone with her on a break from the hardware store. "I held your stack of books for the first time. You were wearing your green hardware store polo with jeans and your usual sneakers covered in tiny doodles. You flitted around the shop like a hummingbird with too many flowers to choose from."

She opened her hazel eyes wide. "I don't know what to say."

"I'm just saying you matter. You'll always matter to me." He cocked his head to the side. Luke wavered. Where did he want the conversation to go? He was leaving Dover, and she was there to stay. Whether he left on the training PCS or his next station, he was out of there—hopefully sooner rather than later. The table rattled, and he gripped his knee to keep his foot from bouncing. He needed get out of Dover, and he had no right to start something with her.

She deserved better.

Chapter Seven

Katy covered a table in the library break room with little orange and white pumpkins and a scattering of rainbow permanent markers. She'd run with Luke's suggestion and had the solar system and a school bus drawn out on the pumpkins.

He'd invaded all her projects and thoughts—even the library pumpkin display had a luminary Air Force logo carved and waiting for evening.

She had to get her body and mind on the same page. Luke Taylor was a bad idea—a proven flight risk and a distraction from what really mattered in her life like the Fall Fair. Her after-school bunch was counting on her.

"Oh, my gosh. The story time kids will go wild." Ava shimmied her shoulders, pointing at the frizzy-haired teacher on the school bus pumpkin.

Katy couldn't blame her. Even as an adult, the childhood cartoon lifted her spirits. "Luke had the idea." Katy added more red coloring to Mars.

"Speaking of Durant Guy…are we okay? I'm sorry I made things weird at the pumpkin patch." Ava fingered the gold pipe cleaner rings around Saturn.

"Did I enjoy being outed about my teenage mortification? No. Did your slipup help clear the air between us? Yeah. I know you didn't mean to." Katy sighed.

"For the record, Durant Guy seemed okay. Not to mention, he's was super cute. I'd only seen him from far away." Ava doodled tiny stars onto one of the pumpkins with a gold marker.

"Cute? He's attractive and all grown up. When I'm with him, sometimes I expect to see a teenager, which sounds so weird out loud." Katy scrunched her nose. They had too much history. If they'd met with a clean slate here in Delaware, without the heavy baggage of her Oklahoma existence, maybe they could have been something special.

Ava narrowed her light-brown eyes. "No, he broke your heart as a teen, so you carried the pain. The *very* attractive man he's grown into wasn't the heartbreaker, though. He seemed content to follow you yesterday. Finding the pumpkin to show his sister was sweet."

"He's a good big brother. He was always looking out for her when we were younger." Katy tossed the bag of pipe cleaners onto the table.

Ava set the pumpkin back in its spot and tilted her head to the side. "When do you see him again?"

"Tonight. I'm helping him wrap books. The school librarian on base, Joshua, booked the school cafeteria, and I think parents are volunteering to help. I'm already working on some collaboration ideas to pitch to Joshua." Katy bit her lip.

"We could build deeper connections with their community. Let me know if I can help. Super Cute Durant Guy shows up for the kids." Ava waggled her eyebrows.

"That's a mouthful of a nickname." Katy clamped her lips together.

"I'm committed. Now, tell me what's what," Ava

said.

"Nothing. We're friends." *Maybe more?* No, *more* was a bad idea. Luke hadn't shown any interest in leaving the friend zone, even after she'd had the mortifying experience of telling him about her high school crush. She sure as heck wouldn't make the first move again…

"Friends who keep sneaking quick glances, hoping nobody will notice. Girl, somebody is always looking. I'm somebody. I need you to give him a chance." Ava pressed her hands together and pouted her lips.

"Nobody is sneaking glances. Seriously, drop the relationship talk." Katy clenched her jaw. She struggled to maintain her boundaries.

"You're fighting your attraction for all the wrong reasons." Ava mimed dropping a mic on her way back to the children's section.

Katy finished the pumpkins and headed back to Darcy's office. She needed to check in with the manager of the Friends of the Library Bookshop. She didn't have time to think about Luke's green eyes or the way he made her feel like melting sometimes. He wasn't a cinnamon roll, and there would be no melty goodness between them.

Mae followed her into the office. "These are lovely." She ran a hand over the fall decorations on Darcy's desk. "How are you progressing with the fair?"

"Social is live and following the schedule Ava created. Her graphics are already pulling in some great organic reach." Katy woke the computer by spinning the mouse.

Darcy's screen filled with a photo of her rescue dog, Fitzwilliam.

"She does excel at all things social. And the book organization?" Mae motioned toward the towering stacks of mass market paperbacks in the corner.

"I'm almost finished putting the price tags on all the books. Instead of pricing the dollar books, I'll organize them on a rolling cart with a sign."

"Oh, I never can skip a bargain bin with books. Let me know if you need help with anything." Mae raised both eyebrows.

Fear of looking like she didn't know what she was doing kept Katy quiet. She should have asked her for help with a schedule for setup and breakdown or how to track the total number of books they sold. Instead, she swallowed loudly in the empty office.

Katy stretched on her way to the storage room. She had a few other projects to work on before she left for the day. Darcy's little office was now book-free—well, mostly. She had her usual books in there, but the tagged books were packed in boxes for the trek over to the Green—a square open lawn Dover converted to small fairgrounds for holidays. She left the storage room with a box of supplies. *Please don't let him see me.*

Isaac was camped out at a longer table with at least twenty titles spread out.

Her favorite Oxford comma T-shirt was bright-white under his hoodie. Was he wearing the shirt for her? Her confusion multiplied.

"Hey." Isaac stood. "Here, I can help."

Katy wanted to speed up and get back to the offices. Why was he offering to carry one box? He'd never offered her help. The realization sank in, and she froze. She'd carried much heavier boxes and wheeled heavy book trollies when they dated.

"I'm good. Thanks." She stepped back.

He adjusted his glasses with his lower lip puffed out. "Will you be out on the floor later? I need to pick your brain about a few other things on my thesis."

Was he angling for her to help him with his paper? Or was he hoping to get back together? He ended things and disappeared for the summer. Now, he was everywhere.

"Well, hey there, Isaac." Ava sauntered over.

The box was getting heavy, so Katy shifted her legs to use her hip. She kept her focus on Isaac. Her heart was racing, but she squared her shoulders. "I think it might be better if you ask a different librarian." Katy maintained eye contact with Isaac.

"Oh, uh, I didn't mean to make you uncomfortable. I miss talking to you." He shuffled his feet.

She swallowed her rising guilt. "I need space."

He jerked his head back.

He'd dumped her out of the blue. What didn't he understand here? Of course, she didn't want to help him write or edit his thesis. A whole different side of his personality was emerging now, and she couldn't un-see the selfishness.

"My thesis is important," Isaac said. "I hope you'll reconsider." He trudged off.

"Come on." Ava held one side of the box and helped carry the load. "I'm proud of you for telling him *no*."

"Not the most professional way to handle him." Katy bit her lip and set the box in Darcy's office.

"Not like you had a choice. You have to set boundaries, especially with *users* like Isaac." Ava popped a hand on her hip.

"How did I not see how selfish he was while we were dating?" Katy whispered.

"When he knew you were starting to get close, he ended the relationship and ghosted. Plus, you have the Pollyanna Syndrome." Ava waved a hand back and forth.

"Pollyanna, what?"

"You see the absolute best in people, even when they show you their worst. Pollyanna was all optimism. Not inherently a bad thing, but the way you see the goodness makes my job as your best friend much harder." She flipped her hair, heading back out to the children's desk.

Elementary school would let out soon, and they had a consistent group of fourth and fifth graders who played games on the computers and read graphic novels after school. Ava adored them. Katy couldn't help but agree. Some of them would be playing tabletop games on Friday night.

Her phone buzzed. Apparently, today was officially sponsored by interruptions. Luke's name popped onto her screen. Maybe she didn't mind *this* one.

—Hey, Katy, you still coming to help me wrap the extra books today? I picked out some wrapping paper for the different reading levels. Jackie helped me over video.—

—I'll be there. If Jackie picked them out, then I know they'll be perfect. She takes color very seriously.—

—That she does. See you in a while.—

She tried not to think about him at a store with his sister on a video call weighing the different options. He was doing a better job of giving his sister reasons to be happy.

Katy did *not* have time for the bubbles dancing in her stomach. Between his deep, rumbling baritone and inherent goodness, she was in real danger of falling for him all over again.

****

Chilly fall wind blew her hair into her face. Katy checked her watch again in the Visitor Center parking lot.

Luke parked his white truck in the lot.

She opened the passenger door as fast as she could.

"You in a hurry?" He cocked an eyebrow. His hand was on the stick from shifting gears.

"The wind is harsh today." Her heart rate slowed as soon as she took a deep breath of Luke's woodsy scent.

"Fall is officially here." His big hand covered her shoulder, and he gently squeezed.

Shivers ran down her arm. Would his touch ever stop making her whole body take notice? "Fair. You ready to wrap some books?" His truck smelled like cedar and mint, and she eased back into her seat.

"I want to make sure you know I'm terrible at wrapping presents. Just want realistic expectations here." Luke chuckled.

"Books are the best for wrapping, though—unlike some gifts with round edges. I believe in you." She patted his arm and did her best to ignore the warmth of his muscles beneath her hand. Lugging equipment sure had filled out the lanky teen she remembered.

He ran a hand over his crew cut. "Thanks for the pep talk. I'll do my best. The wrapping paper is in the back seat."

Rainbow, space, and star wrapping paper were stacked in a tidy pile on the narrow back seat. He'd bought plain craft paper for the older kids.

"Tell Jackie I said she did a good job. Those are great." She rubbed her hands together, ready to get wrap books. His smile warmed her clear to her toes. She whipped her head forward.

He drove through the gate to the tidy housing side of the base. The quiet streets were lined with gray-and-white duplexes. The duplexes had different flags for sports teams from across the country. Most had uncarved pumpkins, and a few had haybales.

Luke parked in the small school lot filled with minivans. "I grew up attending schools like this."

"How many different bases did you live on?" She couldn't remember if he'd ever told her.

"Posts for Army. And five." He raised a hand.

"Right. I'm so excited for these kids to be welcomed with books from the community." Community moments were the best part of being a librarian.

"Our MCL will be a good thing, too." He squared his shoulders.

Heat rose in her cheeks. Ava's words kept rattling around in her head. He had grown up so much since high school, and holding ancient history against him wasn't fair. *Right?*

He wrapped an arm around her with a half hug.

"We're a good team, Taylor." She leaned against him. Her heart fluttered at his nearness.

They followed the signs to a cafeteria bustling with activity.

Joshua, the school librarian, rushed over wearing

an *All the Cool Kids Are Reading* T-shirt. He'd styled his thinning copper hair with gel to add height. "The infamous Katy Caterby." He raised a manicured eyebrow.

"Infamous? That's new, but I'll take it." Her cheeks grew warm.

Joshua hugged her. He hugged Luke, too.

The guy was a big ole hugger.

"I have a few volunteers to help us. Katy and Luke, these are some of the parents on Dover AFB." He introduced them to three parents.

The fourth volunteer stood. She was taller than Luke with her dark hair in a tight low bun. Her bronze skin glowed against her soft gold sweater.

Luke introduced his boss, Major McClain.

"Katy, I've heard good things. Joshua can't stop talking about the great ideas you have for bringing library programming to the kids here at George Welch Elementary School. I didn't realize the library had so many events." Major McClain forced a laugh.

Her tone was clipped, and the space where the other parents shied away started to make sense.

Joshua leaned away.

"Nice to meet you, too. I'm hoping we can provide some great literacy engagement for the kids here." Katy mustered a small smile.

"You should hear about their fun First Friday event." Joshua clapped.

He wore his library science nerd status with pride.

Luke ran a hand through his sandy-brown hair. "Oh yeah, we picked up a bunch of little pumpkins for kids to decorate. Did you make the school bus in space one, Katy?"

She showed them her handiwork on her phone. The parents asked for details, and she was more than happy to share them. Katy recommended several high adventure, middle grade books to a mom sitting kitty-corner. She couldn't imagine a better way to spend an evening. Bookish volunteering was such a win.

Luke set out the wrapping paper and supplies.

One of the moms organized them into different age groups and stations. Community support was alive and well here.

Katy wrapped a copy of *Anne of Green Gables* in the star paper, making crisp lines. She'd spent hours wrapping gifts for people at the hardware store, and the muscle memory kicked in.

"Your edges are all so…so clean." Luke angled to hide his wrapping attempt. "I should be prepping pieces of tape for you all or something."

"You're doing great, and wrapping the books was your idea." She bumped him with a shoulder.

He didn't waver his gaze.

He focused like he needed to memorize every detail—like she was important. Heat creeped over her face again.

"Thanks, Katy. Seriously." He placed a palm over hers.

His touch lingered for longer than a friend's should. Warmth seeped into her skin. She could be brave.

"So, Katy, I need you to tell me all the best teenage Captain Taylor stories." Major McClain raised an eyebrow.

Her tone was a little off. Katy couldn't figure her out. Her topic should be happy, but his boss sounded a little annoyed. Maybe she always sounded put out?

Luke slipped his hand away.

The loss of his warmth rattled her. She craved him in a way she wasn't prepared for. "Oh, gosh. Where to start?" Katy shifted her gaze toward Luke.

"Hey now." Luke waved his hands out.

Major McClain smirked. "You can't blame me for trying. I'm glad you included parents. They're spreading the word about us getting an MCL faster than any flier could. There would be more of us, but as you can see, we have to help with the decorations for the upcoming school musical too." She motioned toward a group of parents stapling a bunch of smaller posters together to create a big pumpkin patch in the back of the room.

The room slowly transformed into the living embodiment of fall spirit. The small raised stage had half a pumpkin patch taped to the back wall. Square construction paper pumpkins dotted the walls around the room, and papier-mâché pumpkins with real sticks for stems covered a table against the wall.

"The kids helped make the set. Brilliant." Katy gazed at the autumnal backdrop.

"My oldest is part of the show for the first time, so I'm learning all about stage productions at the elementary level." Major McClain motioned toward the stage.

When she mentioned her kid, Major McClain's tone softened.

Luke handed her a piece of tape.

"I hope your kiddo has the best performance and a ton of fun." Katy bounced her feet.

"Hey, Monique, can you help us get the last section

145

up?" one of the parents asked.

Luke's boss excused herself to help with the other project in the room.

The group of parents chatted easily once Luke's boss left the table.

"You really pulled off the last-minute wrapping session." Katy patted Luke's hand.

"Joshua did most of the organizing with the parents. I hope the kids like the books and wrapping paper." He added another stack of books to the table.

"You big softy." Their legs brushed, and she couldn't focus on anything else. When her thigh brushed his, she accidentally ripped the wrapping paper.

"Well, obviously. I'm basically a marshmallow man." He was lining pieces of tape in the middle of the table for the others to use.

Katy snorted. "Really?"

"You'd rather I was a prickly pear?" He raised an eyebrow.

"No prickly pears allowed. What would I be then?" Her tone was light.

"A bookworm?" He sat tall.

"I mean, I can't argue. I've read every single book I've wrapped so far. Mr. Price made sure to include literary gold in his selections." She hugged a copy of *Charlotte's Web*.

One of the parents glanced between them and raised an eyebrow.

She eased back. She and Luke were too close.

"He was excited about the project. Kind of caught me by surprise the way all the shop owners automatically said *yes*." Luke rubbed his chin, gazing across the room.

"You thought McKenna wouldn't help? She's pro kids, books, and supporting our troops. Our project is *very* McKenna." Katy couldn't imagine any of the shop owners saying "no" to helping kids on base.

"I didn't realize she was a big reader, but you two are friends so…" He smirked.

"Hey. I don't require reading as a friendship prerequisite." She squinted, pursing her lips.

Their knees brushed again. He was the north to her south magnet, like being close was natural—inevitable. Why was she fighting the way he made her feel?

"Why not? Book people are the best people. Don't you have a shirt saying something similar?" He leaned closer.

His woodsy scent lingered.

Another volunteer asked Luke for more tape.

"I do. But still." She had friends who weren't bookish. Granted, her new friends in Dover were almost all work friends and in a committed relationship with the written word.

He nudged her.

She tried and failed to tamp down her grin. She leaned against him for a moment while wrapping *A Wrinkle in Time*. Knowing the book would be a gift for a new kid on base was like sending a hug out into the universe. She hoped Meg's story inspired them to be themselves and to be brave.

"Hey, Captain, can you help me with the posters?" Major McClain motioned to the top row of background posters for the musical.

"Yeah, of course. I'll be right back." He jumped to help.

Katy admired the way he was always willing to lend a hand. Tall guys came in handy.

His muscular arms held the top row of red, yellow, and orange construction paper trees for the top of the backdrop.

"How long have you known Captain Taylor?" Joshua scooted over to sit in Luke's spot. His copper hair was thinning at the crown of his head. The yellow undertones in his skin were highlighted by his sapphire-blue sweater.

"We were lab partners in high school." Never mind the years they'd spent without contact in the middle. Joshua didn't need to know about their baggage. She'd been ghosted by her childhood friends in a room so similar to this cafeteria. Why wouldn't her closest high school friend do the same?

"Oh, wow. And you both just happened to land in Dover from Oklahoma?"

She couldn't tell if he was making conversation or being nosy. She didn't want to feed the gossip mill if Joshua was the nosy kind. "We did. And we didn't know for the last year. I bet we barely missed each other at the coffee shop every week until there he was standing right behind me. I'm kind of in shock. I'm so far from home. What were the chances of running into anyone from Oklahoma?" She drifted her gaze to Luke again.

"Well, you found each other, and my students will have an MCL. Wins all around." Joshua raised his hands.

He reminded her of gymnasts who nailed the landing at the Olympics.

Joshua smirked.

She didn't like the way he'd raised his eyebrows at the beginning. "The more accessible we make books for kids, the better, especially when they're basically recommending books to each other. Finding common ground builds such wonderful connections." She added another book to the stack of space wrapping paper.

"Absolutely. We do little book groups for the older kids, and they pick which group to go to depending on which book strikes their fancy. Choice makes library time more fun. All the book fun." Joshua did a little shimmy with his shoulders.

Luke's phone buzzed on the table. A big blaring name filled the screen and stole Katy's breath.

Jolie.

Her heart rate spiked. Luke said they'd broken up. Katy had assumed they weren't talking anymore. Her hands trembled. He should have told her if he talked to Jolie after she'd shared the bullying she'd gone through. Why wouldn't he have told her? She gulped. Was she overreacting? Yes. But she couldn't calm down in a room full of strangers. And worst of all—she had to ask for help. "Hey, Joshua? Can I get a ride to my car over at the visitor's center?" She'd been there for over an hour, so she could leave. An hour was a reasonable amount of time to volunteer, right? She didn't know what to say. Her stomach was tangled like a broken butterfly net.

"Oh, sure." Joshua set aside his current wrapping project.

She stood and grabbed her sunflower-yellow bag. "You wouldn't mind?" Tears pricked at the corners of her eyes. She took slow calming breaths. She was not a lonely little girl anymore.

"My keys are in my pocket, and we can leave right now." He stood.

Luke called out her name.

She scooted after Joshua like her life depended on escaping the room. How many times would she run scared?

Joshua drove a cute little compact car with a *Librarian: The Original Search Engine* bumper sticker.

She hopped into the passenger seat and buckled up. His car smelled like peppermint gum. She busied herself finding her keys in her bag.

He joined her in the car. "Just how many books are in your bag?"

"Only two tonight." Acting like she was fine took everything she had. Joshua didn't need to know about any of her backstory.

The drive to the other side of base was easier since they didn't have to stop for ID checks.

"Thank you. I owe you one." She hurried to her car. She didn't think Luke would leave the volunteers and come rushing after her, but she didn't want to take the chance and have to explain herself. She had to find the words. Most of her emotions were tangled in humiliation.

****

Reheating her coffee for the third time the next morning, Katy sat at the chipped black table in the break room with both hands wrapped around a mug of her pumpkin-flavored coffee. She had to get her head back on her job. First Friday was a couple days away, and her countdown clock for the fair was ticking by at an alarming rate.

—*Hey, Katy. Can you let me know if you're*

okay?—

Her phone buzzed with another text from Luke. He sent her several after she'd left the school, but she hadn't responded. What was a breezy way to say she panicked and ran? She needed to figure out how to set the boundaries her heart needed. Her imagination was running amok, and she kept wondering if Jolie had changed her mind and wanted Luke back. Her stomach ached.

Her phone buzzed again. She almost sent him to voicemail, but *Dad* flashed on the screen. "Hey, Dad. I'm on break at work. Everything okay?" She drummed her fingernails along the side of her ceramic *This is How I Roll* book cart mug. She could count on one hand the number of times Dad had called during a work day. The store kept him busy.

"Hey there, Katy Cat. I didn't want anything. Thought I'd call to check in. What's going on?" His gravelly voice had a strong Okie lilt.

Cars roared by in the background. Was he standing at the back of the store waiting for a shipment? She grinned. She'd bet an entire loaf of pumpkin bread. Why be idle when he could accomplish something like check on his only daughter? "Oh, I'm okay. Mostly. Just sort of scrambling to finish prepping for the Fall Fair I told you about." The warmth in her mug seeped into her hands.

"Your first big project. How's the prep?" His tone turned gentle.

"Okay, I think. I asked for help, and the social media stuff is back on track. I don't want to let anyone down." Katy bit her lip. She wanted to tell Dad about everything else, but the words caught in her throat. She sighed.

"Big sigh?" He raised his voice at the end.

"And I'm in a weird place. Remember I told you I was helping Luke Taylor with an MCL project on base? Well, I'm struggling a little with being around him, but I'll be fine." She cringed.

All the repressed memories surfaced with the tiny ways Jolie had embarrassed her for ten years. Tying the laces of her favorite boots led to the memory of Jolie snipping the middle of her brand-new sneakers in fifth grade. Katy had no proof Jolie had done the deed, so she went unpunished. Katy had to wear mismatched shoes from the lost and found for a week until Dad had time to take her shoe shopping. The taunting at school…

"Struggling how? Is he being appropriate?" He hardened his voice.

"He's still talking to Jolie, and I assumed they were done." Her tone was apologetic, but her feelings wouldn't behave.

"Well, bullies leave their marks. I can tell you the name of the kid who always trashed my home lunch at school. Greg Overton. He smashed my little paper bag under his foot because he could. But Luke didn't bully you."

"I know. But he loved her. I don't want any connections or for her to end up popping back into my life because of him. Jolie-free life has been such a relief." She'd thrived in Delaware, starting over with nobody knowing her story. Katy sipped her coffee, searching for comfort. In her head, Dad was giving her his patented wise-dad expression.

"Well, did you ask him if they're friends?"

"I did not as a matter of fact. I ran with my tail between my legs." She examined her brown boots and the scuffed linoleum floor.

"When you were small, you saw signal birds everywhere, especially when there were none to be seen. Take care, Katy Cat, and make sure the bird was really there this time."

His storyteller voice reverberated through her bones like when he shared his mother's stories at community events. He was right. "Did you call to drop some wisdom?" She laughed off the heavy moment.

"I'm old. I drop wisdom without even trying." He chuckled.

Katy gasped. "Dad. You're not old."

"Don't let the dark hair fool you. I've been dyeing the gray for years, so customers don't think I'm too old to know what I'm talking about. You know, in my day, people respected their elders and took their words with the weight they deserved. Now, you take my old dad wisdom to heart and make good choices."

"Love you, Dad."

"*Chi holla li*," Dad said *I love you* in *Chahta Anumpa*, the Choctaw language. He ended the phone call.

The little redheaded woodpecker outside her apartment hadn't shown itself for days. Maybe the danger was all in her head. Her phone buzzed again, and she checked the time. She had a few more minutes of her break left. She bit her lip and decided to be brave.

Chapter Eight

Nothing had gone right all morning, and Luke didn't have his head in the game. Between unloading a C-130 to fix the weight distribution on the aircraft and the aircrew pranking the new duty officer, Luke's left eye twitched again. He stepped into the Air Terminal Operations Center, ATOC.

Major McClain crooked her finger. She didn't make eye contact.

Something was about to go down. He followed her into a sterile conference room full of people from across base.

Major McClain frowned.

Colonel Rodriguez was in his early fifties with thinning hair and bright-brown eyes.

Luke didn't have much experience with him, but he didn't need to be his best friend to see the colonel was not happy. His lips were tight. Luke followed his major into the room, and they both took a seat after the colonel settled into a chair.

Major McClain sat with her shoulders straight and her full attention on the colonel.

Luke followed her example.

The beginning of the meeting covered projects she assisted with, and she handled the questions with grace.

Luke let down his guard.

"What's this I'm hearing about the mini library

project being rejected?" Colonel Rodriguez narrowed his eyes.

Major McClain was the higher ranked of the two, so the colonel ignored Luke. Luke held still. The room existed in slow motion. He focused on Major McClain. Whatever happened next was his fault, and she'd be the one to sit in the room with her peers and accept responsibility.

She tensed her hands into fists. "First we've heard about a problem, Colonel."

Major McClain's voice was deathly calm. Luke's palms were sweaty, and he barely resisted the urge to wipe them.

"The civil engineers' request for a traffic study was ignored." The colonel drew his bushy eyebrows together.

"Sir, I can assure you any missed forms were not intentional." Major McClain leaned back in her seat. "I take full responsibility to fix the forms as fast as possible. I know how important improving literacy is for kids on base."

How did she maintain such a calm exterior in the hot seat? Sweat beaded on his forehead. Were his swallows always so loud?

"I'm disappointed in how the project worked out. Rejected paperwork was not the outcome I expected." The colonel pursed his lips.

"I'll work to rectify my mistake," Major McClain said.

With the issue aired, the colonel continued around the table on several more projects.

White noise filled Luke's ears. After the meeting, Luke followed Major McClain back to ATOC. He dropped behind her after she sped up to get some space. He didn't blame her. Her name was on the project, and the initiative was base-wide, so any issues would get around. He'd made the failure public.

She ushered him into her small office and nearly slammed her door. She slapped the stack of papers on the desk.

Luke stood at attention while she paced back and forth in front of him.

"Did you tell me you had everything covered?" She narrowed her espresso-brown eyes to slits.

"Yes, ma'am." His heart rate accelerated. An angry major wasn't good for anyone. He squared his shoulders and stared straight ahead. He'd take what was coming—what was deserved.

"And were you successful?" Her lips were a thin line.

Luke didn't let himself slump. "No, ma'am."

"We have two choices. Find a way to get an extension to complete the study or a waiver. I am so disappointed in you." She paced and lectured him on the importance of a detailed review of paperwork.

They both searched the paperwork for the request for a traffic study.

She ran across a small notation at the bottom of another form. She gave him a minute to read the paperwork. "Get to work."

He'd completely whiffed and missed the footnote. At his desk, he glanced across ATOC at Major McClain's office and frowned. He would figure out a way to fix his mess. What would he tell Katy? If she even answered his call. He wanted to wait until he had a way to undo his mistake. He checked his phone, but the screen was clear of notifications.

Did he think a traffic study was a waste of resources? Sure. Could he make the argument now without being petty? Not even a little bit. The Air Force had so many forms to wade through. His first stop would be to find the secretary for the commander. As the gatekeeper for the commander, she was the most knowledgeable person on base. She also had an encyclopedia-level understanding of the available forms. The project was for kids on base, and he couldn't fail.

The current secretary was on the phone.

He sat in front of her desk and waited.

"You need help because of the traffic study?" She raised an eyebrow.

He startled. She knew about his mistake? His stomach bottomed out. No wonder the major was furious. "Yes, ma'am. I was hoping to check in with an expert about forms for waiving the traffic study. You're the SME. Any chance you have time to help me? If now isn't a good time, I can come back." He gripped his hat in his hands, squeezing the bill tight.

She steepled her fingers with her head tilted. With a single nod, she typed for a while, not saying a word.

She could be helping him or ignoring him. Luke shifted in his seat. Should he leave?

She sat back and tapped her finger on her lips.

Her dark-brown hair was peppered with what Mom called "glitter."

"I printed a couple forms you can try." She pointed to the printer against the wall, wheezing and whirring to produce a small forest's worth of forms.

"I appreciate your help, ma'am." She might have

saved his bacon. Either way, he would deliver some of McKenna's apple cider donuts as soon as possible. He hurried back to ATOC to review the forms and figure out what he would say to the major to convince her to stick her neck out again for their project.

Ryan maneuvered around the room, keeping everything as close to schedule as possible.

Luke walked toward the major's office.

Major McClain massaged her temples.

His gut told him to walk away.

"Captain. Just the loggie I wanted to see. Step on in." She motioned him forward.

His feet were heavy like they were sinking in quicksand.

"I've heard from almost every officer on the project with some level of disappointment or downright annoyance. Neither of those emotions are ones I like associated with my name." A vein throbbed on her forehead.

"Major, I talked to Mrs. Landing, and I have two options to get the study waived." He held out the forms, stopping her mid-rant.

She snapped the pages away and skimmed them over, letting each one drop onto her tidy desk. She pursed her lips. "We might get the colonel to sign off on the second one. We'll have to get two other signatures. The other one requires the commander's signature, and if the project lands on his desk as a mistake with my name…"

His heart hammered in his chest. His thoughts bounced between worst-case scenarios. The ball was in her court since the meetings necessary to fix his mess were above his pay grade.

She sighed, and the anger rushed out of her face. "Check your email and make yourself available for the meetings. Now, get out there and pick up the slack. Captain Hart shouldn't be doing your job." She turned and opened the tall, beige filing cabinet against the back wall.

"Yes, ma'am." He left the forms and practically jumped over the chair to escape her office.

Ryan struggled to keep ATOC on track. They had a last-minute load requiring rapid planning.

Luke rolled up his sleeves, ready to face something he could handle.

****

Luke stepped outside his office to video call Katy. Salty wind pressed his uniform against his body. He'd almost expected her to send his call straight to voicemail again.

"Hey, I only have a couple minutes left on my break." Her hair was curled into a tight bun.

"Katy. I know you're mad, but I'm in a whole heap of trouble here." He swallowed.

"What's wrong?" She raised her eyebrows.

"I missed a form. I missed one form out of the twenty-some I had to fill out for the MCL. The civil engineers requested a traffic study, like the mini library could cause a traffic jam. But I missed the footnote, and the whole thing was rejected." He stared at his coyote-brown boots. He would fix his mistake.

"What happens now?" she asked.

Luke ran a hand over his face. "Now, we try to defend not needing a traffic study and my stupidity."

"How can I help?" She tilted her head to the side.

The office she was using while her coworker was

on maternity leave had bright posters for several library initiatives on the wall behind her. Her voice was tired, but at least, she offered.

"Luke."

"Listen, I can tell you're not happy with me. You left without saying goodbye. Why did you leave?" He gripped his phone tighter. He wanted to work out whatever had happened at the school.

"Jolie called you, and I had to get out of there. Let's focus on the MCL." She cringed.

He started pacing. "Okay, Katy. I want us to be good. You're important and not because I need your help again."

"How can I help with the MCL?" She bit her plump lower lip.

Ope. He had nowhere to go from there. "Listen, I'll text you with the details. If you can be there as the MCL expert, great. If you can't be there, then can you help me come up with what to say?"

"I'll send you the stats. You know what to say. You were these kids, Luke. Don't discount your experience." She leaned closer to the screen.

Was there hope for their friendship or whatever they were working on? *Whatever?* They were headed straight to Friendsville. Even if he wanted more, Jolie's words rattled around his head like loose change in the dryer. He wasn't good for anything but leaving.

Even without Major McClain's recommendation, he could still be selected for in-person training, and he couldn't guarantee he'd return to Dover. He'd been there for over three years, and he was ready to pack up for a new adventure—mostly. "Thanks, Katy. I'll text you when I know anything." He ended the call, staring at his black phone screen for a moment.

Was Jolie the only big red flag between them?

****

When he stepped into Major McClain's office the next day, Luke wasn't sure what to expect. His initiative to find solutions mollified her, but all of his goodwill had disappeared overnight.

"Captain Taylor." She slapped the *Air Force Times* on her desk. "Check page six."

He flipped to the page and found an article about how different bases were working on literacy initiatives. Good to know literacy was an Air Force-wide focus. He couldn't wait to tell Katy. "The article is a good thing, right?"

"Mrs. Landing called. The commander read the paper and wants to highlight our initiative." Her smile held a wicked gleam.

"So, now the commander knows about the study." The baked pumpkin oatmeal he'd had for breakfast soured in his stomach.

"Correct." She sighed and sat back in her chair. "Which means we'll be meeting with him at 1400 hours to defend ourselves. I've already received approval to include the librarians. Your job is to get them there. We need experts."

Joshua and Katy were both well-educated on literacy, and Katy was passionate about the MCL project in a way nobody else was. If the commander listened for even five minutes, Katy's joy would be too infectious to ignore.

"You'll let them know where to be?"

"Yes, Major." He hurried back to his desk.

Joshua answered on the first ring, and when Luke

mentioned who would be at the meeting, he stuttered his willingness to help.

"Hey, Luke," Katy answered on the second try.

Which was better than not answering at all. "Katy, listen, I need your help again." He toyed with the yellow sticky note detailing the meeting.

"I said I would help."

"Okay." He swallowed. "We have a meeting with the commander. Joshua agreed to help, too, but I was hoping you could be our MCL expert."

"Just text me the time, and I'll meet you at the welcome center. Do you have any idea whether the commander is for or against the project?"

"He wanted to highlight our project after reading about an Air Force-wide focus on student literacy in our schools. That's how he also discovered my ineptitude." He frowned. The first time his name had crossed the commander's desk was not in a positive light.

"Well, if he wanted to highlight the initiative, then we have good common ground to start. I'll prep some data and be prepared. Listen, I need to get back to work."

"Thanks, Katy. I'll make this up to you somehow." He was lucky she cared so much about the kids on base. Maybe when they were together in person, he'd get the chance to fix their friendship. The gaping hole between them was as wide as the Grand Canyon.

****

Luke thrummed his fingers on his steering wheel, heading to the visitor center to pick Katy up for the meeting with the commander. He wished he'd had time to figure out how to fix whatever was broken, but everything had happened so fast.

She was leaning against her car door, waiting. Her hair was in a severe bun, and she wore a black cardigan over a simple black dress.

"Hey, Katy." He hopped out and opened the passenger door. He fidgeted with his hat.

The harshness in her features softened. The grim line of her mouth released. "We can take down the traffic study, Luke. I believe in our project." She rubbed his arm with her head cocked to the side.

He slid a hand over hers on the car door. "How did I get lucky enough to be your partner?"

"I'm here for the kids."

He nodded. How could he have messed things up again? He drove them across the bridge onto base.

Walking toward an office building, he fixed his hat and fidgeted with a clicky pen. The meeting room was on the second floor, so they had to endure both the wait for the elevator and the ride in the new cavernous space. Luke had the wild urge to use the *hold* button on the elevator and make her stay in there and talk. But he couldn't force her into the conversation…or leave the commander waiting.

Joshua waited outside the elevators.

The librarians stood side by side. They were a united front. *How do I get team Katy and Luke back?*

When they reached the room, the librarians snagged the last two chairs together.

The commander entered the room.

Everyone jumped to their feet.

Major McClain kept her expression neutral like they weren't about to sit in the hot seat.

Luke envied her ability to remain unruffled. He sat beside his boss.

"You all know why we're here. I need to know whether the MCL should proceed without a traffic study," the commander said.

The civil engineers presented their concerns. They were flimsy at best, but they were also the experts on stresses on traffic and such.

Luke waited, forcing his leg to hold still. He kept reading his notes, so he wouldn't mess up. Mom would say he was "hearing without listening," which he tried hard never to do.

"Major, I understand you've invited your own experts." The commander motioned toward Katy and Joshua.

They both sat straighter in their chairs.

The room full of officers must have seemed so strange to Katy. Joshua had served in the military before transitioning to civilian life.

"Yes, sir. Joshua Martin is our librarian at George Welch Elementary School, and Katy Caterby is a librarian at Dover Public Library. They've both been assisting with the project after being recruited by Captain Luke Taylor." Major McClain nodded toward Luke.

"The same Captain Taylor who missed the form?" The commander's eyes danced.

Is the commander enjoying this? "Yes, sir." Luke would own his mistakes. Hopefully, they wouldn't take the chance away from the kids on base.

"Well, let's hear what the literacy experts have to say." The commander waved toward the librarians.

"Sir, my name is Katy Caterby, and I've installed Mini Community Libraries, MCLs, in Oklahoma and here in Dover. We use them as an extension of our library services, which I believe Mr. Martin hopes to do at the park near the school."

"So, what would be the value? I won't sanction traffic disruption without a good reason."

The commander's tone was kind. He'd danced with Katy after all.

"I don't know about disrupting traffic." Katy raised an eyebrow at the engineers.

Luke wanted to hug her.

"I don't believe you could find an instance where an MCL caused a traffic situation. The location Mr. Martin helped us pick is at the park. A parking lot is nearby, and families are already there for recreation purposes. We build at parks or places where kids are likely to walk because busy locations increase access to books." She nodded toward Joshua.

"The MCL will invite our kids on base to not only pick a book and read but to recommend a good book to friends at the park. Kids won't have to ask a grown-up to drive them to the library. They can open the doors of the MCL and find books I've maintained." Joshua adjusted his collar.

"Adding an opportunity for the youth on base to find books and offer books to their friends at the MCL will organically increase literacy. The mini library says, 'Our community values books' from the moment you step into the park." Katy clasped her hands together on the table.

Joshua cleared his throat. "The kids coming into my library want to pick their own books to take home to read. The MCL gives them an opportunity in a recreational setting. We're offering a different attitude toward reading. *Choosing* to read will increase their reading. If we're improving literacy, then access to books will always be my top recommendation." Joshua never wavered his gaze from the commander. The school librarian wore a navy button-up and a navy cardigan with suede elbow patches.

"Will the box be near the street? What's the issue?" The commander pointed at the civil engineers at the table.

"I'm not actually sure, sir. Was a location in the report?"

"Second page. The MCL would be built by the benches on the far side. Our box will not be near the street, sir." Luke slid the page across the table. He'd never forgive himself if the whole thing was shut down because he'd missed a single form.

"I want this done by the end of next week." The commander casually signed the form and left the room without a word.

Luke stood with everyone else, sighing with relief.

Katy high-fived Joshua.

"Well, we got lucky." Major McClain picked up the form. "I'll file the paperwork while you take your friend back to the welcome center. Katy, Joshua, thank you both for the support today." The major shot Luke a long look before leaving.

Luke smiled and stepped toward Katy. "You saved our bacon. Both of you. I hope you know how much the major and I appreciate your help."

Joshua clapped him on the shoulder. "You had us at youth literacy initiative, but add in a setting inviting kids to take control of their reading life, and we're ready to defend the MCL. Metaphorically speaking. Well, for me, anyway."

"I'm defensive of our mini libraries." Katy straightened her cardigan sleeves.

Luke pictured a small gaggle of librarians defending MCLs. They'd done a fine job today, though. He followed them out of the room.

"My buddy and I were having a debate about books, and I bet you two can settle the issue once and for all." He pressed the elevator button.

Katy cocked an eyebrow.

"Hey, we can be bookish. We've established I'm on a first-name basis with the local bookshop owner. We can add school librarian and local librarian, so I have some bona fide street cred." He flexed his arms.

"He's got you there." Joshua gently elbowed Katy. "Okay, but spill. What's the question?"

"Are comic books literature? Like could my buddy donate comic books to the MCL?" Luke raised his palms upward. Ryan had a stack of superhero comics, but he didn't think he could donate them to the MCL.

"Yes." Katy relaxed her face into a smile.

"Absolutely." Joshua nodded.

They laughed and stepped onto the elevator.

"I knew you were my people." Katy fist-bumped Joshua. "Luke, comic books and graphic novels absolutely help kids become better readers. I've seen comic books turn even the most reluctant kids into avid readers."

"They can challenge kids to grow their vocabularies, and don't even get me started on the value of visual literacy." Joshua raised his hands high over his head.

"I don't know what 'visual literacy' is, but you're the expert." Luke chuckled. "I figured if kids started reading, then comics had value. Like a gateway book."

"Yes, exactly. Success is all about putting the right book in the right hand at the right moment. Reading is a lifelong journey." Katy hugged herself.

Luke shook hands with the school librarian, and Katy hugged him.

Joshua took off toward his husband's office.

Luke drove Katy back to the welcome center. He shifted the gear into Park. "Katy, can I buy you a cup of coffee tomorrow morning after you do your Friday coffee thing?" Would she say *no*?

"Can you meet early? I have First Friday stuff all day, and I can't be late for work." She bit her plump lower lip.

"I'll see you there." He barely contained the urge to dance a touchdown move. MCL victory and a chance to make things right with one of the most important people in his life? He'd take the wins.

She hesitated again. "If we're lucky, we can get McKenna's cider donuts."

Luke opened her car door. "Well, now, I'll show up when she opens to make sure. Those were good." The fresh donuts melted in his mouth with apples and spiced goodness.

Katy gripped his forearm. "Do not, whatever you do, compare them to the pumpkin patch ones while we're there. McKenna has some kind of issue with the pumpkin patch family. Let's not step in it."

"Good warning. Katy?" He had mostly lived in small towns as a kid. He understood the assignment.

She stepped closer. "Yeah?"

He inhaled her sweet, cinnamon scent. "Thanks for coming today. You and Joshua saved the day." He hesitated before resting a hand on her right shoulder.

Katy didn't step away. "You missed one form, Luke. The commander didn't seem worried once he realized the civil engineers were creating unnecessary red tape."

"You didn't see how mad my major was." He'd worked hard to get on her good side, and now, he had to start over from scratch.

At some point, the MCL project had become more important than his training course. He tucked a strand of her golden-brown hair behind her ear. Finding Katy again had changed everything.

Chapter Nine

The delicious scent of apple cinnamon scones and espresso filled Brewed Awakenings. Katy's Friday act of random kindness was one of the ways she stayed close to Gran. "Do good things, but don't talk about them," she whispered Gran's motto.

Gran's garden filled the fresh food bins at the local food bank, and she usually dropped off breakfasts to a few families experiencing hard times. She'd even paid for a handful of kids to get braces from her paycheck at the dentist's office. Katy hadn't known about the dental donations until those stories were shared at Gran's celebration of life.

Katy was determined to be a force for good like Gran—from big things like securing funds for the summer reading program to small things like a Friday morning pick-me-up for a stranger.

McKenna took the extra money for the next customer. Her dark-blonde hair was twisted in a fancy ponytail. She bustled around.

Katy scooted out of the way. She tried not to pay attention to who she bought coffee for, but sometimes, she snuck a quick peek. Today, an older woman ordered after her. Making someone's day for no other reason than she could gave her a little thrill. She was raised to be the light—to be Choctaw.

She added cinnamon to her latte and then settled in

with Luke's dirty chai. The MCL mattered to Luke. She'd be a fool not to keep him in her life, even if their friendship didn't grow into anything more. She slumped her shoulders again. In the school cafeteria, a tingle of warmth spread across her body like wildfire every time they touched. The wild hope had a life of its own.

"Hey. You're early, too." Luke sat beside her. His big coyote-brown boots stuck out from under the table.

"Good morning. Happy Friday and all that." She cupped her coffee in her hands almost reverently. Would he let things go? Should she just charge ahead and explain herself?

"Are you ready for all the First Friday stuff today? The event sounds like a lot of moving parts." He pressed his lips together into a tight line.

"The activities are all so fun, though. And don't even get me started on the cuteness of the kids after school." Katy clasped a hand against her chest. Community engagement events zoomed by too fast. Her whole body would buzz with excitement from beginning to end.

"Is today the local art show in the bigger multipurpose room?" He leaned back in his chair at ease, even in his starched uniform.

"Good memory. We've had artists in and out of the library all week checking placement and lighting." She'd helped a few display their clay creations and paintings. She wanted to type the stories they'd told her and post them on the library's socials. Storytelling was important.

"I can't wait to see their artwork."

His words caught up with her, and she gazed into his green eyes. "You do *not* have to come to the library on a Friday night, Luke."

"I want to see you in your element." He shifted. "Listen, can we talk about why you left the cafeteria the other night?"

She squared her shoulders and figured she needed to be straight. *Tikba Ihiya*, Dad would tell her, *keep moving forward.* "Are you on and off again with Jolie? When her name flashed on your phone…"

He sat tall now with his back rigid. "Yeah, I'm sorry. I should have told you we text sometimes."

"She was the bully I avoided all through school. I know you see a different side, but I assumed you didn't talk anymore since you broke up. Silly assumption, I know. You clearly ended on good terms since you defended her the other day." Katy bit her lower lip.

"You know she became a special education teacher?" He ran a hand through his short-cropped hair.

She hadn't known. People changed. They grew up. The future didn't change the past, though.

"Do you know why teaching became her dream?" Luke leaned closer.

Katy was speechless. She didn't know what to say. If he hoped she would change her mind about Jolie, he was out of luck. She shook her head.

"She and my sister Jackie really bonded while we dated. I'm glad they've maintained their connection." He picked at the cardboard sleeve on his chai. "Jolie became a special education teacher because she thrives in helping her students grow to become as independent and happy as possible. I'm talking too much. I guess, I'm saying we keep in touch because she's a good friend to my sister." He spread his raised palms.

Katy wasn't sure how to respond. Her thoughts

spiraled. Jolie had never shown remorse for the way she'd treated her. Why hadn't he said something the other day when she'd opened up? She wouldn't cut him out of her life for talking to Jolie. She wasn't the lonely little girl she'd been in Oklahoma.

His cardboard coffee sleeve slipped open. He folded it and set it aside while clearing his throat.

"So, you and Jolie are done?" She wanted to smack a hand over her mouth.

He nodded. "Do you remember AJ Jones? She's been dating him for a few months. He's over at the jewelry store on Main Street. I don't know when she and I fell out of love, but we did. I feel loyal to her, though, and while I won't ever defend her treatment of you, I'll defend the good person she is now."

"Okay, my walls went up. I went into protection mode like old times." Katy's cheeks grew warm.

"I should have told you she and I talk sometimes. I'm sorry." He placed a hand over hers, squeezing gently.

She mustered her best half-smile. "You know Megan and Riley?"

"Jolie's best friends?" Luke raised an eyebrow.

"Before Jolie's family moved to Durant, they were my best friends. We did everything together and were always having sleepovers. And then Jolie was a shiny new person. I don't know why she hated me, Luke. She told Megan and Riley not to be my friends. Our class was small, so I was alone."

He rubbed a warm thumb over her hand.

His green eyes held too much sympathy. She glanced at the door and swallowed. "They didn't say more than a word to me in middle school or high school. They acted like I'd never existed."

"Bullies are a hard thing to deal with. I should have warned you she's in my life, even if our interaction is real limited. I guess I've been kidding myself and making excuses for Jolie. I'm sorry." His thumb rubbed back and forth over her hand.

"Thanks, Luke. I feel silly now." Her throat was dry. She pulled her hand away to pick up her latte.

"No reason to. I feel like a bad friend for not saying anything back then and for letting you be blindsided now." He hung his head. "I showed up to what you thought would be our first date in high school with her. Some friend I am."

Friend. So they were just friends, after all. She slumped her shoulders. "We're good. Now, go buy donuts before they're all gone."

"Yes, ma'am." He mock-saluted on his way to the counter.

She'd never shared the story with anyone. When she was young, she'd struggled to explain what had happened, and then as an adult, the drawn-out drama was too much baggage.

He returned with warm cider donuts.

She clapped, ready for a less intense topic.

"Now, celebration is the appropriate response to my baking." McKenna's purple glasses perched on the tip of her nose like they might fall off at any moment. "I'll see you at the art show tonight."

"Text me when you get there, and I'll meet you. I'll be working, but I can take a break while y'all are there." Katy relaxed her shoulders and eased back into her seat.

"*Y'all.* Your Okie always makes my day."

174

McKenna pressed her hands over her heart.

Katy rolled her eyes. "McKenna."

"What? His accent shows more than yours. How did I not know you were both from Oklahoma? Unreal." McKenna pursed her lips.

Luke tossed his hands up. "I lived there for less time than you did. Maybe the way you talk is a librarian thing? You fixing our grammar while we speak, too?"

"Well, obviously, I correct your grammar while you speak." She huffed. Grammar was serious.

"I feel so judged." McKenna had a bounce in her step on her way back to the counter.

Friday morning regulars were lined out the door.

Luke tsked. "I made a big deal about how great her donuts are, and you had to go and tell her you're the grammar police."

"I don't correct you out loud." She wanted to correct them. *I should get more credit for keeping my edits to myself.*

"Uh-huh. Just silently. But now we know." He had cinnamon sugar crumbs all over his shirt.

She wanted to keep things light. She hadn't meant to tell him about Megan and Riley, but her humiliating story was out there now. "You have some donut crumbs." She motioned toward his Operational Camouflage Pattern, OPC, shirt.

He bit back a laugh. "I think I'm wearing as much of the donut as I actually ate." He used a napkin to dust the crumbs off his shirt. "I'd get a strong talking to about appearance standards at work."

Work was a much safer topic, so she pounced. "Are things better with your boss?"

Luke hung his head. "Not yet. But I'll work hard to

get back on her good side."

"She's being unfair. She missed the form, too." Katy shifted in her seat. Mae would have handled the situation differently. She wouldn't have expected Katy to fix the mess all on her own. Luke's boss had access to the files, and since the whole process was new, she should have checked the forms.

"She assigned me the project and trusted me."

His captain voice was strong and confident. He was being too hard on himself. The civil engineers trudged out of the meeting with their gazes on their shoes.

He rested a hand over hers.

"Technically, you did get the job done." She flipped her hand under his rough palm. Warmth spread down to her toes.

Luke ran his thumb back and forth. "You have time to help me finish building the MCL tomorrow? My buddy Ryan built the main part in his dad's woodshop. His dad and stepmom live a couple towns south of here, so they had all the equipment to build our custom design."

"Wow. Lucky us. I'll meet you tomorrow. No problem. I have the day off. But speaking of work, I need to scoot. First Fridays is here." Her to-do list was dancing in her head while she cleaned their table.

"I'll see you later tonight. If you need me to pick up anything on the way, let me know." He stood to pull his hat out of his pocket.

She tried not to get too focused on how broad his shoulders were in his uniform. She failed. "Coffee?"

"Well, coffee's a given at this point." He chuckled.

His crooked grin left her a little breathless. "Bye, Luke." She stepped out of the coffee shop and took a deep breath of the crisp fall air. The thrum of a woodpecker smashed through her moment of peace. She scanned the trees with wide eyes.

Sure enough, a redheaded woodpecker swooped across the street. The signal bird wasn't close enough to warrant starting over and counting to ten, but she hurried away. Signal birds were everywhere, leaving her unsettled.

****

Katy was riding the high of their successful afterschool activities into her evening events. Her feet ached, but she wouldn't let anything slow her down. She hustled across the library. Her shoes *whooshed* against the blue industrial carpet.

Ava waved from the L-shaped welcome desk. "I'm delightfully tired."

"Same. Did you see how cute the pumpkins were in the craft area?" Katy asked.

"Oh, my gosh. Yes. Did you see the little kitty one?" Ava bounced on her heels.

"With the wild whiskers?" Katy had taken at least twenty photos of the pumpkin with rainbow pipe cleaners sticking out haphazardly to share later.

"Yesssss. So cute. The kids are so proud of their unique creations. I should be more like them. Like the mural I made for the kids to add pumpkins. The bottom is crooked, but my hill is one hundred and ten percent unique."

The pumpkin patch was on a hill—not crooked. "Your pumpkin patch is glorious. You earned the extra ten percent. Okay, let's get the gamer kids all set up. Dom is hanging out with them tonight."

"Yep, he volunteered. I think he secretly loves

tabletop games." Ava giggled.

Katy helped her create a square out of the tables.

Dom helped move the last table into place. "The room is ready. You ladies are the best. Hey, Luke is walking around with coffee."

"Durant Guy sure has your number. If he keeps bringing you coffee, then you'll start associating him with happy warm coffee moments." Ava waggled her eyebrows.

"He has a solid long game." Dom paused in his whiteboard prep and adjusted his glasses.

"Wise words," Ava said.

"Nope. He doesn't have a long game. We're just friends." Katy hugged herself and wanted them both to stop. How could she keep her head in the friend zone if Ava kept pointing her back in the wrong direction? She would not date Luke Taylor. She'd attempted to ask him out once and was humiliated. Friendship was low risk, and safe was where she planned to stay.

"I don't buy *friends* for a minute. Now scoot." Ava shooed her.

Katy threw her hands up in exasperation and left to find Luke.

"Oh, good. There you are." McKenna waved from the library entrance. "Can you take a break?"

"Yep. Thank you both so much for coming out and supporting us." She took her warm coffee.

He tucked an arm around her with a gentle embrace.

Her stomach flipped. What were all the half-hugs about? *Does he like me more than friends?* Dom's words clanked in her head like pots and pans.

"Cheers to a Friday night among friends and

books." Luke raised his travel cup.

So, they *were* just friends. She tapped her cup against his and sipped her favorite Caterby latte, and the corner of her mouth quirked. She had friends who supported her work.

Luke and McKenna both wandered around the room later, talking to artists.

Mae's cousin Barbara was in her element, chatting and storytelling. Her Lenape Tribe of Delaware stories were an act of love and perseverance. She wore a tomato-red ribbon skirt with bright-blue, black, and yellow ribbons trailing from the bottom. Her matching shirt highlighted the bronze undertones in her skin.

"Hi, Barbara. Thank you again for joining us tonight," Katy said.

Luke joined them. His gray button-up made his green eyes stand out.

"This is my friend, Barbara. These are her sculptures." Katy motioned toward the ceramic art pieces on display.

"Oh, wow. Nice to meet you, ma'am. These are amazing. The ballerina took a lot of patience." Luke pointed to the delicate ceramic dancer with tiny little hands stretched toward the sky.

"You know, her hands were a labor of love. Thank you for noticing. The sculpture is of my daughter. The vases are more traditional like my grandmother showed me." Barbara straightened one of her little vases.

"Don't get me wrong—the vases are cool, too. I like the textures and patterns cut into the clay. I think the pottery back home is usually painted with patterns. Right, Katy?" Luke shifted closer.

Katy leaned against his warm shoulder. "You'll see

the patterns cut into the clay back home, too. Cherokee burn horse hair into their pottery. My cousin hosts workshops back home to teach Choctaw kids how to make our pottery." Katy had a bowl in her kitchen her cousin made by hand with a swirling band design like the movements or dance of the sun.

"You know I love teaching my pottery classes, too." Barbara patted Katy's arm with an age-spotted hand.

"I bet you're a great teacher." Luke stepped out of the way for a mom with a double stroller. "All of these artists have such different styles. I'll admit I've never been to an art show, but this is great."

Barbara raised a thin eyebrow. "Our art show is special. These are all community members being brave and showing their work to their neighbors. You're lucky you have a girlfriend like Katy to show you around."

"Oh, we're just friends." Katy shook her head. She'd already been friend zoned since he'd shown up. If only the electricity between them would get the message.

Luke drew his brows together, shifting to create more distance.

"Well, then you are *very* lucky to have a friend like Katy." Barbara pursed her lips.

"Are these young people giving you trouble?" Mae linked an arm with her cousin.

Katy stifled a sigh of relief.

Barbara made a show of glancing around. "Who do you think she's talking to? We're all young here."

Katy led Luke away to give them time to catch up. Her cheeks were warm. Why did she have to blush so hard over the girlfriend comment?

"You want to show me which of these paintings is your favorite?" Luke leaned closer in the crowded room.

His breath was hot on her neck, sending chills zinging across her skin.

He raised an eyebrow.

"Follow me." She tugged on his arm to lead him across the room.

He slipped a hand around hers.

The library meeting room wasn't crowded enough to warrant hanging onto her, but his calloused palm was hard to let go of. She stopped in front of a series of photographs. The patron's nature photo had three dogs running on a beach. The one in the middle was Katy's favorite. He was a boxer mix of some kind and adorable with his spotted tongue hanging out and sheer joy on his jowly face.

"These pups are having a great day," Luke said.

The artist had carefully framed the sunrise, but the dogs stole the show. "Right? So happy. As Ava would say, I want to bring this kind of energy to my everyday life." Katy stepped closer until their shoulders brushed.

"Agreed. My mom never had any posts near the beach, so I'm making the most of living so close to the ocean." He still held her hand.

"We experience the coast in a different way after growing up landlocked. I feel so open and free right by the ocean—unlike anywhere else." Katy sighed, remembering her last trip to read at Seashore State Park.

"What? The vast fields of waving wheat don't give you the same wide-open feeling?" He chuckled.

She rolled her eyes. "Hey, now. The wide-open farmland back home is *majestic*. Driving down a country road is also unlike anything else in the whole world."

"You got me there." He squeezed her hand.

She leaned against him.

"Hey, Katy." Isaac's nasal voice came from behind.

Katy cringed. She took a deep breath and shifted into extra perky mode. How was her ex suddenly everywhere? "Oh, hey, Isaac. I didn't realize you liked art." She jerked away.

Luke held tight.

The stubborn set of his jaw intensified. *Good grief.*

"I wanted to support something you worked on. I know these community events mean a lot to you." Isaac kept frowning at their intertwined hands.

"Thanks." Her tone was flat.

He'd never attended anything at the library, and she'd invited him to every single community event. Even though his thesis was on community and civic engagement, he'd never shown up. Why now?

"Katy, do you have time to show me the pumpkins before you're done with your break?" Luke barely acknowledged Isaac's existence.

"Oh, we better go now, or I won't have time. I need to check on Dom and the gamer room." She waved with a free hand. "He was never so attentive. I don't know what's gotten into him."

"He's realized he made a big dumb mistake. No mystery there." Luke scowled.

"*Right.*"

"Seriously, Katy. Sometimes, guys are big idiots

who don't figure their feelings out until they see their ex with someone else." He raised his eyebrow. "Do we really have time to see your magic pumpkins?"

"We do, but then I need to get back to work. The artists manage the art show themselves, but we always have librarians strategically placed to direct traffic and prevent shenanigans." She shuddered to think of the trouble unsupervised teens could create.

When he spotted her pumpkins, his smile transformed his whole face. "These are the greatest. I'll send photos to Jackie." He let go of her hand to snap photos.

The lack of warmth sent alarm bells ringing in her mind. She searched for a woodpecker in the library. She was too attached for her own good. Was it too late? Was she falling for him again?

Chapter Ten

Luke waited outside Katy's red-brick apartment building. The radio played a song from when they were in high school, and he leaned back to ride the nostalgia wave. He'd done more outside of work in the last few weeks than the previous year combined. Being around her was like waking up on a snow day.

Katy was like the song, "Compass" by Lady A. He was right back in Oklahoma, discovering his best friend. She stepped out dressed for the cooler day in a bright-red jacket. She stopped to tuck stray hair behind her ear.

His breath caught, and his heart raced.

"Hey, thanks for driving." Katy climbed into the cab of his truck.

Being near her was like he'd come up for air. He liked her in his truck—in his life.

Her phone buzzed, and she glared at the bright screen. "How much are we building today?" She crossed her arms.

"Well, my buddy Ryan did most of the actual build. He planned to cut the wood for us, but then I think he kept going." Luke rubbed the back of his neck.

Ryan casually mentioned he'd built all three boxes while they were chasing a safety violation.

"We're lucky he has all those tools to build a custom MCL." Katy forced her phone into her bag.

"Yeah, we'll meet at his dad's house in Harrington." He started the engine.

Katy eased back. "His dad is fine with us taking over his garage?"

"I doubt he'll mind, but you can ask him. And Hunter should be there for a bit." Hunter was their hiking buddy. He was originally from Georgia, and Luke still had no idea why he'd moved to Delaware. They all had their baggage.

She crossed her arms and glanced out the window.

If only he had some kind of translator service for Katy's emotions. Had he done something, or had the message on her phone just thrown her for a loop?

"I can't wait to meet him. You've met all my work friends. And McKenna. So...all of my friends in Dover."

"And Isaac." *Way to keep your inner thoughts to yourself, Taylor.* He glanced over.

"Yeah. You've had the complete experience." She glared at her purse.

Was her ex texting her? He swallowed. He wanted to ask if she was interested in him, but he also had no legitimate reason to ask about her dating life. He was leaving soon, and he couldn't guarantee he'd come back to Dover. He had no business dating her. *Am I trying to date her?*

She glanced out the window when her phone buzzed loudly in the cab.

"You have a good life here." She'd found her people in Dover, excluding Isaac, who bothered Luke for reasons he didn't need to examine too closely.

She leaned back, listening to the upbeat music.

The calm between them was comforting and

familiar, and he was an idiot for letting their friendship go. A mistake he didn't intend to make ever again.

She popped her head to the side. "What's Ryan like outside of work?"

Luke snorted. "Oh, he's grumpy with new people or, well, any people. But when we're volunteering, he'll be the first to offer help and the last to leave. And he likes his cat. We go hiking most weeks with Hunter."

"How did he end up with a cat?" Katy gasped.

"I'll let him tell you the story." He hoped Ryan would share. Luke had seen him ease into a conversation more than once with the cat story. His reaction could go either way, though.

"Well, now I need to know."

"Patience is a virtue." He smiled, enjoying the way her eyes lit up when she talked.

"Have you been hanging out with my dad? I have no chill when it comes to learning new things. Come on. Please?" She batted her eyelashes.

"Aren't librarians supposed to be these calm and wise arbiters of quiet and knowledge?" He pictured her in the tight bun and black dress again—the serious librarian. He flexed his hands on the wheel.

"I am wise and full of knowledge, thank you very much. But also, I need the cat story…to gather more knowledge. Obviously." She sighed. "What's his dad like?"

Sunlight cascaded through the front windshield, bouncing off the gold buttons on her red jacket.

She relaxed her arms and turned toward him.

"His dad is a retired electrician who moved to Delaware with Ryan's stepmom after her mom got sick. They stayed, and when Ryan was stationed here, he helped, too. Dover wasn't even on his wish list—though don't say anything to Ryan's dad." He kept telling her more than he meant to.

"I won't step my foot in the family drama." She mimed zipping her lips with a small whistle.

Luke sighed. "We all have our family baggage."

"Truth."

"We're here." He pointed at the little blue house with white shutters. He parked on the street.

Ryan leaned against his motorcycle drinking a root beer.

Hunter's black hair was freshly shaven in a buzz-cut fade. His dark skin contrasted with his cream-colored Henley.

Hunter laughed and patted Ryan on the shoulder.

"Hey, guys. Hunter, this is my friend Katy," he said.

Katy shook his hand. "Hunter, I've heard good things."

"Good to meet you. You're all the captain here can talk about after you saved his bacon at the meeting." Hunter's voice was deep and steady. "I was just checking on Banjo. I'll get out of your way." His boots crunched the dry leaves in the yard.

"You sure you don't want to stay?" Luke clasped him on the shoulder.

"I have a few bigger animals to check in on down the road. The Harts were on the way. Katy, you keep these two out of trouble." He chuckled on his way to his black SUV.

Katy waved. "Who is Banjo?"

"My dad's dog. He's getting up there in years. Hunter helped my dad build a ramp for the car and another one for the sofa." Ryan shook his head.

"Poor pup. I'm glad he'll have the ramps to help make life easier. Hey, Luke says you built most of the MCL." Katy beamed.

"Oh yeah, I got rolling while I had the time. The MCL still has to get mounted. We should do three posts. One under each box to survive the heavier winds in the fall." Ryan motioned toward the wooden boxes in the yard.

"I'll defer to your expertise. So, we only need to add the doors today?" She fell in step with Ryan, bouncing on her toes.

"The first coat of paint and then the doors." Ryan motioned to the paint and brushes set out. He had the three connected boxes on the grass on an old blue tarp with at least half the rainbow in paint splatters.

Luke counted five or six different paint colors.

"I'll add the rest of the paint after our MCL is installed." Katy circled the tarp, assessing. She tossed her red jacket into the yard with her sunflower-yellow bag.

The bag plunked against the grass. How many books did she have in there today?

"You planning to freehand your characters and designs?" Ryan cocked his head to the side, leaning back.

"Oh yeah, I have doodling skills." Katy inspected the white paint.

Luke chuckled. "She's being modest. The ones she painted back home are works of art. I bet the kids are lured in by the designs."

Katy dug her shoe in the dirt. "We hope so, anyway."

"Has my son offered you all anything to drink?" Mr. Hart waved from the front step.

He was shorter and rounder, but the family resemblance was clear in their faces.

Ryan waved his dad over.

"Hey, Mr. Hart. We just arrived." Luke shook his head. He didn't want Ryan to deal with any violations of Southern hospitality. People argued about whether the lower half of Delaware was Southern, but Luke had spent a good chunk of his childhood in Georgia. Southern social expectations were alive and well here.

"Hey, Dad. Come meet Katy Caterby. She went to high school with Luke." Ryan flipped his khaki baseball hat backward. The patch on the front was custom from his last deployment.

"And you both ended up in Dover? What a good story. Do you want anything to drink? My son should have already offered, but we have tea, lemonade, and root beer."

"My dad makes the root beer. You won't find anything like his brew anywhere else." Ryan motioned to the empty root beer bottle by his chair.

"I do all right. When I retired, I started root beer brewing and baking. I'm only okay with either one, but the family humors me because they have to." Mr. Hart raised his chin.

"He makes the best root beer I've ever had." Luke rubbed his hands together.

Katy shifted her weight back and forth on her feet. "Root beer sounds great. Thank you both so much for helping with the MCL."

"Shouldn't we be thanking you for helping? Luke was assigned the project, and I'm generally assigned to

189

anything he's assigned to by proximity as far as the major's concerned." Ryan rolled his eyes.

Katy clapped. "I don't believe either of you are here on your days off because you were assigned. Not for a minute. And honestly? I'll take any excuse to add another MCL to the map."

" 'Accessible and engaging literary outreach in the community,' " Luke quoted.

"You were listening." She squeezed his arm.

"I'll go get your root beers. Let me know if I can help with anything else." Mr. Hart headed back into the house.

"Your dad is great." Katy glanced at the blue front door.

Ryan pursed his lips. "I think he's stir-crazy with the retirement."

"Well, he's always more than welcome to volunteer at the library. He's a retired electrician, right?" She sat on the tarp, brushing away bright-yellow and red leaves.

"Sure is. Proud International Brotherhood of Electrical Workers, IBEW. Why?" Ryan narrowed his eyes.

"Well, I could set him up in the nonfiction DIY area, and I bet he'd save a bunch of people from catastrophes on a daily basis. Electrical books are dangerous." Katy cringed.

Luke planned to ask for those stories later.

"Who is reading electrical books?" Mr. Hart held two ice-cold bottles of homemade root beer.

Luke stepped forward to take the bottles.

"Patrons come in all the time for electrical books to work on their homes or businesses. If you ever have free time, you'd be an immediate favorite volunteer at the library." Katy took a sip of the creamy soda. The crisp vanilla flavor was strong. "Oh, my gosh. Your root beer is so good."

"Well, thank you. No need to make a fuss. The recipe is from a kit. But I'll think on stopping into the library. The fix-it-myself mess can be a real disaster. I would have figured people used videos online now." Mr. Hart scratched his dimpled chin.

"Oh, they use the Internet, too. But something about checking a book out from the library makes them feel like they went the extra mile." Katy shook her head.

"Hey now, I always like to read a book before I do something new." Ryan joined Katy on the tarp, handing out paintbrushes.

Mr. Hart chuckled. "He has books on backpacking and hiking in a box somewhere. I think we even have a fishing book, even though he learned everything he needed to with me and his grandpa."

"Don't get me wrong. Books are amazing for reference materials. I'm a big believer in reading all the books." Katy smiled.

"We're all giving you a hard time, young lady." Mr. Hart chuckled. "I'll stop by and see what you'd want me to do. I could be useful."

"You're always useful." Ryan cocked his head.

Mr. Hart lifted his chin. "Now, I do want to suggest mounting the larger box on top with the two smaller boxes below on a four-by-four. The winds get strong in the fall and spring, and lower weight is sturdier." He pointed to the larger box.

"We could store the younger reader books down

lower to the ground, too." Luke shrugged.

"Do I need to change the tops on the lower two boxes?" Ryan scrunched his eyebrows, glaring at the mini library.

"No, I think the angled tops will work better underneath the larger one you gave the steepled roof. The more complicated one is gonna get the main focus anyway with the square steeple." Mr. Hart pointed to the fancy roof.

"Will different heights work for the characters you plan to paint on the sides?" Luke rubbed Katy's shoulder.

"I draw by freehand, so any setup will work. I can actually do more characters because I'll have two more sides to work with." Katy tucked a stray strand of hair behind her ear.

"We'll need a different post. Let's get these painted and attach the doors. Then we can run to get a four-by-six post to make it taller. I don't think the one I bought earlier will work for the new design." Luke scratched the back of his head, mentally running their project inventory like any well-trained loggie should.

They started painting the white primer onto the boxes.

Katy was careful to go with the wood grain.

Luke didn't have her level of skill. He preferred efficiency.

"You're making the base coat all fancy. You know nobody will see the primer coat, right?" Ryan smirked.

"When I'm painting the details, I will." Katy pursed her lips.

"Really?" Ryan raised both eyebrows.

"Hey, now. She's doing great." Luke needed to

steer the conversation somewhere safe. "I want to know what characters you think you'll paint."

"Ava keeps giving me new ideas." She waved her paintbrush.

"Who is Ava?" Ryan asked.

"She's a children's librarian and my best friend. But she has all of these amazing ideas, and they change every day." Katy painted another side of her box.

"What's her most recent one? I liked the parade of characters idea she had at the pumpkin patch." Luke painted his last side. White paint caked his fingers.

"We've seen a big movement for picture books about famous scientists, historians, and educators. Or rather, people who should be famous for their contributions to the world. Ava suggested portrait-style paintings of people kids should know. Like Ruth Wakefield, inventor of the chocolate chip cookie." Katy pointed her paintbrush for emphasis.

"Or Stephanie Kwolek. She invented Kevlar." Ryan raised an eyebrow.

Luke liked the idea of offering kids names they might not otherwise know.

"Or Mae Jemison. She was the first black woman in space. She was on my dad's favorite sci-fi show once. He almost fell out of his chair he was so excited about a real astronaut being on the episode." Katy tipped her head back and gazed at the blue sky.

"She'd be a good one to add, too." Ryan rubbed his chin.

Luke's primer wasn't even but covered the whole thing. He evened out the paint so dried globs wouldn't mess with Katy's ability to make the boxes epic.

"More than cool, Katy. Tell Ava I think her idea is

brilliant. Maybe Joshua could stash some books about some of the people you paint in the MCLs on occasion." Luke motioned toward Ryan. "Joshua is the school librarian I told you about."

Ryan rubbed his neck. "Oh, yeah. I think I've met his husband. He's in finance on base."

"Yep. All right, I think we're ready to let these dry. Let's go buy the new posts and joints for the sturdier design." Luke set his paintbrush on the canvas. His mind raced down the list of requirements for the MCL.

"The sturdier, the better." Katy gingerly set her paintbrush aside. Her hands were covered in tiny white paint speckles.

Strong winds picked up, *whooshing* across the front yard and flapping the blue tarp. Ryan grumbled and dropped tools and extra paintbrushes on all four corners. "I'll clean the paint while you're gone."

"Thanks, Ryan. We'll be quick." Luke headed toward the truck. "We better go see your buddy at the hardware store." He bet most people had no idea she was a force to be reckoned with for home improvement and lawn work.

"After all the books he collected, you better believe I'm his customer for life. Or well, don't tell my dad." She stashed her red jacket and bag by her feet in the truck.

In his monochrome cab, she was all sunshine and colors.

She buckled her seat belt.

He revved the truck and backed away from the tidy little house. "How about your only hardware store in Dover?" He pulled onto the main highway. The day was bright and clear without a cloud in the sky. The kind of day made for being outside.

"Delaware. He can have the whole state. I can't possibly get in trouble with my dad for having a favorite hardware store in another state, right?" She fidgeted with the radio.

Luke gripped the wheel. What was she so antsy about? "He'll want the whole state of Oklahoma."

"True. When he heard the local hardware store was helping with the book drive, he was so excited. His day was made." She grinned.

He gulped, studying the stop sign ahead to keep from staring at the way she glowed. "Your dad does all the community events back home. He loves potlucks and parades, right?" Luke couldn't remember a single event where her dad hadn't been in the thick of volunteering.

"His volunteering is why his store has weathered so many tough times. He's so loyal to everyone in town, and they feel the same." She hugged herself.

Dover was showing up for the families on base for similar reasons. The coastal town was getting under his skin. He was a regular at the local coffee shop and bookstore. He had roots here in a way he'd never experienced. In the morning, he would reach the four-year mark in Dover. He'd never lived anywhere for so long.

Would Delaware be so bad if Katy was here?

He shook his head. "My mom will wait a week to get supplies from your dad instead of driving to a larger store in Sherman, so I think you're right. I can't imagine shopping anywhere else back home."

"Thanks, Luke." She tilted her head to the side.

He slid a hand over hers, but remembered he

shouldn't and let go. When he found a parking spot near tidy rows of mums, he'd almost talked himself into telling her about the training.

Katy hopped out.

He met her behind the truck. White paint speckled her cheek. He rubbed the paint away with his thumb.

She leaned into his hand.

Her breath sped up against his skin. He dropped his gaze to her full lips, and he couldn't stop himself.

Her lips parted, and she bit her plump bottom lip.

The trill of a woodpecker nearby snapped them out of the electric chemistry crashing them into each other's gravitation.

He took a step back and showed her the white paint now smudged on his thumb.

"I never could leave a painting project without a solid coat of paint on me." She chuckled and turned her chin up.

Is she searching for the bird? "I won't win any tidy painting awards." He motioned toward his paint-smudged jeans. "I bet Ryan didn't have any paint on him, though."

She tucked a loose strand of her long hair behind her ear.

Had she wanted him to kiss her?

"He's nowhere near as grumpy as you implied." She tugged on his sleeve.

Luke chuckled. She hadn't seen him earlier this week when fleet services had pulled a prank on the new captain. Sure, the stunt was something they did to any new lieutenant, but cleanup slowed them. Ryan turned loads out on time. No excuses.

"Ryan? He was on his best behavior. He must have

already decided to like you, which, by the way, I've never seen." Luke was one of the few people Ryan put up with until Hunter…and now Katy.

"I forgot to ask him about his cat." She gasped.

He chuckled. "Just wait until we get back. The paint should be dry by then."

"Painting projects?" Mr. Zhang rubbed his hands together. "Are you working on the mini library?"

"Yes, sir. We're here to get a sturdier base." Luke shook his hand.

The owner helped them get the wood while telling them all about how close he'd gotten to collecting more books than the bookstore.

"Just return the other wood." Mr. Zhang nodded like everything was settled.

"Are you sure we can't pay for the supplies?" Luke asked again.

"Same answer as last time. I'm happy to donate. My daughter was very proud. She might call you to ask about MCLs." He clapped Katy on the shoulder.

"I'd love to help her in any way I can." She beamed. If she could spend every day working to launch new MCLs and drinking cinnamon lattes, then she'd be living her dream.

"Well, you're lucky to have such a knowledgeable girlfriend." Mr. Zhang pointed his thumb at her.

"Oh, we're just friends." Katy tucked a stray hair behind her ear.

She shut the chance for anything more down without batting an eye. He had no right to be bothered. He had one foot out the door in Dover. Even if he'd almost kissed her earlier, he would not start anything with anyone. Jolie's words ricocheted in his head. He was only good for leaving, anyway.

"Oh, sure, sure." Mr. Zhang raised his eyebrows and pursed his lips.

Message received.

****

Back at Mr. Hart's, Luke parked and walked around to open the tailgate. He leaned against his truck. The autumn day had turned colder.

Ryan lounged in a lawn chair, drinking another root beer.

"Rough life." Luke chuckled.

"Well, someone had to hold down the fort." Ryan stood, folding away his chair. "I need to get to work in a bit."

Katy widened her eyes. "Oh, wait, but you can't go. I'd love to hear the cat story."

Ryan sighed. "Why do you always tell people I have a cat story?" He narrowed his eyes.

"I was explaining how we met Hunter." Luke shifted toward Katy, moving to stand between them.

"Well, you can tell her. I'm not entertainment." Ryan pasted on a smile. "He's the better storyteller anyway." He took off after helping them load the MCL parts and pieces into the back of Luke's truck.

Luke turned the heat on in his truck.

"Okay, so now I've seen the grumpier side. What happened?" Katy toyed with the radio, flipping through stations for something more upbeat than the sad country song crooning over the speakers.

"His fiancée broke his heart. After traveling twenty-two hours to be home, he found an empty apartment. She'd moved out without telling him while he was still deployed. Only thing left in the whole place was a cat in his bathtub. Little gray kitten no bigger than his bike helmet."

"And he kept the cat?" She opened her eyes wide.

He didn't blame her. Ryan hardly seemed like the warm and fuzzy type. He wasn't, really. "Well, yeah. He'd been chosen. He checked with Hunter to see if the cat was chipped."

"You met Hunter because of the cat?" Her hand fell from the radio.

"Ghost brought us all together." Luke smirked. The cat now had plush beds in every window of Ryan's apartment, but he would probably freeze him out if Luke shared those details.

"The bathtub cat." Katy let her head fall back against the seat and drummed her fingers on the console between them.

He'd never been so aware of anyone. "Yep. Hunter named her Ghost."

"I would have enjoyed him explaining how he kept a cat who literally invaded his home." She softened her gaze.

"He was weird about Ghost earlier." He raised his eyebrows. His chances of stopping her were slim, but he enjoyed his partnership with Ryan on the flight line. He didn't want to lose their bond to Ryan's annoyance. He'd seen Ryan cut people off for less.

"Like he doesn't want to be seen as a cat guy? Or he doesn't want people to know he cares about anything, let alone a cat?" Katy stretched her legs.

"All of the above?" Luke winced.

"Noted." She bobbed her head.

He called a first-floor apartment home, so they could set up on his patio table. He unlocked his door and waited.

Katy beelined for his bookshelf.

His little apartment was warmer and brighter—more *something*. "I don't have homemade root beer, but how about a pot of coffee?" He crossed the beige living room to the open-concept kitchen.

"I'm always available for coffee." She stood on her toes for the top shelf.

His tiny kitchen was packed with faded white appliances from the 1980s. The coffeepot gurgled while his hardwood floors creaked under her.

What did she think of his home library? "Go ahead and snoop on my books while I get the pot going."

"Me? Curious about books?" She pressed her fingers to her chest and batted her long eyelashes.

Sometimes, her eyes were so brown they had an almost indigo tint in certain lights. The hazel hid away in those moments. He searched her face for the girl he'd known so well in high school. Her cheeks had narrowed, and her frame had changed from thin to graceful. What would high school Katy think of the confident and accomplished woman in front of him?

She held one of his Agatha Christie books. She'd pulled her golden-brown hair back from her face into a low ponytail.

He pointed toward the book. "Those were all my aunt's books. She handed them to me, and I sort of started the whole mystery reading track."

"What an Air Force way to say Agatha sparked your love of reading. Did your mom read to you when you were a kid?" She slipped the book back onto the shelf and followed him outside.

"Oh, yeah. No matter where we lived, I could

count on reading time." His mom and sister still read together at least a few times a week.

"I want every kid to have a grown-up willing to spend time reading. How many kids had a chance to ask someone to read to them because they found a book at their park or on their way home from school? MCLs are so important." She ran her slender hand along the roof of the largest MCL box.

"Well, let's get the doors on these. And then I get to buy you dinner for spending your entire day helping me with our project." She deserved a meal at the very least. Feeding her was his only motivation. The dinner had nothing to do with the way her eyes derailed his thoughts.

"You think so, huh?" She tilted her head to the side and bit back a small smile.

He lingered his gaze there. He was losing his mind. "Yep. I think I had you at breadsticks." He'd never know how he pulled off a casual tone. The teasing light in her eyes made his breath catch.

"Sounds about right." She laughed.

He'd expected her to put up a fight. She wanted to spend even more time with him? He would never get enough of her.

Chapter Eleven

Maybe agreeing to dinner was a terrible idea. Katy stared in the floor-length mirror in her bedroom, raised her chin, squared her shoulders, and reminded herself she could be brave. She'd changed into a dark-green sweater dress, her favorite charcoal leggings, and a pair of cowgirl boots she'd had since high school.

She added a pair of Gran's earrings. Her outfit was a patchwork of her old and new life. She bought the dress with Ava from a crafts sale to support a couple of their library patrons with a knitting business. Maybe her relationship with Luke could blend new and old, too. They had their friendship to build the foundation for something special. She was getting ahead of herself, but when they touched, her skin tingled. Her phone rang, jolting her upright.

"How'd the day go with Durant Guy?" Ava asked. A TV blared in the background.

"Good. We attached the doors on the MCLs and finished the first coats of paint. I'll paint the characters after they're in the ground." Katy ran a hand over her soft wool sweater.

"I wasn't asking about the mini library. I mean, I'm happy the project is coming together. But do I get to live vicariously through your new dating life or not?" A screen door slid open and closed, muting the noise.

Katy started pacing. "He asked me to dinner after

spending all morning with me. I met his other best friend. I'm freaking out about whether he meant dinner as a *date*."

"Well, how did he ask?" Ava raised her voice an octave.

"He told me he was taking me to dinner for helping him all day. So friend zone, right?" She frowned. Did she want to date Luke? She slumped her shoulders. Yes, she really did.

"Was he leaning into you again? You two were cozy at First Fridays. He was holding your hand at one point. Guys don't hold hands with just friends. Are you ready to be more?" The porch swing on Ava's grandmother's balcony creaked in the background.

Katy wished she was sitting there beside Ava as she had so many times before. "I think so. No, I know so. But I can't shake the fear of him taking off again. I know I'm being ridiculous. The teen drama was a million years ago." She sighed. Why did the worst moments live in bold colors in her mind? Their horrible would-be date lived in slow motion in her memory.

"You like him. You like him so much. And the heartache was a long time ago. Give him a chance. He seems like a good guy."

They talked about what Katy was wearing, and Ava updated her on her grandmother's health. Ava must have mentioned moving into senior living for the TV to be so loud. Her grandmother aggressively increased the volume to drown out unwanted conversation. They ended the call with plans to get coffee the next morning early enough for McKenna to sit with them for a while.

Luke knocked on her door.

She let him in. He filled her doorway in a button-up shirt and nice brown shoes. At least her clothing choices matched his. "Hey, long time no see."

He furrowed his eyebrows. "I was expecting a lot more books." He slumped his shoulders.

She grabbed his arm and led him to her library nook. Four packed bookshelves clustered in a corner with a small bench covered in bright-blue pillows and a knitted yellow blanket.

"Yeah, much better." He took a seat on her reading bench. "I was worried there for a minute." He brushed his long fingers over the velvety blanket.

"Sorry to worry you." She sat beside him, admiring the corner bookshelf where her favorite books waited for a reread. She slowly breathed in the book nook air. "The little nook is why I picked the apartment."

"Sounds about right. You ready to head out? I made a reservation at a little Italian restaurant near base." His hand barely brushed against hers.

Reservation sounded date-like. Two checks in the date column. She grabbed her purse and locked up after him. She didn't stop to search for a woodpecker.

****

Dark cherry wood and mood lighting permeated the restaurant. Soft shadows danced over Katy's skin. The swanky bar had tall shelves with mirrors. A bright mural covered one wall with landscape and cityscape scenes of Italy.

A few couples were tucked into quiet booths.

"Roma is so cute. I've never been in here." She gazed around the room.

"Mr. Hart recommended the place. He said the cannoli is the best he's ever had." Luke pulled out her chair.

His deep voice filled her with the urge to lean closer. She cleared her throat and slipped into the offered chair. "His root beer was so good. Do you think he'd share the recipe?"

"Are you kidding? You'd end up with the root beer kit and all his secrets. He's so proud of his home brew. At first, he was driving Ryan and his stepmom crazy with his retirement, and then overnight, he decided to learn all these different things."

"Lifelong learning is such a great journey. I'll ask him for his root beer secrets. I want to make Gran's root beer float cake with homemade pop." She could practically taste the moist cake with vanilla frosting.

"Wait, I need details. What is a root beer float cake, and when do I get a slice?" He leaned in, and his green eyes sparked at the mere mention of cake.

Some things hadn't changed. He made the same face at bake sales in high school. "I always pick root beer cake for my birthday. I'll make you one. Maybe." She squinted, secretly planning to buy the ingredients as soon as possible.

"Just tell me what I need to do to earn one."

The server stopped by and took their orders.

Katy chewed on her lower lip. The restaurant screamed *date*. Candles were lit in the center of the table with faux fall leaves scattered under them, and bright-red mini roses rested in petite crystal vases.

"Do you go back for holidays? I visit when I get the chance—usually at a random time of the year." He crossed and uncrossed his arms again.

Was he nervous, too? She'd been quiet for too long. "Christmas and then in the spring for my dad's wild onion dinner."

"I'd never had wild onions with scrambled eggs until we lived in Oklahoma." His lips were in a flat line.

Maybe he hadn't liked them? "Wild onions are about spring and hope—about saying goodbye to the days when we're too cold to be outside with neighbors. Wild onions mean the days will soon be warmer, and everyone can get together again."

Dad usually made a big pot of chili while family and neighbors filled the house with potluck deliciousness.

She sighed happily. Their kitchen counters would be covered in her favorite foods: Choctaw fry bread, pickled okra, and grape dumplings with vanilla ice cream. Her stomach grumbled.

Luke sat back and nodded. "The food was so good at the wild onion community thing in high school."

"Community is all about the food. I don't care what culture. The food brings everyone together." She waved at the cozy restaurant where couples leaned closer under the dim lighting.

"I can't argue with the truth." His grin was lopsided.

The server returned with their orders.

Katy wished she'd known about the restaurant sooner. "I love being here." She took a bite of her pumpkin ravioli, savoring the creamy filling.

"The breadsticks, right?"

Oh, he meant the food. The food was fresh and well-seasoned, but she'd meant dinner *with him*. She bit her lip. "Well, yeah. Thanks for inviting me. I actually—" She lost her nerve. "I'm sad I didn't know about Roma for the last year. Think of all the breadsticks I could have eaten." She picked her fork back up and focused on turning invisible.

"Well, I'm game any time you want to get your breadstick fix." He took her free hand, rubbing his thumb back and forth.

His calloused skin created delicious friction. She forgot about the rest of the world. She was almost convinced they were on a date.

"Hey, Captain." A man with a crew cut stopped at their table.

"Major Owens, good to see you. Major, meet my friend from back home, Katy Caterby. She's a local librarian helping us with the literacy initiative." Luke sat straighter, shifting his hand away to shake hands.

"Nice to meet you, Major Owens." Her cheeks warmed.

"Oh, we're off base. Please call me Greg. Listen, I didn't want to interrupt your dinner, but I did want to congratulate you on the Squadron Officer Training PCS. I saw the recommendation Major McClain wrote you. I hope you get to go in person." Greg rubbed his hands together.

In any other setting, Katy would have liked him. But as his words jangled in her head, the meaning hit her. He'd needed a work recommendation—needed the volunteering—to leave town, and she'd unwittingly helped.

"Thanks, sir. I'm lucky to have Major McClain's rec." Luke cleared his throat.

"Every little bit helps. Now you two enjoy your evening." The officer patted Luke on the shoulder and left.

Katy held very still. PCS meant he'd be transferred

to a new base. Was he leaving and hadn't told her? "You're moving?" She pitched her voice extra perky, and she winced.

Luke widened his eyes, and he sat taller. "The training is not a sure thing. Before the literacy initiative, Major McClain told me I had a shot at in-person Squadron Officer Training."

"And in person is a big deal?" Katy tried so hard to understand. She swallowed, unsteady. She set her fork beside her plate and leaned against the back of the chair.

"Going in person is a game-changer for anyone who gets to attend...sort of a career jump start. Not many people get selected to go in person, and even Major McClain did hers online." He rested a hand on the table.

She crossed her arms. She couldn't think straight with his touch. He'd invited her on a date while working hard to leave town at the same time. *What are we even doing here?*

"I'd kind of assumed the in-person training wouldn't happen. I didn't even know she wrote me a recommendation after I messed up the paperwork for the MCL." He drew his eyebrows together. He clenched his square jaw.

Katy tightened her lips. "When would you go?"

"I don't know. The whole thing is a long shot." He swallowed loudly.

"But you knew the whole time we've been *hanging out*?" She wanted to take back those words. Phantom teenage mortification settled like a full encyclopedia set in her stomach. He'd almost kissed her outside the hardware store. Hadn't he? Why start something if he was only working on the MCL project to get a recommendation?

"I should have told you. I guess I didn't want a wall between us when the PCS might not happen—or to jinx my chances." He rubbed the back of his neck.

"Was the recommendation why you were so crushed over the traffic study?" Had the MCL been for some kind of work opportunity? Had he cared about the kids...and their project?

Luke shifted in his seat. "Partly. I also just plain want to be on her good side, so my boss doesn't treat me like I'm gum stuck to the bottom of her shoe."

"Was her recommendation tied to the MCL project?" Katy had to get the connection clear in her mind. Had he been using her to get a ticket out of Dover? Like Isaac used her to write a better thesis? Why did she keep picking men who wanted something but didn't want *her*?

"Kind of. Going in person is not guaranteed. But I will leave Dover at some point. Moving is part of being in the Air Force." He narrowed his eyes.

But he'd been using her to leave Dover while holding her hand and inviting her out to romantic restaurants. *What did the hand-holding and dinner invite all mean?*

A server refilled their water glasses.

"But you're actively working to leave earlier." She slid her gaze to the mural. She wasn't prepared, but she should have known. Everyone left or chose someone else. She was completely leave-able.

"For a six-week training, then I'd either come back here or move to a new base. I don't have a say over what happens next."

His tone was overly calm, but he'd been hiding things. Not telling her he talked to Jolie was one thing. But hustling to leave town while inviting her out to a date-ish dinner?

He cleared his throat.

"Why didn't you tell me?" She ran her fingers along the edge of her cloth napkin. The seam was rough. If she'd known he was determined to leave Dover as soon as possible, she wouldn't have held his hand. She wouldn't be sitting here now.

"Never the right time, I guess? No. I didn't want you looking at me like I'm already gone." He drew his eyebrows together.

Her pulse throbbed in her throat. "You had one foot out the door while you were encouraging me to spend more and more time with you." The last part left a bitter taste in her mouth. Was she overreacting out of her own insecurities? Maybe.

Luke threw up his hands. "My time here was always on a countdown."

"Eventually getting orders to a new base is different from *actively* working to leave, but here's the thing." Her head pounded. "If I'd been applying for jobs in different cities or even training programs or whatever and I didn't tell you, then you'd feel a little betrayed, too." She'd been sure he was starting something with the fancy dinner. All her wild hope was one-sided. He was Isaac all over again. He'd needed someone to make him look good to advance in his career. She blinked rapidly, begging her heart to hold back the torrent of disappointment until she was safely home.

"I didn't mean to keep anything from you." He

offered a hand.

She ignored his passive attempt to placate her. She didn't want to pretend like everything was fine. Nothing was fine. She'd taken a chance on him, and he was actively working on a project so he could leave. "Can you take me home, please?" She bit her lip, wishing she'd driven. All the times he'd called them "friends" were on a skipping record player.

In the windy parking lot, the *whoosh* of cars on the highway crashed over them like waves. The sun slipped out of sight. Katy closed her eyes and took a deep breath. She couldn't control what Luke did, but she could walk away with her head held high. She could quiet her heart and be his friend. If she had to say goodbye, she would cheer and wish him well, knowing she'd never see him again. Chance brought them together—not Luke. If the universe hadn't intervened, he would have walked away forever after high school.

He kept opening and closing his mouth on the way home, but he didn't say anything.

The silence made her skin crawl, and she squashed the urge to fill the gaping hole between them. She breathed deeply after climbing from the cab of his truck. "What are you doing?"

"Walking you to your door. We might be ending the night on bad terms, but my mom didn't raise me to sit and wait in the truck. I don't care how mad you are." He stuck his hands into his pockets.

She scowled but kept her even pace. She was not running scared, so she had no reason to hurry.

"Good night, Katy," Luke said.

She took slow, even breaths. Mental brick by brick, she erected walls to protect her heart. He'd been

211

encouraging her to trust fall while he had one foot ready to step away. She started making long-term plans, and the rug was ripped out from under her. "Night, Luke. Thanks for the ride." She covered her polite bases. She was an Oklahoma girl, after all.

He lingered for a moment.

She shut her door firmly. Her heart hammered. Leaning back against the wall, she tried a few more measured breaths. The first hot tear slipped down her cheek.

In the kitchen, she made apple cider, simmering the cider in a saucepan and filling the apartment with the aroma of cinnamon and spice. She nestled into her reading nook with her cider and a favorite Jane Austen. If the officer hadn't popped their little bubble of hot air, she would have fallen even harder, and when he'd walked her to the door, they might have shared their first kiss. She raised her fingertips to her lips, imagining.

Her phone buzzed, and she half expected her screen to flash with *Luke*. But Ava's name flashed on her screen.

—So is dinner a date?—

—Doesn't matter. Some other officer stopped by our table and congratulated him on the new post he's been trying to get.—

Her fingers shook.

—Wait, what?—

Katy wasn't sure she had the words yet.

—Stopping for wine. Be there soon. Xoxo—

She was certain her best friend would show up with a bottle of Malbec. They almost always shared a glass of wine on Mondays and talked over their goals for the week. Their Monday planning sessions were one of Katy's absolute favorite traditions. They were both goal-getting queens.

Sure enough, Ava brought a bottle of wine and candy bars. "I bring comfort food." Ava opened her arms wide.

Katy hugged her friend back and took a deep breath. Ava smelled like grapefruit and citrus—like summer and sunshine. Her face was makeup-free. She wore yoga pants and a sweatshirt. Katy needed out of her cute date outfit and excused herself to find her comfy clothing. The evening's heartache called for pajamas. She returned in her softest navy flannel set with tiny pumpkins dotting the fabric.

Ava had already poured their wine and lined the candy bars like a tasting menu on the coffee table.

"You're the best." Katy dropped onto the ecru sofa in her living room.

"So spill already."

She caught Ava up on everything.

Ava sipped and listened without interrupting.

Presenting her case made Katy feel better about her reaction. He kept quiet on something pretty big.

"So we're mad because he was clearly starting something while having one foot out the door?" Ava set her wineglass on the long bookshelf coffee table Katy's dad built.

"In a nutshell." Katy crossed her ankles. "But also, maybe we weren't on a date, and I'm overreacting."

"Well, let's review the facts objectively. He held your hand at the art show. He asked you to dinner tonight. Where did he take you?" Ava mussed her bangs.

"The cute Italian place near base." Katy picked at the fringe on her gold pillow and took a bite of the rich dark chocolate.

"The most date-ish restaurant in town? So holding hands and Saturday nights at romantic restaurants doesn't sound like you're overreacting. Maybe you're underreacting." Ava raised an eyebrow.

Katy dropped her half-eaten chocolate bar. "I made him take me home."

"Good. Lies by omission are still lies. I was rooting for him, too. He better hope he never has to see me again." Ava held up her fist. "He doesn't want to hear what I have to say."

"I like him. Again. And he won't check *yes* to go out with me." Katy swirled her wineglass like the burgundy liquid might offer insight.

"What?" Ava frowned.

Katy chuckled. "You know like the notes you pass in school?"

"Uh, maybe leave middle school references behind." Ava took another sip of her wine and rolled her eyes.

"You already pictured the notes. You know exactly what I'm talking about." Katy plopped a pillow on Ava's legs.

She snatched the cushion away for the nest she always built on wine nights. "Did you tell him how you feel?"

"No. I told him to take me home." Katy bit her lip.

"Oof. How'd the ride home go?" Ava smoothed the hair slowly escaping from her messy bun. Even relaxed for the weekend, her friend was color coordinated down to her pink scrunchy and socks.

"He was quiet." Katy winced, picturing the painfully quiet ride home.

"Nope. Don't guys know silence makes everything worse?" Ava wrinkled her nose.

"Apparently not." Katy's phone buzzed, and Isaac's name popped up. She scowled.

"Did you want the call to be from Durant Guy? Or are we back to High School Heartbreak? No, maybe he's no longer deserving of my nicknames. Maybe he's just *Luke*." Ava gently put her wineglass down.

Katy nearly defended him but swallowed instead. She set her phone face down on her coffee table. "I can't figure out what Isaac wants. I cared about him, you know?"

He'd texted her every day, sending grammar memes and manatee videos.

They had a steady back-and-forth while dating, but Katy hadn't responded lately. She didn't want to give him the wrong impression.

"I know. And the way he ended things was weird. You're not seriously considering giving him another chance?" Ava shook her head.

"I don't know. Yesterday was the first time he came to one of our events." Katy bit her lip.

Ava's fingers flew to her parted lips. "Really?"

"Really, really. I don't want a guy who only supports my job when he's jealous." Katy sipped the peppery wine.

"Or maybe he's showing up because he's realized you're what he wants?" Ava waggled her eyebrows.

While Katy appreciated talking problems through from every angle, she was done with Isaac. Mostly. Her phone buzzed again.

"Answer and find out what he wants. Tonight is getting juicy." Ava mimed eating popcorn from a bowl.

Katy checked her phone.

—Hey, Katy, can you meet me to talk? I'm at the Lobby House.—

—I'm with a friend. Coffee tomorrow morning?—

McKenna's was the safest place to meet. With her friend present, she was much less likely to do something foolish like take him back on the spot.

—Brewed Awakenings. 10 okay?—

She sent him a thumbs-up and then returned her phone to the table. "Okay, but do I want to start dating him again? Will he ask me to give him another chance?"

His repeated questions about his thesis blared in her memory. What were the chances he'd get her back to read his thesis and then ditch her again?

"Well, he'd have to be an absolute idiot not to want you back. But he's already proved to be a flight risk. If he'd texted yesterday before you knew Luke was leaving, would you feel differently?" Ava tilted her head to the side.

Katy eased back.

Ava passed her another candy bar.

These kinds of decisions required chocolate—copious amounts of chocolate. The sweet aroma filled Katy's small living room. "Yesterday, I wouldn't have even considered trying again with Isaac. When I felt like Luke and I were headed somewhere, I wanted Isaac to stay away. But we were good together. He's already planning to apply for city jobs here in Dover, so we have a future in the same city."

"But Luke's in the Air Force, so he would leave

eventually." Ava sighed. "And I still say Isaac is a user. He's not good enough."

"If orders shipped Luke to a new base, the assignment wouldn't have anything to do with our project. He worked on the MCL project *because* of his recommendation. He asked me to help him leave Dover, and he wasn't honest. Just like Isaac and his thesis." Hot tears streamed down her cheeks.

"Okay, so we're mad he lied. Do you think the whole MCL project was about the recommendation, though?" Ava ripped open another chocolate bar.

He'd brainstormed and worked hard to go beyond the project with wrapping books for new kids on base. Someone out for a recommendation wouldn't dive all in. "No, I don't. I know he's a good guy, and I want to be his friend. But I guess I'm a little…"

"Heartbroken?" Ava's brown eyes shimmered. "You hurt. I hurt."

Katy slumped back onto the sofa. "I don't want to be, though. He never really said anything to lead me on."

"He held your hand in public and took you on a date. He led you on. Don't make excuses." Ava waved a finger in Katy's face.

"Okay, okay." She leaned against Ava.

Friendship was good medicine. She had everything she needed between her job and the best friends she'd ever had. Katy breathed in deep. She was better off alone.

****

Brewed Awakenings bustled with customers lined almost to the door. Katy hopped in line. The shop smelled like pumpkin spice lattes and apple turnovers.

"Well, hey there. How's my favorite Okie?" McKenna slid an arm around Katy's shoulder.

Katy half hugged her back. "I bet you say that to all the Okies in your life." Her smile faltered. The other Oklahoma transplant wasn't someone she wanted to think about.

"You meeting Luke?" McKenna raised her eyebrows.

"Nope. Isaac." Katy bit her lip.

"You need to hang around after coffee with Isaac." McKenna narrowed her eyes.

Katy couldn't escape explaining everything again. Talking with Ava was enough. If McKenna hadn't been babysitting her niece, she'd have joined them for wine and chocolate. "McKenna."

"Katy." McKenna motioned to her barista. "Get her a latte going on the house. I can see worry lines you didn't have last time, so I know you need caffeine." McKenna fixed the bow on her apron and motioned for another barista to take customer orders.

"I always need caffeine." Katy adjusted her bag on her shoulder.

"Don't we all? Now go get the last table, or you'll be standing around for whatever awkwardness you're entertaining with Isaac." She hung her head.

"McKenna."

"I said what I said." She raised a shoulder and left to talk to other patrons.

Katy snagged the table by the big windows at the front of the café. She and Luke had gravitated toward the same spot to work on the MCL project.

"Hey, you okay?" Isaac set his ever-present messenger bag at his feet. "Can I go order your cinnamon latte?"

Since when did he know her coffee order? She sat taller. So many little things pieced together. *Ugh, hindsight.*

McKenna saved her with a large red mug. The latte had a pretty little leaf in the milk and a light dusting of cinnamon powder.

Katy inhaled the sweet and spicy aroma. "You get me."

"I do." McKenna's dark-blue eyes twinkled. "Isaac, you better go hop in line. We're about to get another wave."

Isaac scooted over to the line and kept glancing back.

McKenna plopped into the chair beside Katy and nudged her with an elbow.

"What? He asked me if we could talk. I'm guessing he wants to brainstorm about his thesis." She couldn't meet McKenna's gaze.

"That man does not have his academics on his mind. He even wore his date-night sneakers." She motioned toward the newer black high tops without scuffs on the white soles.

"He does not have date-night sneakers." Katy slumped her shoulders. He absolutely did. But she didn't want to add fuel to the fire in McKenna's eyes.

Even his graph paper-patterned collar shirt screamed date. He'd made extra effort. Her stomach was full of lead.

"Just remember, I was here when he pulled the rug out from under you, and if he acts up, I won't hesitate to throw him out." She glared in his direction. She stood, making the chair screech across the floor.

"I love you."

"I know." McKenna smirked. She jumped back into the mix to help her employees.

—Well?—

Her phone buzzed with a new text from Ava. Her friends needed to get their own drama, so they weren't quite so invested in Katy's.

—Chill. He's just ordering.—

Katy's phone lit up with dots while Ava worked on a witty reply and then stopped. Katy scowled, willing her phone to distract her from worrying over the multitude of ways the coffee meetup could go. Part of her hoped his new interest was purely academic.

He sat beside her, adjusted his dark-framed glasses, and kissed her cheek.

His lips were dry on her skin. No telltale trail of electricity zinged across her skin like she'd come to expect with Luke.

"Thanks for meeting me. I miss this." His dimple popped out with his smile.

"The last time we had coffee here, you broke up with me. What exactly are we doing here again?" She wouldn't sit with her worry anymore. *Time to get some answers.*

"I made a mistake." He raised his voice.

Several people from other tables glanced over.

Color crept over his pale skin. He ran a hand through his dark-brown hair. "I had a timeline for my life. I wasn't supposed to meet you yet, and I panicked and ran."

"T-timeline?" She cupped both hands around her latte, seeking warmth. He never mentioned anything. Did he really think life happened on schedule? Like a map all charted out?

"Well, yeah. I was supposed to finish school and start my first job without balancing my career with a relationship. First jobs set the tone for your whole career." He cleared his throat.

"You dumped me so I wouldn't slow your career?" She slipped her hands under the table to hide their shaking. Why start dating her at all if a relationship was too early for his precious timeline?

He blanched but nodded. "I was stupid, but panic isn't a rational emotion. Losing you made me realize I was wrong. I'm ready to be together. You're the one I want to be with."

His words were almost romantic if she ignored the lack of excitement in his tone. His attempt to rekindle their relationship failed to inspire her confidence in their future.

He glanced at the counter when they called out his order, but he stayed at the table.

"You dumped me out of nowhere. We'd been doing so well, and then we weren't. I need some time to think. I'm not sure I want what you want anymore." Luke popped into her mind. She didn't need to be making big decisions right away. She sipped her creamy latte.

"Because of the Air Force guy?"

His sullen tone made her spine go rigid. She supposed the new nickname was better than Durant Guy but not by much. She'd introduced them, so Isaac was being willfully obtuse—which was on brand.

A barista brought Isaac his coffee.

"Did your feelings change because I spent time with someone else?" She didn't owe him any explanation about who she spent time with after they'd broken up.

He pressed a hand over hers, rubbing his thumb.

Isaac made sense for her future, but his touch wouldn't linger for days. She sighed, sliding her hand away. "I need time to think." She owed him some consideration at the very least.

They were good together. *Weren't they?*

Chapter Twelve

Luke carried an MCL post from the back of the truck. The three blue boxes were ready to be attached, but he wanted to wait until the posts were in the ground. The afternoon sun peeked through the thick tree cover surrounding the park.

"Why do you look like somebody turned your goat loose?" Ryan asked.

"My goat what?" He was lost and not just from Ryan's sayings. When he'd seen the text from McKenna to stop by for a latte, he'd hustled to Brewed Awakenings on Sunday. The sight of Isaac and Katy nestled together still made his stomach clench. He left without even stepping foot inside.

"Man, I thought Oklahoma gave you some Southern sensibilities. What has you all bummed out? You have a fight with Katy?" Ryan dropped the post with a thud.

"My mood has nothing to do with Katy Caterby." Luke slammed the door shut on his truck and stomped.

"Oh, man. Her full name. Well, tell Uncle Ryan what's wrong. I'll do my best to pretend to have a heart and listen." Ryan adjusted his OPC patrol cap with the flat top and leveled Luke with his full attention.

They'd picked a shaded spot for the MCL, and shadows from the swaying branches swept over them.

Luke took a deep breath. The bitter wind made his

eyes water. "You're all heart, Captain Hart." He leaned on his shovel.

"Come on." Ryan nudged him.

"She found out about the training PCS." Luke always expected to install the MCL with Katy. He texted to see if she wanted to help them, but she hadn't responded. The unanswered text was the loudest silence of his life.

Ryan motioned for him to keep talking.

"From someone else."

"So she thinks you lied?" Ryan widened his eyes.

They hadn't bothered changing after work, so they were both in their OPCs, failing to blend in with the quiet park in the khaki camo. "Didn't I, though? I didn't tell her about the training and how much I thought I wanted to go." In the beginning, the move hadn't seemed like a big deal. But now, he was tumbling down a rabbit hole falling for her.

Ryan lifted his hat and adjusted the bill. "You don't want to leave because you have a girl?"

"She's not mine." The way her face had fallen at the restaurant tied him up in knots.

"Well, whose fault is that?" Ryan asked. "You two have deep roots from being friends so long ago. She's not the kind of girl you let go."

"Didn't you swear off relationships after…" Luke paused, not wanting to say his ex's name out loud and make Ryan difficult to be around. Red and yellow leaves swirled across the ground. Luke shifted, and his boots crunched over the dried grass.

"Mina was never the staying kind. We didn't have friendship as a foundation, and she cut and ran when the long distance made everything harder. Can you ever imagine Katy taking off while you're overseas?" Ryan grimaced.

"No. She's the weekly package and daily email kind of woman." His chest ached. She was the one he should never have let go, and he'd gone and hurt her again. The three-door MCL was Katy's brainchild. The little wooden box would help so many kids and brighten the playground. She'd turned his life upside down from all work to something more. He hadn't even known how much he'd needed someone to wake him up. Being "the job" was easier, but he couldn't go back. She made him want more.

"Exactly. So what are you doing?" Ryan raised his shoulders.

Luke shook his head. All of his reasons for not starting something were just as real now as they were before Katy popped back into his life. "I could be leaving now. Major McClain sent in a recommendation after everything worked out." He had a bitter taste in his mouth.

"So? Ask Katy to find a library job in Montgomery. Ask her to do long distance while you're at training. You could come back here. You don't know. And you won't know until you try."

"Big motivating speeches from Captain Hart. What is the world coming to?" Luke swore he would never hurt her again. She had to come first.

"Man, if you let her go without a fight, then I'll remind you every chance I get for the rest of forever." Ryan glared.

"Thanks, man. You're real kind." Maybe he should try again? At the very least, he had to apologize. His stomach clenched. What if she wouldn't accept his apology? What if he'd ruined everything?

"I'm a sweetheart." Ryan's big fake smile showed teeth. He carried the posthole digger like live ammunition.

"You have a lot of experience with posthole diggers?" Luke asked.

"My dad made me dig all the posts at their house in Tennessee. I'd pulled some stupid teenage stunt with my buddies, and to teach me a lesson, he had me dig all the holes for their new fence. They had a big yard. My arms hurt for weeks." Ryan held the posthole digger at arm's length.

"I bet the lesson was effective, though." Luke bit back a laugh, but his friend wasn't making the situation easy.

"Well, yeah. I didn't exactly have time to get into any more trouble. The next summer, though." Ryan wiped his forehead and readjusted his hat.

Luke chuckled. They'd already had the area marked for power lines and cables, so he'd checked all the safety boxes. He'd carefully reviewed all the requirements and forms for the MCL. He wouldn't cause any more trouble.

By the time they had the post packed in and ready, Ryan attached the lower boxes and added the top one last.

The MCL was officially ready for Katy to do her artistic thing.

"Well, you have to get her to talk to you now. Otherwise, one of us will have to add some stick figures on here, and nobody wants to see our creative capabilities." Ryan cringed.

"I know, I know." Luke squared his shoulders. He

planned to take a cinnamon latte to the library. If she wouldn't call him back, then he'd have to change tactics.

****

Luke breathed in the pumpkin and spicy chai air at Brewed Awakenings. He leaned against the counter to order a cinnamon latte, wishing Katy would walk in to join him.

Order forms were spread out in front of McKenna, and she was using the downtime to work on her inventory. Her dark-blonde hair was tied back in a braid.

"So this is how the magic happens. Order forms."

"What did you do? Katy might get back with Isaac, and I'm blaming you." She slapped her pencil on the counter and adjusted her purple glasses.

He took a step back, wary of the angry coffee shop owner. "I made a mistake. But I'm not giving up."

She prepared Katy's drink of choice, slamming the empty cup and banging the espresso harder than necessary. "I need more details."

McKenna's facial expressions shifted into a hard mask after he told her what he'd told Ryan. He never wanted to disappoint anyone, let alone the coffee shop owner who had become his friend. He'd never been on a first-name basis with any shop owners at his other bases. Dover was getting dangerously close to feeling like home.

"So you're taking a cinnamon latte, and you're prepared to grovel. You better make this right." She frowned and handed over the latte.

"I hear you." He was ready for his friends to quit making him feel even worse than he already did.

"Isaac wasn't ever good enough, and we all saw he was a user except Katy. He never brought her coffee, attended her events, or even learned what she read for fun. He was all about him and his thesis. If I hear she takes him back because you broke her heart, we will have *words*." She clenched her jaw.

"Yes, ma'am." He would protect Katy, even if she didn't give him a chance. He couldn't deny he wanted her to try. Ryan's words echoed in his mind. Katy was the one to keep.

****

Luke worked out what to say on the drive over to the library, changed his mind, and searched for another way to explain the mess of things running through his mind. By the time he parked, he had no clue. He found her at the welcome desk.

When she spotted him, she slumped her shoulders and frowned.

Last week, she would have jumped up and given him a hug. He wanted the big smile back, too.

Her golden-brown hair hung in loose waves down her shoulders, and she had a mechanical pencil tucked behind her ear.

He caught his gaze on the connection to the girl she'd been so long ago. "One Caterby latte, with McKenna's best regards, and she said to tell you she's sorry I'm such an idiot. Her words, but they're true."

"Let me see if I can take a break."

Her tone was resigned. She hadn't even reacted to the jab he'd thrown.

Ava took Katy's place.

Luke stood there, holding Katy's latte, not sure what to do while he waited.

Ava glared.

He shifted his weight between his feet. His apology tour was growing again—like he didn't feel bad enough already.

Katy led him outside and sat on a bench.

Chilly October air danced through the red and gold trees. The leaves were a bright backdrop for a sad conversation. "I messed up." He handed her the latte.

She took the lid off like she always did to check for cinnamon powder. She blew across the top.

"One latte won't fix what I did, but I do want the chance to make things right."

"I don't want to talk about everything yet." She gripped her latte.

He frowned. He'd had all these ideas for how the conversation could go, but she'd shut him down. "I'm sorry, Katy."

"I can see you're trying to make things right. And I will talk, but not on a break when you've shown up at my work." She tightened her burgundy cardigan around her stomach.

Realizing he'd put her on the spot, he flinched. "I didn't mean to ambush you. I'll follow your lead." He searched her eyes for some clue. How could he explain? At first, he'd kept the PCS to himself to keep his expectations low. After a while, though, his reasons became selfish. He'd always known on some level his determination to leave would ruin everything.

"Okay." She eased against the bench. "I know I need to paint the MCL. Did you and Ryan install the posts?"

He wanted to hug her. "Yes, ma'am. Our MCL is *planted* and waiting."

She checked her phone calendar. "Do you work tomorrow?"

"No, I have tomorrow off."

"A Monday for a Saturday is tough." She bit her lip.

He pried his gaze away from her full lips. Teasing was a good sign, right? Maybe she'd hear him out after all. "I should have told you. I almost did a bunch of times, but *almost* doesn't excuse my silence." Maybe if he apologized, she'd let him back in. He doubted fixing his mess would be so straightforward though.

Isaac strolled toward them with his canvas messenger bag and oversized water bottle covered in too many university stickers. The guy took academic to the next level as a lifestyle.

Luke had taken a slow and steady route to college, earning his degree with online classes while serving as enlisted. He wasn't academic like Katy and Isaac.

"Hey, Katy, you able to take a lunch break with me?" Isaac gripped the strap of his messenger bag.

Katy stood.

Luke followed, standing shoulder to shoulder. He wasn't ready for her to go back to work, but he was lucky she could take a break in the first place.

She stepped away.

The urge to protect her stormed through his blood.

"I'm not sure, Isaac. I have a lot to do for the fair." She checked her phone.

"Didn't you already put stickers on all of those books?" Isaac threw a hand in the air.

Luke barely kept himself from stepping between them. She'd worked hours and hours on the used book sale, and Isaac boiled her project down to sticking prices on books?

"You know the project is a lot more than stickers." Katy straightened her shoulders.

Luke recognized the warning signs. He'd made her mad enough lately to instinctively take a step back when her tone shifted low and hard.

"But you had time to read over the pages I sent you, right?" Isaac drew his brows together.

Luke took deep breaths. Users were his least favorite kind of so-called friends. He didn't need to fight the battle for Katy, but what was he supposed to do if she didn't recognize the battle?

"Not until next week."

Her tone flipped to overly calm like she was talking to an irate child. Luke resisted the urge to whistle. Nothing good ever happened when Katy used that tone.

Isaac took a small step back. "I thought you were kidding."

"Isaac, I told you the fair and the MCL are my priorities." She hugged the latte closer to her chest.

She had more patience than Luke could have mustered.

"I—" Isaac opened his mouth.

"I can't wait to see the fall sale. I'm hoping to get a stack of books to mail back home to my mom and sister. They're real proud of all the work you've done." Luke angled between Katy and Isaac to block her line of sight.

Her hazel eyes lit up. "I found the perfect book for Jackie. She collects coins, right?"

If he ignored Isaac standing there, then her reaction was what he'd been hoping for. Their connection was deep, running back along the years to two kids who knew each other's families and had inside jokes. She'd known him at his worst when he'd been a mess of teenage hormones, dealing with a newly present parent, and she'd stuck with him.

She took a sip of her latte.

He leaned in. A joyful Katy was a gravitational force. "She does. Just point me in the right direction on Friday."

"Well, I have to go edit my draft. The deadline is next week." Isaac huffed and almost slammed into the sliding glass doors at the entrance. He stepped back and rose to his tallest, waiting for the automatic doors to open.

How could she not see who he really was? Luke chuckled. He wanted to call the user out, but he was there to apologize not antagonize. He swallowed back his opinion of her ex. The wind *whooshed* past them, and Katy's long brown hair danced across her shoulders.

"He's stressed about his thesis." Katy nudged her shoe into the sidewalk.

"Did he volunteer to help?" Luke didn't want her to make excuses. Isaac didn't deserve her.

"He has to finish by next week." She studied her dark-blue suede flats.

"Well, you're stuck with me. I'm signed up to volunteer every day, and I'll help with whatever else you need, even if you're just after my truck." He wagged his eyebrows.

She smirked. "Your truck is handy."

"Uh-huh. Well, my truck and I are both at your service. I took the whole weekend off, so I'm game for whatever." He would move mountains to prove he was worth her time. Their friendship mattered more than he could admit.

"What? You shouldn't have messed up your schedule." She stiffened.

"Are you kidding me? I'm spending the weekend with you and books. What more could I need?" He tucked a strand of her silky hair behind her ear.

She blushed.

Was Ryan right? Was he being an idiot? He didn't want the answer. She was the once-in-a-lifetime kind of woman. Could he be enough?

With plans to meet the next afternoon, he hoped he could fix their friendship, and if he was lucky, she'd give him a chance at something more. They could try long distance, or he could request returning to Dover. He was getting ahead of himself. He had to tell her how he felt first and convince her Isaac wasn't worth taking back.

****

Luke missed having Katy in his truck, fiddling with the radio until she found a song with a good beat. He pulled into the visitor's center parking lot the next morning.

Katy always parked her red compact in the same spot, and she leaned against her car like waiting for a pickup at the front of Dover AFB was an everyday occurrence. Her shirt had paint splatters, and blue paint stretched across the left sleeve.

She was ready to work, which made her even more perfect in his estimation. He couldn't imagine Jolie having any shirts with paint in her dresser. She'd have borrowed a shirt, rather than risk her own clothes. He sucked in a breath. Comparing the two women was wrong.

She climbed into the cab of his truck with a tight smile.

"Welcome back. I have all the paints you sent me, and I'll come back and paint the top layer you mentioned tomorrow. I had to print all the paint names. How do they pick the names?" His favorite was choco-latte with rockin' red as a close second.

"Someone's job is to name the colors. Can you imagine?" She mustered a lackluster smile.

"Just come up with puns for colors? Maybe I'll retire and work for a paint company. Though, I can't think of anything for green. I'm always kind of amazed at how many different shades of green I see when I'm hiking." He was rambling, but he could not, for the life of him, stop.

"You'd come up with something." She pulled on her shirt sleeve.

He drove across base, parked, and followed her over to the MCLs with the box of paint supplies. The posts were level, and the shadows from the trees played over the mini libraries.

In the late afternoon, a few kids were playing on the equipment.

He nodded to their parents.

Katy sketched out her design on a couple of pieces of scratch paper.

He marveled at how she filled all the spaces to tell a story.

"I'll paint historical figures all around and add the reading age group on the front of the coordinating box." She pointed to the figures on her sketch.

"You're incredible. I only know some of the people, though." Luke pointed to Amelia Earhart.

"Well, you can research them later or ask Joshua for the books he's compiling. The kids will know them all soon. Ava helped me brainstorm ideas for each of the boxes." Katy set her sketchbook aside.

"Ava is the expert. I'll have to send her another thank-you. Both of you have made our project work. I'd have suggested something lame on my own." He would have built a blue box without any embellishments.

Katy sketched her plan over the MCL with her pencil. "You'd have reached out to Joshua at the school, and he would not have allowed anything short of extraordinary for his students."

"Yeah, but does he have MCLs on his mind all the time? The park needed one. You're the MCL whisperer."

She bit her lower lip. "The MCL Whisperer is the name of my next band."

"I'd buy their album." He laughed, realizing she'd made a reference to a running joke of theirs from high school. Whenever the lesson included something weird or ridiculous, the other would say the new term was the name of their next band—even though neither of them could play an instrument.

Katy kept a list at the back of her notebook and sometimes even doodled band logos if the name was worthy. He had missed so many notes while watching her sketch.

Quantum Flavors was his favorite. Their science teacher taught a section about flavors, and the lessons never had anything to do with food. "We should have showed Mr. Wegman the list of band names." Luke tracked the graceful curve of her hand as she sketched.

"I think a couple had definite disco vibes he would have appreciated." Katy switched to painting black outlines over her pencil marks.

"I'm sorry I let our friendship go after graduation. I can't believe we lost so much time." His heart beat wildly. Riding the wave of nostalgia created too many strong emotions to sort through. The main one was regret.

She stopped painting and nibbled on the corner of her lip. The paintbrush hung suspended over her cupped palm, dripping tiny drops of black paint.

"I guess I have a lot to say sorry for. I should have told you about the possibility of the training PCS. I was a chicken, and I'm sorry." He hung his head. How many times would he have to apologize? *Until she believed him.*

"PCS Chicken is the name of my next band. I don't like how you kept the real reason you started volunteering on the MCL project from me, but I understand. Kind of." She painted historical figures in fancy little frames with their names beneath.

Her brush strokes were almost hypnotic. A clip held her hair, revealing the long line of her neck.

"The worst part is you were starting something. Something more than friends, but you were also hoping the project we were working on would be your ticket out of Dover." She kept painting.

"I told myself I wouldn't start anything because I might be leaving. I didn't want to hurt you. But you're right, my actions didn't exactly line up with my intent." He stuck his free hand into his pocket. "I can only promise not to keep anything from you again. The second I know anything about the PCS, then you'll know about the PCS."

"I'm glad we're *friends* again, Luke."

That word again. He couldn't shake Ryan's advice. "Whatever we've got between us deserves a chance."

She added another framed historical figure to the main box. "I think friendship is all I have to offer. You're leaving soon or at some point."

Her voice sounded so final at the end. The moment was exactly what he'd been afraid of and part of why he'd kept the PCS a secret. Jolie was right. He was only good for leaving. A woodpecker trilled in the distance.

Katy jolted at the rhythmic thrum.

"I never meant to get so close, but I don't regret a single minute. If friendship is what you can give me, then I'm game. I can't imagine life without you now." He brushed a strand of her soft brown hair away from her face. His breath caught. "The PCS isn't guaranteed. I could be here completing the training online and bothering you to meet me for coffee and a bookstore visit every week."

"I'm not saying I don't…" she whispered. She set her paintbrush on the box by her feet. She narrowed her eyes. "Look, I know being in the Air Force means moving. And I'm not sure—" She sighed. "What if I follow you somewhere and our relationship falls apart? I need to be sure, like *really* sure, about us."

"You need to trust me." He'd broken her trust too many times. He would never give up. Katy was *the one*.

Chapter Thirteen

The housing side of base rolled into view from the passenger window of Luke's truck. Katy did her best to stay in the present. The little ceremony for the MCL Grand Opening would begin soon. She was overjoyed a librarian would be curating the book selections, and Joshua had the MCL fever.

He already visited her other MCLs in town and texted her all about his first impressions. His encouragement boosted her in a way she'd needed after everything had gone sideways with Luke. She'd been too invested in him.

"You're awfully quiet." Luke nudged her with his elbow.

The chat while they'd painted had helped, but the finality of her decision to remain friends made things uneasy. She'd almost tripped over herself, checking out his blue uniform. Had she drooled? She touched her lips. "Will the kickoff be very big?"

He shook his head.

Today was not about her and Luke and the big "what might have been" hanging over them. Today was about a community connecting over books.

"We're expecting a lot of the families, and someone from the *Air Force Times* should be there. A few credential requests crossed my desk, but the flight line has been busy, so I didn't get a chance to check."

"What are credential requests?" The learning curve for Luke's military lingo was as steep as her to-be-read list of books, but Katy was determined to file away every new word.

"Sorry. That just means someone from an outside organization wanted a pass to get through security for the event." He adjusted the rearview mirror.

"Got it." She tapped the art case on her lap. "And they're okay with me doing the face painting?"

Luke chuckled. "Are you kidding? Major wanted me to ask if you are secretly a magical nanny or something."

"Well, I lack the talking umbrella and carpet bag, but I think magic nanny is officially my Halloween costume." She could already picture the pressed white shirt, red bowtie, and black hat. Finding a carpet bag would be a trick, though.

"Only if I get to be your favorite chimney sweep," Luke said.

"You'd be a great sidekick." Another wave of sadness crashed over her. She should not be making future plans with Luke. He'd have looked dapper in a black vest and old-fashioned cap.

"Well, costumes are settled then." His smile was wide.

He couldn't guarantee he'd be there at the end of the month. Though, as Ava had reminded her several times, dating someone in the military meant she had to accept moving around. Luke's life was a call to service. She wasn't sure what to do. She wasn't tied to Dover, but she'd found her people here—friends who chose her.

He parked and rushed around to open her door.

Katy gulped at the size of the crowd. Families and Air Force personnel filled the park and spilled over into the elementary school parking lot.

Luke's boss called him over.

Katy found Joshua with a box of books. She snuck a glance back at Luke and bit her lower lip. His blue uniform was her new favorite.

"Well, hey there. The crowd is huge. My bookish heart is growing three sizes." Joshua clapped a hand over his heart.

She fully approved of his soft cotton blazer and bookish T-shirt combo for the day. She was covered in all of her library gear. She hoped she'd see some of the families at the library soon. "We have a big crowd, and they're in for a bookish treat." She motioned toward the open box.

"School librarians have the inside track on popular books, so I was born to shepherd our MCL." He mimed flipping long hair over his shoulder, even though his copper hair was thinning and short.

"Yes, you were." The bright glow of their success warmed her to her toes.

"Come on, I'm supposed to stock the books before they do the speeches." Joshua picked up the box at his feet.

"Aren't you talking, too?" Katy carried the second box filled with picture books.

"If by speech, you mean I plan to gush over your artwork and the books now available, then yes." Joshua smiled.

"I'm glad you like my little paintings." She was humbled all over again.

The books inside were the real stars of the show.

She and Joshua lined the books for each reading level into their MCL boxes.

Katy admired the finished product. The MCLs were official filled to the brim with books. The vibrant spines added another element, inviting kids to open the doors and dive right in. "Now they're MCLs." She stepped back with the empty box. Joshua had known the exact number of books to fill each one.

Several boxes with wrapped books sat under the bench, and the plan was for each kid to go home with a new book gifted by the Dover community.

"I had no idea I could love a little box of books so much." Joshua ran a hand across the steepled roof on the central box.

She and Joshua joined the crowd.

Luke turned on the microphone. Because they were outside, he wore his slim blue hat.

She checked him out in his blue service dress uniform, distracted by his broad shoulders. Heat flooded her cheeks, and she bit her lower lip. *Friends. We are nothing more than two old high school buddies.* The boundary she'd set was harder than she'd imagined.

"Thank you all for being here today. The MCL project, like all projects, took many hands to make and wouldn't have been possible without Major Gabriela McClain."

Everyone clapped for his boss.

"When she first heard about the literacy initiative, Major McClain knew we needed to consult with experts. Two of our experts are here today—Joshua Martin, our school librarian, and Katy Caterby, a Dover Public Library librarian."

Joshua grew two inches.

Katy stepped behind him. Her heart pounded as the size of the crowd felt like it doubled when everyone's attention was focused in her direction. She wiped a clammy palm on her jeans.

"I was lucky enough to grow up with Ms. Caterby in Oklahoma, and she answered the call when I needed an expert. You might have seen other Mini Community Libraries around town Katy built and painted. She's the Mini Community Library Whisperer, and we're lucky to have her as a part of our community. She's seen the way these mini libraries put the right book in the right hand at the right time and spark a lifelong love of reading. I'm excited to introduce them to Dover AFB."

Luke's deep rumbling voice crashed over her like a warm wave.

Joshua ushered her forward, and everyone clapped.

Her cheeks heated. She wished Luke would start talking again so everyone would stop cheering.

"Mr. Joshua Martin, our librarian here at George Welch Elementary School, will explain how the Mini Community Library works." Luke handed Joshua the microphone on his way to the crowd.

Luke stepped a little closer than necessary. "My lucky library brought you back into my life," he whispered.

The feel of his breath against her neck made her lose all sense of time and place.

His hand slipped around hers.

She let him, even though she shouldn't. She should be defending her boundaries and not letting her guard down all over again.

After the ceremony, some of the kids picked out

the first books while someone with media credentials snapped photos.

"A rep from Mini Community Library is here to show their support for our literacy initiative." Luke pointed across the crowd.

The rep had smooth mahogany skin and a vintage-style polka dot dress highlighting her curves. All she needed was a cardigan, and she'd fit right in at any library. Her purse was shaped like a book with red leather, matching her red dress with white and black polka dots.

Another man stopped beside Joshua. "I bet the commander is in hog heaven."

Joshua's face lit up at the sight of the newcomer.

"And you must be Katy." The man had sandy-blond hair buzzed high and tight.

"And you must be Chris." She shook his offered hand.

He raised his thick blond eyebrows. "Are we that obvious?"

Joshua's joy was infectious from his glowing face to the way he was bouncing on his feet.

Chris smiled.

"'There could have been no two hearts so open,'" she quoted.

" 'No tastes so similar, no feelings so in unison.' Austen." Joshua clapped his hands together and leaned against his husband.

Chris raised an eyebrow. "You have any idea what they're talking about?"

"They're bonding over books." Luke smirked.

"Ah, as you were then." Chris straightened and surveyed the crowd. Joshua's husband was tall and lean.

They posed for photos, and the commander raised his chin, reminding Katy so much of Dad. He had the universal I'm-proud-of-you dad expression.

"I appreciate the way you gave your time to our project." The commander shook her hand. "Sometimes, we forget to be part of the community around the base which is clearly a mistake."

"Every shop owner we talked to was overjoyed to help with the book donations. Our city is incredibly proud of Dover AFB." She beamed.

"I understand a number of the captain's coworkers have volunteered to help you in return?" He raised an eyebrow.

Katy grinned. "They sure have. I cannot explain how much their help means. All the proceeds from the used book sale will fund our new summer reading program. We'll do more than offer reading suggestions. Every kid will get a free book to kick off the summer, and then we'll have prizes to support them as they achieve their reading goals. I'm so excited."

He rubbed his chin. "Well, summer reading sounds like a fine program. I always did notice a change in reading habits when pizza was on the line for my own kids. Though, they're in college now."

"Pizza is evergreen for motivation." She'd lived for those little personal pizzas in elementary school. The little star stickers on her daily reading circles glittered in her memory.

"I agree. Please keep us informed about other volunteering opportunities."

His eyes sparked like when he'd danced with her without telling her who he was. "Absolutely. Thank you for the support. I should go get my face-painting station set up." Katy sighed in relief. She wasn't even in the Air Force, and he made her feel like she was in the principal's office or something. She found a little table for face painting and unrolled the smock.

Another officer had balloons for the occasion. The black organizer bag around her waist didn't fit with her OPCs. Her bag had small pockets full of rainbow-colored balloons and two air pumps.

"Thanks for volunteering your time." The brunette motioned toward Katy's face paints.

"Shouldn't I be thanking you for your service *and* for volunteering your time?" Katy's eyes flashed wide. "The least I can do is paint a few rainbows."

"When I learned how to make balloon animals as part of my mom's clown act, I never in a million years imagined I'd be making balloon swords as an Air Force officer. But I have fun, even if my teenager is mortified I'm doing this in public—again." She nodded toward a teen near the MCL.

"Someday, they won't mind the memory." Katy gazed in the indicated direction.

Her teenager edged closer to the MCL.

"Well, let's hope." The woman made a daisy for one of the kids.

"Do you want a matching daisy?" Katy asked.

The little girl clutched her balloon flower and nodded.

Katy caught sight of Luke in his blue service uniform across the park. He stood tall in the crowd with his gaze locked on her. Shivers ran down her spine. Why did her body always react like a lightning bolt whenever he paid even the slightest attention?

****

When her line dwindled to nothing, Katy was free from face painting. She packed her supplies and wiped glitter from her hands. The autumn wind was gentle, cooling the sunny day.

Luke and the MCL rep he'd pointed out earlier started toward her.

"Katy, I'd like to introduce Ginny Dean from Mini Community Library." Luke excused himself to talk to his boss.

"Well, hello. Now, you'll have to remind me. Are you with the elementary school here?" Ginny was all red, black, and white in her clothing and accessories.

"I'm a librarian at the Dover Public Library." Katy motioned toward Joshua across the sunny park. "Joshua Martin is the librarian here on base. He'll be the one curating the books in the MCL."

"I always appreciate when the MCLs are partnered with a librarian. I started out as a librarian many, many, years ago." Ginny smoothed her dark hair.

"Where was your library?" She wanted to know her entire story. She was living proof Katy's dream job was real, and she wanted the entire road map to get there someday.

"In a small town outside of Savannah, Georgia. My career was a bit of a journey, but with Mini Community Library, I get to travel all over to visit communities and help support them." Ginny beamed.

"You've just described my dream job. I actually worked on an MCL project during my masters." Katy rubbed at a stubborn glob of green face paint on her palm. Of course, she had glittery paint all over.

"Oh, right. The captain mentioned you'd done

other MCLs. I need to visit the park to see your other artwork." She opened the MCL app on her phone and found the bright-orange dots. "I can't wait to see them. I'm guessing the MCL was your suggestion?"

"MCLs are always my first thought for increasing literacy." Katy waved toward the park.

A little girl grabbed a teenager's hand, dragging her to the bench and pushing a book into the teen's hands.

"Books out in the wild and in the community." Ginny followed her gaze. "Moments like these are something special. You let me know if you have any other MCLs in the works. I'll follow your career now. We MCL lovers have to stick together."

"When I build the next one, I'll call you first." Katy would find ways to keep in touch.

"I like how you said *when* and not *if*." Ginny handed Katy her card and wandered back over to the press.

Luke nudged her shoulder. "She seemed cool."

"She's living proof my dream job is out there." She grabbed his forearm. "I didn't mean to say anything out loud."

"My mom would say you didn't mean to use your outside voice." Luke rubbed her arm. "But don't worry. Your secret is safe. Though really, anyone who has ever heard you talk about the MCLs knows where your heart belongs."

"My obsession is obvious, huh?" She grinned.

Luke chuckled. "Yep."

"Well, don't tell Mae. I need my job." She frowned. Mae had taken such a chance on her, and she wouldn't repay her faith by accepting another job when she'd barely been there a year.

"Your boss thinks you're great. She gave you the whole Fall Fair sale because she knew you could handle the project." He bumped against her shoulder.

Katy winced at how much work the setup would require. If even one volunteer no-showed, she'd be in a bind. She swallowed, easing closer.

"You worried about tomorrow?" He wrapped an arm around her shoulders.

"The fair is a lot. I've never managed a sale before, so the setup and breakdown each day feel daunting." She thinned her lips. Someday, she wouldn't share every random thought when Luke was around. She followed him to the parking lot.

"Ryan and I will help set up and pack all weekend—and anything else you need. You have a lot of people who will drop whatever and help. Your flier was posted at McKenna's, and I bet the sale will be a big success." He waved to his boss when she walked past them.

"You're right. I need to chill out." Katy released a slow, deep breath.

"Ava and all of the librarians are volunteering, right?" Luke scanned her face.

Katy hugged her arms across her chest. "They will. I don't want to disappoint anyone."

"You work too hard to let anyone down. The books are organized. The regular volunteers from the store will be there, running the sales. You've got this." He squeezed her shoulder.

She wished she shared his faith. "Thanks." She studied her sneakers.

Joshua bounded up. "I just had one of the top five

afternoons of my life. Kids who drag their feet into my library were hugging books. *Hugging* books. I'm making you an MCL Whisperer button to wear everywhere."

"Everywhere?" Katy eased away from Luke. She had no problem wearing a pin from her new librarian friend. Pins and buttons were a weakness. She already had too many on her lanyard at work. What was one more?

"Yes, obviously everyone needs to know. You have superpowers." Joshua struck a superhero pose with his hands on both hips.

"He's not wrong." Luke shifted to stand shoulder to shoulder with Joshua.

Katy rolled her eyes. They were being ridiculous.

"Hey, did you volunteer to help with the used book sale?" Luke asked.

"I'll be there on Saturday, and Chris is volunteering with me." Joshua smiled.

"Okay, okay. Just making sure." Luke adjusted his narrow flight cap.

"Thank you both so much." Libraries depended on community engagement and support, and she couldn't explain how much their help mattered. Deep gratitude warmed her to her toes.

"Come on, I'll get you back to your car. Are you working tonight?" Luke started toward his truck.

"I have a few more things to get ready for tomorrow. I want to double-check the volunteer hours and maybe find a little basket to keep the bookmark gifts in by the cash wrap." Her mental list kept growing, and her heart rate picked up speed. How did Mae and Darcy always make these events appear so effortless?

"McKenna has all of those baskets over where she lets people share community fliers and local business info. She'd let you borrow one for a weekend. They'd be about the right size." He opened the passenger door.

"She might." Katy lit up at the idea, climbing into the cab.

"Text her, and I'll grab the basket. I can help sort the bookmarks or whatever."

She swallowed. Spending a whole evening with him didn't seem like a great idea. Her feelings were all over the place. "Ava and Mae will help. You don't have to."

"I know I don't *have* to. I want to. Did you see how well our mini library launched back there? The success was all you. You took time away from your First Friday and Fall Fair to help kids on base, so you better believe I'm spending all tonight helping you." He started the truck and took off his slim blue hat.

She brushed a loose strand of wavy hair from her face and texted McKenna about the basket. "McKenna is game for loaning the library a basket. You don't mind?"

"I'll bring coffee, too." He ran a hand through his rumpled hat hair.

"Are you bartering friendship for cinnamon lattes?" She pursed her lips. She couldn't convince herself he'd only been concerned with the career boost. He'd been those kids, and now, he was helping them. Literacy for kids on base mattered far more than a possible advance in his career.

"Is the coffee working?" His fingers tapped the steering wheel, and he bit his lower lip.

She laughed. "Getting me to associate you with my

favorite latte is a strong game plan."

****

Katy returned to the library with a spring in her step. The MCL had gone so well, and she had a new connection to the organization with Ginny. Someday down the road, she would earn her dream job.

Mae paced in the narrow library office hallway between two bright-red, yellow, and black paintings. "Katy, oh, good. I was hoping you'd be back soon. How did the MCL event go?" She turned her lips into a tight frown.

"Great. I snapped photos with permission to share on our social. What's wrong?" Katy's heart hammered in her chest.

Mae furrowed her dark eyebrows. "The vendor who runs our sales system has a bug."

"A bug?" Katy was sure she was supposed to be following, but she was lost.

"We had to close the Friends of the Library store today. Our sales system is down." Mae checked her screen again.

The words echoed in Katy's mind. "What?"

"They're not sure when they'll have the app back online, and now, nobody is answering my calls. I won't tell you how many voicemails I've left." Mae glared at her phone. "We might have to cancel the sale."

Katy paced in the tight hallway. She wiped her clammy hands on her jeans and took a slow breath, hoping to calm her racing heart. She couldn't let the after-school crew down, and Mae was counting on her. The blue industrial carpet scratched under her white sneakers. "Wait. There has to be another way to run sales. Another vendor?"

Mae slumped her shoulders. "We have to get county permission to enter into contracts. If I could call another vendor and switch, I would. I don't have a backup plan for the summer program funding." She stared at her phone.

Where were her ever-present pencil, notebook, and lanyard? "Okay." Katy swallowed. "Do we have time for a staff meeting? Maybe a brainstorming session will help?" The after-school crew was already excited about the program. They'd helped come up with some of the prizes. Canceling the program would crush them.

Mae tapped her chin. "Get Ava to collaborate, but you'll have to meet near her desk. I need her on the floor."

"We'll figure the sales out." Katy forced as much bravado into her voice as possible. Mae had lifted her spirits countless times. Katy could return her kindness. Everyone would jump in with both feet. She was not alone here, but she had to find a way. She picked up the bookmarks and her lanyard. The button from Joshua shifted in her pocket.

"Hey there. How did the MCL thing go?" Ava scanned her computer screen, wearing orange and red with a matching scarf braided into her hair.

"Good, but listen, did you hear they had to close the bookstore?" Katy paced on the round, primary-colored rug in front of the desk.

"Oh yeah, the volunteers all left. What's up?" Ava clicked the computer mouse.

"The sales system crashed." Katy gulped. Hearing the words out loud made the situation real.

Ava's expression shifted in slow motion with her brows knitting together.

Katy's phone buzzed.

—Your coffee order has arrived.—

—Hey, Mr. Persistent. Follow the yellow brick carpet.—

"Let's work over here." Katy motioned to the round table with an alphabet monster activity. She filled the monster tub with all the alphabet bottle caps to clear the table.

Luke joined them, holding a drink tray with four coffee drinks. "Well, you all look serious. You ladies ready to sort some bookmarks?" He handed Katy her cinnamon latte. "Can we drink these out here?"

"We allow drinks in the library." Ava waved a hand. "And we're in crisis mode here, Durant Guy. You have something for me?" She took the lid off her cup. "Hot cider? Yum."

"McKenna said you were working. She made a drink for your boss, too." He motioned toward the third drink—Mae's hazelnut latte.

"McKenna is a rock star." Ava took the fourth drink back toward the offices.

"What's the crisis?" Luke sat in a youth-sized plastic chair. His knees were up past the tabletop. He was still dressed in his service dress uniform. His blue tie was perfectly centered.

His deep voice melted Katy's nerves like butter in a frying pan. Lifting the lid, Katy breathed in the cinnamon goodness of her latte. Steam rose into the air. She belatedly worried she might have glittery rainbow paint smeared on her face.

Luke took a sip of his drink.

"Our sales system is down. They're not even answering Mae's calls anymore, so I'm not sure if the computers will turn on tomorrow." She bounced her knees. She had to start problem-solving.

He sat back in the tiny chair. "Well, you can do paper sales, right? You don't need software for money."

Air whooshed back into her lungs. "You're right. But who carries cash these days?" She'd have to count everything—multiple times. Someone else would have to count, too. Would the cash register even work without the computer system? Her eyes blurred with unshed tears.

"For a Fall Fair? Everybody has cash for festivals. You have to have cash for the games and a lot of the food at these things." Luke motioned for Ava to jump in.

"What games?" Ava plunked into a tiny, blue plastic chair.

"Like I just told Katy, some of the games and food at the fair are cash only. A lot of people will have money for those." He raised his eyebrows.

Luke sounded so reasonable.

"I'll have cash for the food. Oh, man, I hope the taco truck is there." Ava rubbed her hands together.

"Focus." Katy snapped her fingers in Ava's face.

Ava gently smacked her hand away.

"Luke thinks we can get by with cash only." Katy's throat dried.

"I mean…we'll lose some sales." Ava sipped her apple cider. "But he's not wrong. I'll have cash to buy from the vendors in case they don't take credit. Some of the vendor's social posts say *cash only*."

The sweet spices wafted across the table. "We don't have *cash only* on any of our stuff. What if patrons are frustrated we weren't up front about needing cash?" Katy sorted the bookmarks and stacked them again.

"A ten-second explanation covers the situation, and if they can't accept software crashes, then they have problems." Ava pursed her lips.

How was she so calm?

Dom took a seat at the table.

He wasn't even supposed to be working. Katy raised her eyebrows.

"Ava texted me about the crisis mode. I'm here. What's what?" Dom glanced around the tot-sized table.

The tall librarian fit about as well as Luke did in the little chairs. Katy caught him up.

Dom lifted his Delaware State Hornets hat and readjusted its angle. He'd played for them during college and still went to most of the games at his HBCU undergrad. "Cash sounds like a straightforward solution." Dom pointed toward the bookstore. "The shop will have petty cash for change anyway, right?"

"Yeah, they were managing the money side. But they weren't planning on cash only." Could cash earn enough sales to fund the summer program?

"McKenna says you can print credit card slips and write the customer's info. You know, the old-fashioned way? We can log the sales when the system is running." Ava scrolled on her phone. "I told her thank you for the cider. She didn't know you would be here, or she'd have sent you a drink too, Dom."

"Good to know I have drink status with McKenna." Dom adjusted his bright-blue DSU hat. "So we print slips of paper, and the store volunteers manually enter the sales later. We can help."

"We used those forms when I was little at the

hardware store. I'll ask my dad later. The bookstore volunteers trained me on the sales system last week. I can tackle the backlog." Katy sorted the bookmarks a different way. "We'll have to clear everything with Mae." Katy's heart rate was too fast, making her hands tremble.

Luke collected the bookmarks and slipped them into a basket. He raised his eyebrows with a crisp nod.

Their plan could go wrong in so many different ways. At least, she wasn't alone.

Chapter Fourteen

A sliver of golden light crested the horizon behind the Dover Public Library. The parking lot shimmered with dew under the tall lampposts. Luke sipped piping hot coffee in his truck and tried to wake up.

Ryan had his vintage red Ford pickup, and he'd even cleaned out the truck bed.

Luke wasn't sure he'd ever seen the thing without a coat of dirt.

"I'm here." Katy's long brown hair was pulled into a bun. Her shirt had the library logo, and her red jacket was bright in the early light. "Let me go unlock the bay doors. Can you drive around?"

He'd forgotten about the back dock. He needed another cup of coffee and to cut Ryan more slack for the early hour.

Around back, he waited until the truck doors opened with an exaggerated groan. The library truck was already loaded, so they grabbed the remaining tables and loaded them into their trucks.

Ryan had an impressive collection of cables, and he had the boxes of books all secured in no time.

"Wow, hanging out with loggie guys has real advantages." Katy leaned back.

Ryan lifted his chin in the air with a small grin.

"You want to ride with me?" Luke asked. "I need help keeping McKenna's to-go box of coffee from falling over."

"Sure. I'll see you there." She waved at Ava and Ryan after locking the library.

Luke caravanned behind the staffer driving the library truck. They were as ready as they could be.

"McKenna packed two to-go boxes of coffee?" Katy held one on her lap.

The cab smelled like freshly brewed nutty coffee and surprise apple cider donuts. "She let me stop by early to get them. I wanted to make sure your volunteers were caffeinated."

"And you, too." Katy motioned toward his cup.

"She packed her new roast. She likes you." He took a sip.

"Let's drink all the coffee before we get there." She bounced her knee, sloshing the coffee back and forth in the cardboard holder.

He gripped the steering wheel to keep from resting a hand on her knee. "She sent another surprise." He handed her a small white pastry box with the purple Brewed Awakenings logo.

"She didn't." She offered him a donut. "Mmm." She licked the sugar from her thumb.

"Hey, the sales will all work out." He bit into the fluffy cider donut. The cinnamon burst on his tongue. "You coaxed the commander back on board with the MCL, even though I messed up the endgame. We'll get these sales done with or without the software."

Katy chuckled. "When did you become the Pollyanna in our duo?"

"I must be spending too much time with you. Or less time with Ryan." He plucked another donut from the box.

"Ryan's not so grumpy." Katy set the empty box in the backseat.

Luke shook his head. "You didn't see him with Ava."

"Oh, opposites attracting?" She raised her eyebrow.

He scowled. "More like uncaffeinated Ryan could not handle the energy Ava wakes up with." They'd gotten on each other's bad sides fast over the best way to load his truck.

"I want her morning mojo." Katy sighed. "I couldn't sleep after finding out about the sales system and then needed a lot of coffee at home before I even met you at the library."

"Coffee is like duct tape for the mind." Luke nodded.

"Duct Tape Coffee is the name of my new band. I should start writing these down." She pulled a blue notebook from her sunflower-yellow bag and doodled on a page at the back.

"The real question is if you were dancing to disco." He pictured her in her kitchen, dancing around. What he wouldn't give to be with her to dance along…

"My jams"—she shimmied—"shall remain a mystery for all time."

He told his phone to play the disco tune he'd downloaded earlier and goofily danced in his truck while he sipped his coffee.

Katy laughed so hard tears streamed down her face. "Mr. Wegman would be so proud right now." She wiped away a tear.

She had color in her cheeks now. Sometimes, a little goofy sacrifice was necessary.

****

Under the white tent marked with a small number eight, Luke helped unpack the tables, carts, and bookshelves for the sale.

Katy set out a brightly decorated chalkboard sign, advertising the library's book sale. When she turned on the tablet to run the software, the screen remained black until an error message popped up. She dropped her chin.

Luke wrapped his arm around her. "Where are McKenna's slips?"

She showed the volunteers how to use them and where they should go in the cash register.

The tiny space filled with the smell of paper and glue.

"Good morning, my favorite people." McKenna was covered in Brewed Awakenings brand gear. Even her earrings were coffee cups.

Katy hugged her and thanked her for the coffee donation.

Ryan stopped beside him. "I need to head out." He nodded toward Katy. "You fix all that yet?"

"No, but he's trying," Ava said.

Where had she come from? Luke scanned for any other sneaky librarians.

"Well, trying is a good place to start." Ryan tipped the bill of his hat like a cowboy on his way out.

"He's a complicated one." Ava furrowed her brow.

"Hmm." Luke cleared his throat.

Katy hugged herself.

"The system might start again before we open." Ava blew out a breath. "And we have a work-around. We shouldn't lose too many sales."

"The book sales will all work out fine." Mae adjusted her cardigan. "Oh, I've startled you. Don't you have situational awareness training, Luke Taylor?"

So much for his training to be focused on his surroundings. Were any librarians left at the actual library? "I did, ma'am. Seems like I might be needing a refresher course." He didn't mention librarians were sneaky.

"He's focused." Ava patted his shoulder.

He cocked an eyebrow. Wasn't she mad?

She half shrugged. "We have all the books set up, and Katy is about to finish the photo booth."

"Wonderful. I'm counting on you to take photos. We'll want to replicate everything for next year. Your setup is charming." Mae waved at the stall behind them. "I wanted to wish Katy luck before heading into work." She narrowed her eyes. "Shouldn't you be on your way to the library to start your shift?"

"I should." Ava ran over to hug Katy and took off.

Luke was impressed at the level of command execution. "You run a tight ship."

"Librarians know how to get the job done, and we've researched to make sure we know the best way currently available." She sashayed away to join Katy and McKenna.

His alarm buzzed with a reminder to text Jackie to see if she wanted to video chat. Sometimes, she wasn't up for calls, which was always fine with Luke. For him, he needed her to know he wanted to chat. If she'd had a hard day or was overstimulated, he understood.

—Video call still okay?—

She called him with the video activated, glancing sideways at the screen. She worked through the initial questions she always asked.

"Here's the tent." He swung around to give her a good look.

"Did they figure out the computer issue?" Jackie twisted and turned a pink-and-green fidget cord.

Her tone was flat, which was standard. Her volume of questions always told him her excitement level.

A volunteer ducked under Luke's phone, staying off-screen.

"Not yet, but they have a way to accept cash or credit." Luke showed her the old-school cash register.

Katy opened the drawer so Jackie could see what change they had prepared.

"That's good. I always make sure I have enough quarters when my shift starts. Check your quarters." Jackie adjusted her noise-canceling headphones.

He wasn't sure how it was comfortable to have her wireless earbuds underneath, but Jackie always wore them together. "I will. Katy is here."

Jackie might say *no*. Video calls were better than phone calls for her, if he could show her new spaces, but he hadn't warned her about Katy.

Jackie sucked in a breath, taking a long pause. "Hi, Katy."

Katy answered her initial questions and shared her favorite Agatha Christie quote from the photo booth.

"Which book is that from?"

Katy identified the book and chapter. By the time Jackie ran out of questions, Katy was smiling from ear to ear.

She joined in Jackie's endless curiosity because hers was just as vast. Jolie was patient with Jackie, but Katy opened up and shared her passion. He shook his head to quit with the comparisons.

When she finished her questions, Jackie ended the call.

She rarely said goodbye on calls. Luke preferred Jackie's method to Mom's Midwestern twenty-minute end-of-call nonsense. Goodbyes were even worse in person. At least ten hugs and a few false goodbyes were involved before he could leave a visit with Mom in Oklahoma.

"She's doing okay?" Katy rested her palm on his bicep.

Luke nodded. "She'll need to start getting ready for her shift at work."

Katy pressed a hand to her heart. "I'm so glad her job makes her happy. Not everyone gets as lucky as we are."

"Truth." Luke helped one of the volunteers restack some of the overstock books. His phone buzzed. "Captain Taylor," he said because the phone number was Air Force.

"Captain, good. I caught you."

Major McClain's voice was hoarse.

"I know you were supposed to have the morning off, but I need both you and Captain Hart to report in until at least early afternoon."

Adrenaline spiked under his skin like an electrical current. "Yes, ma'am. Do you want me to call Captain Hart?"

"Yes, I have to keep moving." She ended the call.

He found Katy fidgeting with the tablet again. He placed a hand on the small of her back to shake her laser focus.

She leaned against him.

He rested his chin gently against the crown of her silky brown hair. He inhaled a deep grounding breath of her cinnamon-and-sugar scent and stepped back. "I don't think staring will start the system. You have a good backup plan." Her soft, slender hand grazed his, sending electricity zipping up his arm.

"Maybe the system will reboot before we open the stall?" She sighed.

Her little frown made Luke's protectiveness spike. "Listen, Major McClain called, and I'm headed back to work for a while."

"Oh, I hope everything is okay." She knit her eyebrows together.

He shook his head. "I won't know until I get there. Ryan and I can handle the situation."

Katy stiffened. "She called both of you in on your days off?"

"Yeah, something is up. Listen, text me if you need moral support, and I'll be back as soon as possible." When he hugged her, he took comfort in the cinnamon scent of his favorite librarian. He didn't like leaving when she was so panicked.

****

Luke pulled into ATOC's parking lot in time to spot Ryan by his old truck. He pulled on his hat and rushed over. The sky broke into bright shades of orange with the sunrise. The morning was crisp, but Katy couldn't have ordered better weather for a fair. He hoped she sold all of her books. He beelined toward the building.

"You know what's happening?" Ryan fell in beside him.

Luke opened the door to the sand-colored office

building. "No, Major was in a hurry."

"Not good." Ryan sighed and tucked his hat back into his pocket.

"Nope." ATOC was packed with Major McClain hurrying back and forth between airmen. Their counterparts, the current duty officers, had bloodshot eyes.

The newest officer waved them over. "Buckle up. We've been here for twelve hours, and nobody will go home anytime soon." She rubbed a hand over her face.

By midafternoon, he must have walked ten miles, working double-time to find the parts needed for a mission. The next shift started with a fresh crew wandering into ATOC.

Major McClain surveyed the room. "If you've been here for more than ten hours, clear out." She pointed at Luke and Ryan. "You two aren't even supposed to be here today. Head home. We found the parts. You should be proud, Captain Hart. Quick thinking earlier."

"Tracking those parts was a team effort, ma'am." Ryan squared his shoulders.

"Well, get going." She disappeared into her office.

Ryan rubbed his face. "You heard the boss. We have library equipment to pack up tonight."

"You sure you're good to help?" Luke shuffled the papers on his desk.

"I don't back out of commitments." Ryan frowned.

Luke logged out of his computer. "Thanks, Ryan."

"You know a bunch of my team at the rec center spend time after school at the library. The summer program helps them, too. I'd do about anything to help those kids." Ryan grabbed his keys.

"They're lucky to have you as a coach." He figured

even curmudgeons deserved some praise. He followed Ryan out of the building only to be blasted by the chilly fall air in the parking lot.

"Don't ask them. You might not like the answer." Ryan wandered toward his truck.

Luke shook his head. He'd helped out a time or two when Ryan had needed a second adult. Coach Hart hung the moon to those kids.

"You fix things with Katy? She leaned on you this morning." Ryan adjusted his hat.

"I'm working on it."

"You figure out your endgame yet?" Ryan raised an eyebrow.

Luke gulped. "I'm going all in."

"Finally." Ryan slammed his truck door and peeled out of the parking lot.

Luke had to find the right time to tell Katy how he felt and hope she felt the same.

****

Luke froze outside the library stall. The world around him muted, and all he could hear was his heart in his throat. The afternoon sun blazed down on him.

Isaac had on a button-up and a newsboy hat. He crowded Katy.

Luke swallowed the comments he wanted to make.

McKenna nudged his shoulder. "He's been here for thirty minutes." She glowered at Isaac.

At least, he wasn't the only one who had very strong opinions about Katy's ex.

"A whole year of volunteer opportunities, and the guy doesn't show up until he smells competition." She crossed her arms.

"You think he's here because I'm here?" Luke

widened his eyes.

"Clearly." She threw her hands in the air. "So, what will you do?"

He wished he had an answer. "Are they back together?" He didn't go after women with boyfriends, but as Katy's friend, he also didn't want to stand by while she dated the dud again. The idea of her with someone else made his heart jump into his throat.

"Not yet." Ava stood beside McKenna. "But we wish it was you. You'd be better for her."

"She lights up when she's around you," McKenna said. "We're counting on you."

"So march back over there and convince her to take a break with you and leave Isaac behind." Ava shooed him away.

"Easy, huh?" He lifted his eyebrows.

In unison, the two women popped their free hands on their hips.

"Okay, okay." He raised his hands in surrender and took a deep breath. Weight settled in his stomach. *Now or never.*

"Hey, hey." Dom helped another customer. "Things sorted on base?"

Luke leaned his head back. "Ryan and I handled the situation. Thanks."

"Look who's back, Katy." Dom stepped between Katy and Isaac. "Hey, man, help me get a few more boxes to replenish the tables." Dom ushered Isaac toward the back of the tent where they had overstock waiting.

Katy slid her gaze between them.

"Hi." Luke hugged her just because he could. She smelled like books and cinnamon.

"I'm glad things are okay on base. I was worried." She wrinkled her brow.

"The situation is handled. Ryan will be back to pack up later, too." Luke swallowed. Had he ever had friends off base worry about him before?

She stepped away. "You guys sure do volunteer when you say you will."

"For a good cause, you can always count on us. Listen, you have coverage here. Can you take a break? I need caffeine." Would she say *no*? Luke held still.

"You good if I take a break?" Katy leaned away.

Dom shelved a stack of books. "You're not even scheduled to be here right now. Bring me back a cider."

"Will do." Katy raised two thumbs-up.

Isaac stepped around Dom, forcing his way into Katy's line of sight. "You said you'd stay while I volunteer."

His puppy dog expression was what Mom would call over the top, OTT. Luke took a deep breath. He would let Katy handle her ex. She was more than capable.

"I'm taking a break, Isaac." Katy took a step back.

Her tone was dangerously calm. Luke blanched.

"I should get going then," Isaac said.

"But you're scheduled to help for another half an hour." Katy bit her lower lip.

She must have seen a different person. He had to stay out of her issues with Isaac. Katy wasn't a damsel in distress, but the urge to protect her from her ex made him feel reckless. Luke shifted his boots, staring at the ground.

"My thesis is due in a week." Isaac stood taller.

"Nobody made you sign up." Katy gazed into

Isaac's eyes with narrowed brows.

Luke covered his smirk with a cough.

"Katy, you know my degree is the priority." Isaac adjusted his glasses.

"Your only priority," she whispered.

His pale skin heated berry-pink to his ears. He rushed out of the tent.

"Good riddance." Dom wiped his hands.

"Hear, hear," another volunteer said.

Luke couldn't remember their name, but he'd met them during morning setup.

"I should stay." Katy tracked Isaac's retreating form with her gaze.

Dom adjusted his hat. "No, the fair won't be busy again until people end their workdays. Go take a break while you can."

"I'm the only volunteer in the store all the time, Ms. Katy. We'll be fine. And you won't have to listen to us talk about Del State football for a while. Doesn't a break sound lovely?" the older person told Katy with a sparkle of mischief in their eyes.

Katy laughed. "A break sounds great."

Luke took her hand and headed to McKenna's coffee cart.

"My Okies. You need the usual?" McKenna waved.

"I need two extra shots in my chai tea latte." The hours spent scrolling computer screens weighed on his brain.

"Poor Captain." McKenna made the magic happen. "And look at you, actually taking a break."

Katy cupped a hand around her ear. "I know you're not giving me a hard time for overworking."

"What? And be a total hypocrite? Never." McKenna smirked. "The sale going okay?"

"I didn't have a chance to tell you. The software started working around noon, so everything is working out. Thank you again for the idea of using the credit card slips." Katy hugged her.

Luke sighed in relief. Those slips would have been a mess to keep organized.

"I'm taking a break soon. You'll take photos of me and Katy in her bookish photo booth, right?" McKenna pleaded with her hands clasped.

"You got it." He stepped out of the way for the long line forming behind them.

"We'll see you later." Katy waved, turning toward a long aisle of booths decked out in bright orange decorations.

"So Isaac." He bumped her shoulder.

"Yeah, Isaac." She wrinkled her brow. "I didn't even know he'd signed up."

Luke rolled his eyes. He led them to the first row of white tents. "But then he wouldn't stay to finish."

"Listen. I know McKenna and Ava don't like him." She hugged her latte to her chest.

"And a few others." Luke kept his voice soft.

She stepped around a mom and toddler in matching red flannel. "Okay, I don't know any of my friends who like Isaac. But we were good together."

Luke spread his legs like he was ready to stand his ground. He needed her to say she wasn't taking Isaac back. Even if she wasn't with Luke, he needed her to see she was way too good for her ex. "Not if he never supported your work before." His tone was harder than he intended.

"He's been busy." She grabbed Luke's arm.

He didn't budge. "He had time to hang out at a bar with his friends."

"That's not fair." She pressed her lips into a thin line.

He stuck his free hand into his pocket so he didn't try to hold hers again. "Seems fair."

She took a deep breath.

"Katy, if a guy acted the same way toward Ava or McKenna…" He needed another tactic. *How could she not see he was a user?*

"I'd tell them to cut him loose." Katy ran her fingers over a creamy handmade cardigan at the entrance to a small stall.

He lifted a shoulder.

"I haven't taken him back. I don't have anything to cut loose." She pressed a hand to her stomach.

His heart accelerated, and he did his best to hide his relief. He would never have forgiven himself if she'd gone back to Isaac. "So you're not together?" His tone was soft.

She rocked on her heels. "What?"

"You were holding hands at Brewed Awakenings." He studied his coyote-brown boots. Just the memory made his stomach heavy. He entwined their fingers, pressing his palm against hers to reassure himself.

"Oh, well. Yeah. But holding hands doesn't mean I'm in a relationship with someone. We hold hands all the time." She lifted their hands as proof.

"I like holding your hand. But then I'd like to be in a relationship." He dropped his jaw. *Way to go all in, Taylor.* He planned to be slow and smooth. In reality, he was more like a bull in a china closet.

"Luke, you're planning to leave." She slipped into another stall, leaving him behind.

"For a temporary training. I might even come back and be stationed here again." He'd do whatever it took to be wherever she was.

The tables in the small white tent were packed with bright-red, orange, and yellow ceramics.

"But you might not. You can't guarantee you'll stay in Dover for very long." She picked up a small clay pumpkin.

"I think we could make it work." He blew out a breath. *What a mess*. Orange and red decorations covered every stall. If he wasn't so terrible at communicating, he could be holding her hand and making her laugh. The next stall had quilts and quilted pot holders. He trailed behind her, grasping for the right words.

She returned a custom puzzle set to the table in a stall with wooden models and pumpkins.

"I would request coming back here if you'd try," he whispered. Living in one town would still be an adventure if he was with her.

"Well, hey, guys." Ava carried bags of homemade goodies outside the wooden model stall. "Oh, I've interrupted something." She stepped back.

"You didn't interrupt anything. I was about to introduce Luke to my favorite vendors at the Fall Fair." Katy rushed out of the stall.

"Make sure you take him to get some kettle corn." Ava held a bag filled with golden goodness.

"The fair has kettle corn, and nobody told me?" His light tone was forced. Miles stretched between them, and he wasn't sure how to close the distance.

"You should have seen Luke when he spotted the kettle corn at our homecoming dance in high school. I think you must have eaten an entire batch." Katy shook her head.

"I didn't feel right for days, but I had zero regrets." He smirked. Ten out of ten, he would overeat again.

"A mom and daughter team own the business, and I bet their kettle corn is way better than anything you have back in Oklahoma." Ava hugged the bag.

"I need to buy a bag to prove you wrong." Luke tossed his empty coffee cup into a nearby trash can.

"To prove me wrong, I'd have to compare the two." Ava tapped her finger against her chin.

"I bet my mom would mail me some." Luke rubbed his hands together.

"You two are ridiculous. Kettle corn tastes the same in every town." Katy chuckled.

Ava gasped. "I'll pretend you didn't say anything because I adore you and don't want to end our friendship. See you later." She breezed into the puzzle stall.

Luke opened his mouth.

Joshua and his husband stepped out from a white tent with pumpkin-shaped lights strung across the entrance.

Luke bit the inside of his cheek. They couldn't take two steps without running into someone.

"Well, hey, guys." Katy gave them both a hug. "I was about to introduce Luke to the best kettle corn in the world."

Luke waved. He wasn't on hugging terms yet.

"What? Delaware has been holding out." Joshua waved ahead. "Lead the way."

Luke fell back beside Chris while Katy and Joshua lost track of time in library talk.

"I'm glad he found someone here to talk shop with," Chris said. "I don't mind listening while he works out problems. But having someone who can actually suggest solutions has been exciting."

"Moving has to be tough for the spouses. I didn't know any better as a kid." He paused. Was he asking too much of Katy?

"You're an Army brat, too? New posts were normal for us growing up. All of the kids we ran with lived the same life." Chris shrugged.

"Where all did you live?" Luke raised his eyebrows.

"My dad was Army, so we were all over. I think we spent the longest time in California." Chris rubbed the back of his neck.

"My mom was Army, too. We spent most of our time in Oklahoma and Georgia." Luke's time in Oklahoma was complicated, but he'd met Katy. He'd endure hard transitions and awkward exes to have her in his life now.

"What are you two talking about?" Joshua rubbed his husband's back.

"Turns out, we're both Army brats." Luke smirked.

"A military childhood is an experience I bet you have to live through to understand." Katy waved toward a stall with a short line.

Luke smelled the sweet kettle corn from where they stood, and he was already talking himself out of buying the whole stall's worth. The butter and caramel smelled like movie nights with Mom and Jackie. He sent a photo of the stand to their group text.

"The captain is getting his corn." Joshua laughed but was close behind him.

Luke slid into the line. He had no doubt the golden goodness was completely worth the wait.

Katy waved at the woman working the register.

"Well, hey, Katy. How's my second-favorite librarian?" The raven-haired woman high-fived Katy. She wore a bright-orange T-shirt with the kettle corn company logo across the chest. Her name, *Emily*, was embroidered above the logo.

"Second favorite?" Luke asked.

"Her first favorite is Mae Adams, my boss. And I have to say, she's my favorite librarian too." Katy grinned.

"Mae is one of a kind." Luke's favorite librarian was standing beside him, though.

"You've met Mae? She's my cousin, so I'm biased. Cousins are like siblings, but you can actually get along." Emily rubbed her hands together. "So, what will it be today?"

"These guys have never had your kettle corn. And at least two of them are fanatics. Luke has been known to set records for eating kettle corn." Katy motioned with her thumb.

"Records, huh? Well, I have a military discount to get you started." Emily tapped the price board.

Luke swallowed. "Thank you, ma'am."

"My son's in the Air Force. I always like to chip in and help support. Even if my support is a discount on your popcorn." A little dimple appeared on her cheek.

"We appreciate the support. Kettle corn earns me extra husband points." Chris nodded toward Joshua.

A younger version of the woman joined them.

"Mom, the line."

"Angie, Katy is here, and I'm supporting our troops. Even out of uniform, those haircuts give you away every time." She chuckled.

Luke didn't mind being pegged, correctly, as military. He ordered as many bags as he could carry.

"Hey, Katy. I'll stop by and catch up soon. Lily has been dying to find a new graphic novel." Angie hustled to bag their orders.

"Sounds great," Katy said.

Luke figured she was already making lists of books for the woman's daughter. She'd have a stack set aside before the end of her next workday.

Luke ordered drinks at a different stand with Chris while Katy and Joshua guarded the bench they'd found. Luke fidgeted with his bag of kettle corn. He needed to apologize again and ask her to give him a chance—long distance or otherwise.

Katy happily accepted the apple cider slushy he'd ordered.

At least, the moment of truth was as good as Katy had promised. "I don't want to lose the bet with Ava." He slumped his shoulders. "She'll have bragging rights from here on out. My poor Oklahoma corn." He exaggerated his reaction to make Katy smile.

"California has better kettle corn." Joshua smirked, waving a hand.

"Where?" Luke needed to know and maybe travel there.

Joshua mimed mouse ears. "A magical theme park."

"Well, no surprise there. When are we headed to California?" Luke turned his puppy dog expression on

Katy.

She burst into laughter. "Only you would travel clear across the country for corn." When her alarm buzzed, Katy stood. "I should get back."

He fell in beside her, exchanging waves with the guys as he walked away. "How's the sale going, anyway?" Luke held his corn and the two bags she'd bought at another stall with pumpkin and ghost-covered cotton book sleeves.

"We're on target for where Darcy thought sales should be." She bounced with a little dance. "We'll buy the best books and prizes for the summer reading program. I can just picture the carts full of books now."

"Darcy is the librarian you're covering for?" He leaned closer as they walked.

"Yep. Mae has been keeping her little dog, Fitzwilliam. I think she'll stop by later with her little dog, Coco. Fitzwilliam is a rescue terrier mix, and Coco is a Frenchie."

"They should attract a ton of book buyers." Luke nodded. Cute dogs were always a strong sales strategy.

"Brilliant. I bet she'll let them hang around for a while." Katy rubbed her hands together in excitement.

Dom waved from the tent. "I hope you have a bag of corn in there for me. Ava already told me I have to buy my own. Wouldn't even share with her hungry coworker." He adjusted his hat.

Luke handed over one of his smaller bags. He could go back the next day and buy more.

"You're totally reassuring yourself you can buy more, aren't you?" Katy laughed.

"Delaware has the best kettle corn I've ever had." Luke angled his other bags out of Dom's reach.

Dom opened his bag. "I restocked the tables, so you should be good. The book you claimed is under the checkout table."

"I found a book on rare coins Jackie might like." She bent to retrieve a tiny hardback.

He leaned back on his heels. He should have known she'd not only care about Jackie's areas of interest but support them. Luke stashed his corn under a side table. He held the book with Katy's handwritten sticky note, and the realization hit him all over again. He had to keep trying for a chance with her. He snapped a photo of the book for Jackie.

"Katy, can we talk?" Isaac only took one step into the stall.

His expression was stormy. Luke squinted at Katy's ex. He couldn't believe he came back after stomping away in an embarrassing tantrum earlier. The guy acted like nobody had ever told him *no*. Where was a red flag when Luke needed one?

She bit her lower lip. "Are you good here for a minute? The booth is slow."

"Yeah, you do what you need to do. *I'll* be here." Luke rubbed her shoulder.

Katy dragged her feet behind Isaac.

Mae followed two dogs into the stall.

"You must be Fitzwilliam and Coco." Luke knelt to give them both a scratch.

"They're famous," Mae said. "They're getting along so well I might have to get a friend for Coco. She's been so happy."

"Friends make life a heck of a lot better." Luke's throat was dry. He tracked Katy with his gaze. Luke wished he could hear what they were saying. Katy said they weren't together, but what if she gave him another chance? Was he already too late?

"I hope she's showing him the door." The man beside Mae craned his neck for a better view. His black beard and hair were the same trimmed length and slowly turning silver. His light mahogany skin had deep laugh lines around his eyes.

"Carter," Mae gasped. "Luke, this very opinionated man is my husband, Carter Adams."

Luke shook his hand. "Pleasure to meet you, sir."

"Well, I've heard all about you, Captain." Carter smiled.

"All good things, of course." Mae pursed her lips.

Carter widened his eyes. "And you both agree."

"Not the point, dear." Mae smoothed her dark hair.

"Well, she's stepping back, at least." Carter drew his bushy eyebrows together. "But now she's hugging him. I don't want to see any hugging."

Luke's heart sank.

Chapter Fifteen

Katy waved at Luke on the last day of the Fall Fair. He'd been uncharacteristically distant at setup, and she hadn't had time to corner him. He was in his khaki-and-olive-green OPC uniform, heading straight to work to help with another crisis on base. Katy hugged her arms across her stomach. Something about the physical distance he'd kept made her feel cold.

"Luke and Ryan hustled out of here this morning." Ava stood beside her with a soft orange cardigan over her cream library T-shirt.

"They had to get back to base again today. Some kind of emergency, but they can't talk about Air Force cargo." Katy leaned against Ava's shoulder. How could he just take off? She'd been the one to set the friend boundary, though, so she had no right to be bothered by his indifference. She wanted to be his friend…right?

Ava sipped her hot apple cider. "Having friends with security clearance is complicated. Like, I want to ask *all* the questions, but I can't."

Katy chuckled. She was lucky Luke and Ryan kept their commitment. Their trucks, and both of them, were a huge part of her plan. She could count on Luke. *Trust.* Realization slammed into her, and she widened her eyes.

"Whoa, big thoughts just crossed your face." Ava leaned closer. "I don't think you've had enough coffee yet."

"I trust him," she whispered. Why hadn't she noticed earlier? Luke was someone who would work double time, trying not to let her down. He showed up for her because he wanted to and not because he had an ulterior motive.

"Uh-huh." Ava narrowed her eyes. "I need more details. And you better not be talking about Isaac."

"No, Isaac knows I'm not interested in getting back together. I swear he came back to get me to read his thesis." She'd fully accepted the reality of the situation. Isaac didn't matter, though. Luke's green eyes and deep rumbling voice were all she could think about.

"I warned you everything was about him and his research." Ava pursed her lips.

Katy sighed. "Okay, I hear you. I don't trust Isaac. I *trust* Luke." Saying the words out loud lifted a weight off her chest.

"Well, he sure showed to set up and break down the stall all weekend. Even when major drama is going down on base, he keeps his promises. I like loyalty in a guy." She pressed a hand to her chest.

"I need to forgive him for keeping the training from me," Katy said. "I told him I understood, but his silence hurt."

"He's worked to get back in your good graces. Are you saying you'll give him a chance? He does want a relationship, right?" Ava clutched her hands together.

"Yes. Maybe?" Katy reshelved two thin paperback books. She'd welcomed the intrusions, at first—she needed to think. His words about wishing they were together played on repeat. Why had he winced after he said them?

McKenna joined them, wiping her hands on a black-and-white apron covered in tiny, white, heart-shaped coffeepots. Her long blonde hair was in a messy bun. "What are we talking about?" She glanced between them.

"Katy might give Durant Guy another chance." Ava smirked.

"No more High School Heartbreak? He's earned Durant Guy status again?" McKenna raised an eyebrow.

"He grows on you." Ava cocked her head to the side. Her glance turned impish. "And you know you love my nicknames."

Her friends' voices faded into the background. Katy had a lump in her throat. Her mind whirled. Was she really going for it? Could she and Luke make a relationship work?

"Well, you have to give him a chance. I haven't seen a guy work so hard to apologize in my entire life." McKenna raised a hand to her chest in an oh-my-heart gesture.

"A good man who can apologize is impossible to find. My *abuela* always says you have to watch how they treat your friends and their friends. Luke passes all of those tests with flying colors. *Abuela* would approve." Ava flipped her dark hair over her shoulder.

"You're not wrong. My gran adored him when we were younger." He had grandma-approved written all over his Southern way of opening doors and jumping in to offer help at the drop of a hat. Katy's pulse throbbed in her throat. Luke was one of a kind, and she'd let him walk away. What if she'd blown her chance?

"Okay, so go talk to him." Ava threw her hands in

the air.

Katy couldn't help but smile. Ava was so different, making lightning-fast decisions and sticking with them. Katy was slow and changed her mind several times before committing. They kept each other in check. She breathed deeply. Liking Luke was one question she'd never wavered on. If the chance was real, she wanted him. "And what if he's stationed somewhere else?" Katy bit her lip.

"Then we'll video call and drink coffee together in the morning. Friendships don't stop just because people live in different cities. Your feelings won't go away because he's not in Dover, either." McKenna wrapped a strong arm around Katy's shoulders.

"And wine and chocolate nights will continue over video calls, too. Those are unstoppable." Ava squeezed Katy's arm. "I know I'm the best friend you've ever had, but I won't be the reason you hold yourself back from finding your person."

"Um, I make the cinnamon lattes. I'm the best friend she's ever had." McKenna stepped back and fluffed her messy bun.

"Competitive, much? You both know you're the best friends I've ever had. Don't you have to get back to the long line of coffee lovers? I bet they're already in place. The fair opens in five minutes." Katy stuck her hands into her pockets to hide their trembling. Was she ready to say goodbye to seeing Ava and McKenna? If Luke was stationed somewhere else, then she'd go with him. Her heart hammered in her chest. She'd built such a good life here, but she'd never forgive herself if she didn't give what she felt for him a real chance.

Ava hugged her on her way out of the white tent.

"He's worth the risk." McKenna slipped from the bookstall.

The sweet scent of apple spice followed in her wake. Katy picked up a stack of books to reshelve so she wouldn't think about not seeing McKenna and Ava all the time anymore. She didn't need to be sobbing while selling used books.

A familiar ache lodged in her chest. She'd never had friends like Ava and McKenna. When she'd tried to keep her distance, they'd waltzed right on through her fears and had shown her what true friendship looked like.

Was a chance with Luke worth losing the closeness she shared with her friends? The thought of moving away from them and her job made her dizzy. Her eyes stung with unshed tears. And yet, her heart leaped into her throat when she thought about life without Luke.

****

Around midmorning, Mae joined Katy in the white tent to volunteer, and her husband had Coco and Fitzwilliam on matching red leashes. She pinned tiny bows with sunflowers in the center on Coco's collar.

Katy suppressed the urge to check her phone. Luke hadn't responded to her call or texts, and she was determined to hide how all over the place her emotions were. The sale was a success, and she should be riding high on not failing. But the day moved at a snail's pace, and her frustration was like a live wire under her skin.

"Darcy might stop by with baby Charlie in a bit. She's also ready for Fitz to come home, so I might have to visit the local shelter for a friend for Coco. This little guy fit right into our house. Who knew?" Mae beamed.

"Me! I knew." Carter raised a hand. "I've wanted

another dog for the last year. Coco is a social dog. She needs a friend when we're at work."

Mae shook her head. "Well, you were right. I needed to know taking care of two dogs was doable."

"I can't wait to see Darcy and the baby," Katy said. "When I dropped off dinner the other day, I held him so she could take a break. Charlie isn't the greatest sleeper, but they're developing sleep schedules."

"He's just the cutest." Mae pointed at the front of the stall. "Now go stand so people see the pups. Shoppers flocked to them on Friday."

"Come on, pups. You're marketing for the library now. Look cute." He kept talking to the dogs on his way to the entrance of the tent.

"Did Luke help this morning?" Mae raised an eyebrow.

Her Cheshire cat smile made Katy gulp. "He sure did." Katy held in a sigh. She'd come so close to not thinking about him for a whole minute. "He, um, should be back when we break everything down tonight." Katy turned away before Mae could ask more questions.

Ginny Dean trailed a finger over their mystery section. She twirled her floral-orange scarf around her finger.

"Ginny, good to see you." Katy waved.

"I was hoping you'd be here. I've already found two books." She raised two cozy mysteries in the air like trophies.

"Both of those are great." Katy grinned. "And all the proceeds from the sale support our summer reading program at the library."

"Well, summer reading is my jam, so let me find a few more books." Ginny ran a hand over a stack of food-themed mysteries.

"Mine, too. Have you had a good trip to Dover?" Katy reorganized the remaining children's picture books, leaving a cover facing out with a scarecrow and a little red dog.

Ginny searched along the makeshift shelves. "These little coastal towns never disappoint. I stopped by the other two MCLs you set up, so there should be photos on the main social accounts. Everyone was impressed."

"Thank you. We'll share them from the library's social media. We libraries have to stick together." Katy smiled. Had Ginny shown them to her coworkers?

"I couldn't agree more." Ginny patted her short curly hair. "While you're here, I wanted to talk about you coming to work on my team. I have an opening, and I know you would be a perfect fit. You already know the process, and you've been doing the work since grad school. I asked around, and the libraries you did in Oklahoma have been the benchmark for future projects."

"I'm not sure what to say." *Where is Mae?* Katy scanned the tent. She was being offered her dream job in front of her current boss. Mae had taken such a big chance hiring Katy straight out of grad school, and she didn't want to let her down by leaving so soon after taking the position.

"She says she'd be happy to hear more about the opportunity." Mae crossed the short distance from the front cash register to stand beside Ginny. "I'm Mae Adams, the director at the Dover Public Library, and you must be Ginny Dean from MCL."

"Mae was my Indigenous Library Project mentor

when I worked on the MCL projects in Oklahoma." Katy shifted from foot to foot. She couldn't find any traces of anger or annoyance on Mae's face. Was she really okay with Ginny offering her a job? Right in front of her?

"I've heard your name attached to other MCL projects. I don't mean to poach your top talent, but you can't blame me for wanting Katy on my team." Ginny laughed.

"You'd be very lucky to have her, and I would be happy to write a reference." Mae shook Ginny's hand. She raised her eyebrows at Katy with a smile.

Was she a bad employee? Did Mae want her to leave? Katy's stomach bottomed out. Mae's smile was genuine, though. Katy blew out a deep breath.

Mae walked to the back of the deep tent to help another customer.

The autumn wind picked up, flapping book covers and moving fliers. Katy forced the corners of her lips up and focused on Ginny.

"Well, let me buy these books, and then you better call me on Monday so we can talk." Ginny patted her purse. "You have my card?"

"I do, and thank you so much. I'm looking forward to learning more about the position." Katy's tone was polite, bordering on overly formal. She had to hold in her happy dance until she was out of sight. Her dream job was real. She could travel the country and help organizations set up new MCLs or visit communities where an MCL was abandoned. Her days would be filled with meeting volunteers and filling MCLs with books. She checked Ginny out in a haze, trying to pay attention, but the daydream was too big.

Ginny left with five books stacked inside her canvas tote.

Mae tidied the area around the cash register, humming a Dolly Parton song with a grin.

"I won't apply for the job." She wouldn't repay Mae's trust with disloyalty, even if she had to wait a little longer for her dream. She wished Gran was alive. Gran would tell her to follow her heart and be brave, but her heart was torn between doing right by Mae and her love of MCLs.

Mae widened her eyes. "What on earth are you talking about? Of course, you'll apply. You're all but guaranteed the job." She wrapped an arm around Katy. "I know you think I took a chance on you when I hired you last year, but I was recruiting *top talent*. And now, you have the chance to do your dream job. Don't forget I was there when you built those three MCLs in Oklahoma. You need to follow your true north. Don't stay here in Delaware out of misplaced loyalty."

"I don't know what to say. You were there when I almost quit my master's program, and you never let me give up. I discovered MCLs because of you. I could never explain how much your support has changed my life for the better." Katy's vision swam with unshed tears.

"Well, I'm counting on you to pay it forward. We all need people who want us to *thrive*." Mae stepped away to help a customer check out.

Katy swallowed back the conflicting emotions and settled on profound gratitude. She moved to the back of the tent, restacking books on the tables that formed a U-shape and stretched to the back of the tent. She froze her hand over *Anne of Green Gables*. Mae wouldn't have offered a recommendation to Ginny unless she meant it. She was living her dream, and now, Katy had a chance to live hers. Gratitude swelled within her. Mae was a true friend, and Katy was lucky to have her in her corner.

"What did I miss?" Ava raised an eyebrow.

Katy jumped. She hadn't noticed anyone around her. She was due for a break, so she and Ava found a bench down the grassy aisle from their book sale. As quickly as she could, she caught Ava up on the potential job.

"Nothing is standing in your way with Durant Guy." Ava settled against the back of the bench, fiddling with the buttons on her orange cardigan.

"He won't be here until we break down the sale at the end." Katy checked her watch. Three more hours to figure out what to say. Would she give Luke a chance? She gulped.

"So, call him and ask him to meet you." Ava pursed her lips.

Was he too busy to check his phone, or was he ignoring her? What if something terrible had happened on base? Katy had texted him earlier but never got a response. She glared at her phone. She'd reached the limit on texts before she made things weird.

Ava's phone buzzed. "My shift starts soon. Go take a walk and clear your head."

Katy wandered over to McKenna's coffee cart. People walked by with their cinnamon hot cocoas and apple cider scents wafting from their white Brewed Awakenings cups. Katy took a deep breath, grounding herself in the present.

"Well, hey there." McKenna stepped around her

coffee cart for a hug. "You just missed Luke and Ryan."

"They're here?" Why hadn't he told her?

"Ryan volunteers every week at the rec center, I guess. He and Luke are staffing the rec's table for a while before they help you at the end." McKenna shrugged.

"He didn't tell me he was here," Katy said.

"Hmm. I'm surprised Luke didn't tell you he'd be around. They didn't have time to get coffee or tea. You want to be the hero and take him one for a change? I'm not sure what Ryan drinks, though." McKenna pressed her lips together.

"Coffee or coffee-flavored coffee as he likes to call his order." Katy chuckled. He would grump if she brought him a latte or something frothy.

"Black coffee." McKenna smirked. "Why am I not surprised in the least? You know, I find people drink black coffee sometimes because they don't want to be a bother, like asking for more, even milk, would be too much."

"Oh, man, you think?" Katy frowned.

"Who knows? Maybe he likes to judge the rest of us and our milky coffees?" McKenna tapped the espresso before starting a latte for Katy.

"Just let him try to judge my cinnamon lattes." Katy mimed like she was clutching her nonexistent pearls.

McKenna made the drinks and gave Katy a drink carrier.

She wove through the crowds filling the wide grass paths between the white tents. She wasn't sure how Luke would react when she showed up. He'd ignored her texts. Knowing he hadn't even been on base for part of the day made it all even more confusing. The silver cuff bracelet Gran had given her caught the afternoon sun. Diamonds within two parallel bands shimmered. Gran always said the design showed their respect for the world around them—healthy dirt, green plants, and clean water. Wearing the bracelet kept Gran's memory as close as possible. She needed to channel her fearless ancestor.

How would she even find the words? She'd been so determined to draw a line in the sand... Had she already ruined everything? She found the rec center tent. Her heart jumped to a quick staccato rhythm.

Luke helped kids spin a prize wheel to win a rubber bracelet, a finger flashlight, or a pencil. He smiled at each kid, asking for their names and repeating them. He was so good at making other people feel seen and important.

Katy sighed. He was good with kids, too. One more reason to adore him. Katy set the coffees on the little table where the volunteers had other drinks.

Luke froze mid-sentence, swallowed, and then helped a toddler pick out her prize. When the line disappeared, Luke picked up his chai tea with espresso and took a long sip. "McKenna likes us."

"I do, too." Katy raised an eyebrow. "Don't I get delivery credit?"

"Delivery credit counts big around here." Ryan raised his black coffee to her and graced her with a crisp nod. "Thanks for the joe."

"I didn't realize you guys were volunteering over here today. I would have brought you caffeine sooner." She chewed on her lower lip. Something was still off with Luke. He was a couple feet away and made no move to get closer. Was he upset? Or was he respecting the friendship boundaries she'd foolishly set?

Ryan tipped his head toward Luke with a tight frown.

Was Ryan annoyed with Luke?

"Well, we're covered, so you should take a break." Ryan narrowed his eyes at Luke.

Yeah, Ryan is definitely not happy.

"You sure?" Luke rubbed the back of his neck and didn't even glance at Katy.

"Hey, you want to go for a walk? I haven't had dinner yet." She figured feeding Luke was always a good place to start. Nothing like a crowded fair to work up the nerve to tell someone you wanted a relationship, after all…

"I can always eat."

His tone was almost hopeful, and his half-smile made her want the real deal even more. She took a deep breath and shook her diamond-patterned bracelet for courage. The familiar weight of the silver bangle settled the butterflies in her stomach. With steam rising from their drinks, Katy slid her free hand into his.

He jolted at the contact. His calloused thumb slid over hers. "I, uh… You and Isaac…"

Was he being distant because of Isaac? Katy was sick of talking about her ex. She needed to clear the air and tell him she was falling in love before she lost her nerve. "I told him I needed a clean break yesterday. I'm not interested in getting back together."

Luke squeezed her hand and stopped walking.

Relief washed over her like a wave. Katy leaned against him, swallowing a lump in her throat. Why couldn't she just blurt out her feelings? She would *not* chicken out. The ceramic pumpkins booth where he'd told her he wanted to be in a relationship was behind him like a neon sign.

"Well, okay then. Let's get you some dinner." Luke had a bounce in his step.

****

They sat together at a picnic table while Katy worked up the courage to tell him everything she'd been holding back. "Ginny from MCL stopped by the tent a while ago." She pushed the paper bowl filled with chicken tacos away. Her nerves were too loud to eat.

"Is that what you were texting me about? I had to keep helping Ryan with those kids. We had a never-ending line." He licked barbeque sauce from his thumb.

Katy was momentarily mesmerized by his full lips. "Y-yeah, actually. She basically offered me a job doing what she does: traveling, helping to set up new MCLs, and rescuing orphaned locations."

He beamed. "What? Katy, you're describing your dream job." He let out a *whoop*.

A few people glanced over.

Katy smiled at the strangers, hoping they would lose interest. "Mae was there. But she was actually the one to tell Ginny I'd *love* to hear more about the job." Her eyes stung from the quiet determination her boss had tried to infuse into her words. She believed Katy was the best person for the job.

"She wants you to be happy." Luke rested his warm hand over hers.

"She does. I can't even find the words for how excited I am. But, Luke, the job also means I could be based out of *anywhere*." Katy needed to say she wanted to be with him, but the words still wouldn't come. She was sitting at a picnic table with their thighs touching and his hand covering hers, and she still couldn't be brave.

He slid his food away and leaned closer. "Major called. I get to do the training in person." He frowned.

"Are you kidding? Congratulations. So, where is the training? Do you know when you'll go?" She would not ruin this for him. He deserved a career boost and for his friends to support him. Katy shoved all of her misgivings to the back of her mind and smiled.

"I won't have the particulars for another week or so, but the training is in Alabama." He scrunched his eyebrows together and pulled his hand back.

"I'm so happy for you." She waited to see what he'd say next. Her food sat untouched. He would move away, and they would only be friends. She would spend the rest of her life knowing he was the one who got away.

He cleared their spot without a word.

What was he thinking? His facial expression was neutral. Katy stood from the bench and waited. Should she say something? Her eyes stung. Her moment was slipping through her fingers, and she couldn't muster the courage to admit her feelings.

"You probably need to get back to the book sale." Luke offered her his hand.

Holding hands was a good sign, right? "Um, yeah. I guess my break is over. Do you—"

"What?" Luke stopped and released her hand to text someone.

The chilly autumn breeze filled her empty hand. She crossed her arms, waiting for him. The text exchange lasted long enough to give her a third-wheel sensation. She didn't want to walk away from him, though.

"You ready?" He tucked his phone away.

The sky filled with reds and pinks as the sun slowly hid behind the tent line. "Luke, about what you said yesterday." Katy took a deep breath of the caramel corn and apple spiced festival air.

"Well, hey!" Ava pointed at their linked hands and jumped. She stepped outside of the library stall by the dollar deal cart.

Dom poked his head out of the stall before ducking back in. At least, someone was still helping customers.

Ava motioned them to the side and out of the way of the photo booth where a family was taking goofy photos.

"Luke was selected for the training program he was hoping for." Katy's hands trembled. She was so close to finally spilling her feelings for him.

"Wow. We'll miss you here in Dover, though." Ava squeezed Katy's arm.

"Going in person is a big deal. We'll host a little party." Katy leaned against him, soaking up his warmth while she could.

"And if you're lucky, we'll video chat from Brewed Awakenings so you can live vicariously." Ava flipped her dark hair over her shoulder.

"Where is McKenna, anyway?" Luke scanned the booth.

Katy frowned. Why would McKenna be at the library stall? She had a coffee cart to run.

"Oh, hey, the hayride was filling up, so I bought you both tickets. You better head over." Ava offered the pumpkin-shaped printouts.

He rubbed his thumb over the back of Katy's hand, leading her away from the library booth.

She squeezed his hand. Was he on the same page for what they could mean to each other? "Now I know who you were texting." Katy leaned against his shoulder. A fall hayride was the perfect place to tell him.

"Guilty as charged. I figured you'd want to go. Is this okay?"

Like a hayride would ever be a bad thing. "I haven't been on a hayride since high school. Did you ever go to the pumpkin patch about an hour from town with the long hayride? I used to go with Dad and Gran every year."

He shook his head. "You'll have to take me next time we're back visiting our parents."

She lifted her gaze. "You planning to travel together?" The urge to overanalyze joint travel plans was overwhelming.

He squeezed her hand. "As much as you'll let me." He stopped when they reached the line for the hayride.

Her breath caught. Hope flared deep in her chest. Visiting their parents together had to mean something. "I want to be where you are—"

"I heard you two were over here." Mae shared a knowing glance with Barbara.

"I never stopped by your stall, Barbara. I'm so sorry." Katy covered her mouth.

"You had a big book sale to run. Besides, you support me at First Fridays and at my summer booth. Did you know my husband runs the hayride?" Barbara motioned toward the hayride ahead.

They were the first in the next group for the hayride. "I didn't." Katy turned toward the green tractor.

"Hayrides give him something extra to do with his tractor, and driving his green machine is all he wants in life." Barbara chuckled.

She had the best laugh lines on her face, and Katy hoped she'd be the same way someday. Mae and Barbara were easy to mistake for sisters. Barbara was twenty years older than Mae, but age hadn't slowed her down.

"Well, you two enjoy your ride." Mae joined the next group in line.

The line didn't stretch back far. Katy counted eight people behind them. She'd been surprised the line wasn't longer. Hayrides were one of the best events of the fall.

"Mae knows everyone." Luke shook his head.

"No kidding." The green tractor kicked up dust while parking in front of Katy.

Two families climbed down from the flat trailer. A toddler in a pink-flannel jacket gave the tractor a pat-pat like it was a good pony.

Katy grinned.

"I was hoping you'd stop by." Mr. Brooks hopped off his tractor.

Katy hugged him. He was tall with the lightest-blue eyes Katy had ever seen.

"Well, you two climb into the back," he said. "We have blankets back there, in case you get cold. We'll go around the square a couple times."

"Oh, don't we need to wait for the others?" Katy glanced back at the line. She didn't feel right making anyone wait extra time.

Mae and Barbara were nowhere to be seen.

"Let's take a ride for two." Mr. Brooks winked.

Luke led her to the back of the trailer. Tidy rows of hay bales lined the back with loose hay covering the wooden bottom. Luke scooted to the very back so they could see the fair as they rode around the square.

"A ride for two, huh?" She leaned against him, breathing in his woodsy scent.

"I'd like to claim credit, but Mae, Barbara, and Ava are the masterminds. I think they've forgiven me." He pulled her close.

"You're back in their good graces. And mine, too." She rested her head on his broad shoulder.

"Thank you." The tractor started with a brief jostle, and Luke held them both steady.

The sun hung low over the horizon, and the lights hanging on the stalls twinkled in the early dusk. The square was magical. His shoulder was so warm, but she needed to tell him how she felt. She hadn't seen a signal bird for days, and she was ready to stop worrying about them.

Luke shifted his long legs on the short haystack.

Katy sat up, shifting to make eye contact with him. *Be brave.* "So, with the new job, I could be based out of anywhere." Her pulse hammered in her chest. What if he still left her behind? Doubts rushed through her mind, but she hushed them. He was worth the risk— worth being vulnerable and saying she was all in.

Luke swallowed. He'd rolled the sleeves up on his olive-green button-up at some point, and he tensed his forearms.

She didn't want to let him go. His silence grew

louder. Should she say more? She took a deep breath, preparing to say the words building up inside her. "I tried so hard not to fall in love, but I didn't stand a chance. You're kind and hardworking and one of my oldest friends. You *see* me when usually I feel invisible. You went above and beyond for kids on base—most of whom you'll probably never meet. Showing up before the sun was up and staying after the sun went down, you made this book sale a success. I love what a great team we make."

"I love you, too. If you want an invitation to Alabama, consider yourself invited. If you want to wait to see where I'm stationed after training, then I'll wait. I want to be where you are." He pulled her closer and rubbed his warm hand down her arm.

She shivered from his touch. "I feel the same way, like being with you is the *home* feeling I've been searching for. Alabama sounds like an adventure." Her eyes glistened. She wouldn't be left behind.

He leaned over and kissed her.

Delicious tingles spread to her toes. She leaned into the kiss and slipped a hand over his lightly stubbled cheek, enjoying the friction of his five-o'clock shadow. Ever since their almost-kiss in the hardware store parking lot, she'd wondered what his lips would taste like. His full lips were soft and sweet.

He pulled her closer until his thigh pressed against hers.

She smiled and pulled back to gaze into his green eyes. She trusted him. He wasn't the kind of guy to leave her behind anymore. He'd grown up into the kind of man she could count on, and he wanted *her*.

"You're my kind of adventure." He tucked a loose

strand of hair behind her ear. "Who knew one tiny library would be the start of something so right? Being with you feels like I've finally found my home."

"Never underestimate a library." She kissed him again just because she could. She pictured them exploring new towns and cities when he changed bases. New bookstores, libraries, and coffee shops were out there waiting, and she would discover them with Luke by her side.

Epilogue

The ocean breeze whipped Katy's hair across her face. Virginia Beach was slowly filling with locals and tourists. The water was too cold to swim, but the warm day was perfect for a beachside picnic. After three months in Alabama for Luke's training, Katy was ready to settle down for longer in Virginia. They might get lucky with as many as four years in this vibrant seaside town.

Luke rubbed his warm hand in small circles across her back. His white linen button-up made his tan skin shine. He was dressed up in crisp khaki shorts, but he'd already rolled up his sleeves and ditched his flip-flops.

Goose bumps trailed after his fingertips. Her light blue sundress had a cutout back, leaving plenty of skin available for her boyfriend's touch. "Do you see them yet?" She blocked the sun from her eyes with an outstretched hand.

"There." Luke pointed across the sandy expanse.

McKenna barely beat Ava as she ran across the beach. She dropped her purple beach bag and crashed into Katy's outstretched arms.

Ava jogged up a second later and tried to encompass both of them in her petite arms.

"Ladies, you just saw each other over video five days ago." Luke chuckled. He moved their bags next to his cooler and claimed more space for the group by spreading out a green beach blanket.

He slowly built a square perimeter of space before all the open sand was swallowed up by beachgoers.

"But not in person for months—not since you stole her away." Ava pouted her lower lip.

Luke grinned. "I can't imagine moving around without her."

Who knew Luke Taylor was a romantic? His words were healing in a way she hadn't known she needed. Katy beamed.

"We forgive you." McKenna let go of Katy to offer Luke a half-hug.

Katy still had an arm around Ava. She wasn't ready to let her go. Her life with Luke and the Mini Community Libraries was a dream, but being in person with all three of her favorite people was next-level.

"Well, now that you're stationed so close, get used to visits." McKenna sniffed with her eyes glistening. She turned to rifle through her purple beach bag.

"We were so worried you'd end up somewhere too far to drive, like *Texas*." Ava squeezed her arm tighter around Katy.

"I don't have much say in where I end up." Luke stuck his hands into his pockets.

Katy let go of Ava to reach for Luke. He never needed to apologize for the military lifestyle.

He shifted to hold her hand. When the new orders had come through, he'd delivered them with a flourish: candlelit dinner, special-order McKenna coffee, and a map printed to show the route to Delaware from Virginia Beach.

Ava flung out her yellow towel and dropped down. Her bright-pink-and-orange maxi dress billowed in the light breeze. "But now, you're an easy day trip away."

If someone had told her six months earlier that she'd live in Virginia Beach with Luke Taylor, she would never have believed them. And yet, Alabama and now Virginia were easily the best months of her life. Katy's cheeks burned from smiling so hard.

McKenna narrowed her eyes at Luke and waved her hand in a go-ahead motion.

What was going on? Katy switched her gaze between them.

Ava held up her phone with the camera pointed at Katy. Her smile could have powered entire cities from the wattage.

Was Ava recording?

Luke dropped to one knee.

No, he couldn't be…

He lifted an opened small black box.

Inside was a beautiful princess-cut diamond ring. Katy gasped and raised a hand to cover her mouth. She had to be dreaming.

"Katy Cooper Caterby, this life we're building together is the greatest adventure I've ever known. Will you do me the honor of becoming my wife?" Luke's eyes were misty.

His tone was weirdly serious, like he was afraid she would say *no*. The white button-up finally made sense. He'd dressed up to ask her to *marry* him. The world around them disappeared. A life with Luke would be filled with travel and quiet moments like their Sunday brunches. He brought her coffee in the morning when he could, sent e-books when she traveled, and called her just to hear her voice. Maybe they would bring their kids to Virginia Beach someday to show them where their dad proposed.

Luke shifted in the sand.

Katy's heart pounded in her ears. "Yes!"

He slipped the ring onto her ring finger.

"Your grandmother's ring?" She'd seen photos of the vintage two-tone engagement ring when they'd visited his aunt and uncle. The only family heirloom Luke owned glistened in the afternoon light on her finger. How had he known her size?

"I picked it up at my aunt's when we drove through Georgia. Don't let me forget to call her later." His grin was lopsided.

She joined Luke on her knees and threw her arms around his shoulders. The sand shifted beneath her.

"I call dibs on baking a wedding cake." McKenna had tears streaming down her cheeks.

Ava still had her phone camera out. "Any chance we can talk you two into a destination wedding? You know, in glamorous Dover, Delaware?"

Luke gazed into Katy's eyes as he grinned. "What do you say, Katy?"

"Dover sounds perfect." Katy shared a short, sweet kiss with Luke, aware Ava had her camera aimed at them.

"Where we took the leap." Luke brushed her hair back.

"Where my coffee shop brought you together," McKenna said.

Luke wiped a tear from Katy's cheek.

"Okay, one more kiss for the video." Ava made kissy noises.

Luke brushed her lips with a slow, gentle kiss.

"Perfection." Ava packed her phone away and

stood.

Luke pulled Katy to her feet. "And I'm forever grateful for that random act of kindness."

Katy squeezed his hand. If only she could go back in time to tell the lonely nine-year-old girl she'd once been that her life would be so much better than she ever dreamed. She leaned into her future husband and took a deep breath of salty air, looking out at the expansive ocean.

Luke planted a kiss in her hair. "No signal birds?"

Katy shook her head. She hadn't so much as heard the trill of a woodpecker since she'd kissed Luke at the Fall Fair. "All clear, Mr. Persistent. I think you scared them off."

He shifted to stand in front of her, stealing another kiss. "We'll keep each other out of danger. And maybe find an adventure or two."

She cupped his cheek in her hand and gazed into his bright green eyes. She had a partner, now and forever. "*Together.*"

A word about the author...

J.R. Boles is a fantasy and romance writer from Kansas City. J.R. is a lawyer-turned-novelist, a full-time book editor, and a sometimes crochet blanket-maker. You can usually find her writing, editing, or trying new coffee shops.

Visit her website jrboles.com to find her next event and follow her bookish adventures on Instagram and TikTok at @jrbolesauthor.

www.ingramcontent.com/pod-product-compliance
Lightning Source LLC
Chambersburg PA
CBHW072114020726
47501CB00003B/810